PRAISE FOR

Princess of the Silver Woods

"The stories of Red Riding Hood and Robin Hood get a twist as Petunia and her many sisters take on bandits, grannies, and the new King Under Stone to end their family curse once and for all." —Teenreads.com

"A fast and addictive read. Expect to feel the need to read the whole thing in one sitting." —Cracking the Cover

PRAISE FOR

Princess of Glass

"In a clever reworking of the Cinderella story, George once again proves adept at spinning her own magical tale. Fans of Donna Jo Napoli's retellings will cheer loudly as George proves her own mettle." —*Booklist*

"George delivers another satisfying fairytale retelling. . . . As with [her] other retellings, be prepared for plenty of twists." —*VOYA*

PRAISE FOR

Princess of the Midnight Ball

"A well-realized and fast-paced fantasy-romance." —*Booklist*

"Fans of fairy-tale retellings like Robin McKinley's *Beauty* or Gail Carson Levine's *Ella Enchanted* will enjoy this story for its magic, humor, and touch of romance." —*SLJ*

Princess
of the
Silver
Woods

Jessica Day George

BLOOMSBURY
NEW YORK   LONDON   NEW DELHI   SYDNEY

First published in the United States of America in December 2012
by Bloomsbury Children's Books
Paperback edition published in December 2013
www.bloomsbury.com

For information about permission to reproduce selections from this book, write to
Permissions, Bloomsbury Children's Books, 1385 Broadway, New York, New York 10018
Bloomsbury books may be purchased for business or promotional use. For information on bulk
purchases please contact Macmillan Corporate and Premium Sales Department at
specialmarkets@macmillan.com

The Library of Congress has cataloged the hardcover edition as follows:
George, Jessica Day.
Princess of the silver woods / by Jessica Day George. — 1st U.S. ed.
p.   cm.
Summary: When Petunia, youngest of the dancing princesses, is ambushed by bandits in wolf
masks on her way to visit an elderly neighbor, the line between enemies and friends becomes
blurred as she and her sisters get a chance to end their family's curse once and for all.
ISBN 978-1-59990-646-1 (hardcover)
[1. Fairy tales. 2. Princesses—Fiction. 3. Robbers and outlaws—Fiction. 4. Blessing and
cursing—Fiction. 5. Magic—Fiction.] I. Twelve dancing princesses. English. II. Title.
PZ8.G3295Prm 2012   [Fic]—dc23   2012011230

ISBN 978-1-61963-126-7 (paperback)

Book design by Donna Mark
Typeset by Westchester Book Composition
Printed and bound in the U.S.A. by Thomson-Shore Inc., Dexter, Michigan
2 4 6 8 10 9 7 5 3 1

All papers used by Bloomsbury Publishing, Inc., are natural, recyclable products
made from wood grown in well-managed forests. The manufacturing processes
conform to the environmental regulations of the country of origin.

For Amy Jameson,
friend and agent

Princess
of the
Silver
Woods

Prologue

You promised us brides!"

"I grow weary of your whining, Kestilan," said the King Under Stone. The king, who had once been Rionin, third-born son of Wolfram von Aue, gripped the arms of his throne, and the black stone made a thin cracking noise.

"Do you see?" Kestilan pointed to the throne, though no fracture was visible. "Our home crumbles around us! Something must be done!"

"Do you think I merely sit here night after night and gloat over my kingdom?" The King Under Stone's chill voice would have done their father proud. "I am not blind." The king gestured at the ballroom with a broad sweep of his long arm.

The marble floor had lost its sheen and there were shallow dips worn into it from a hundred thousand dances. The gilt was peeling from the mirror frames, and the velvet upholstery had faded from black and purple to gray and lavender.

Blathen murmured something, and the king's head turned sharply. "What was that, dear brother?"

At first Blathen looked as though he would demur, but then he squared his shoulders. "Our father ruled for centuries, yet the palace was ever new," he said again.

The King Under Stone nodded. "Very true. And you think that it decays now because I am not as strong as our father."

None of his brothers moved or spoke, afraid to agree or disagree with this statement. Whatever his strength in comparison to their father's, the new king could still kill any of them as easily as breathe.

The King Under Stone got to his feet, smiling as his brothers moved away. They stepped down off the dais, making him appear taller though they were all the same height. He took the opportunity to loom over them, and his smile became even more terrifying.

"I assure you this is not the case," he said. "The truth of the matter is that the Kingdom Under Stone is dying because it was meant to contain our father, and our father is gone."

"So we can leave?" Tirolian's voice was rich with relief.

The king paused for a while, mulling over how best to tell his remaining brothers the news. "Not yet," he admitted. "The kingdom is dying," he went on at last. "Dying with us trapped inside. Like a birdcage smashed beneath a stone. The door to the cage is still locked and there is no way for us to fly out." His smile became even more terrifying as he saw his words sink in.

"Then what do we do?" Blathen folded his arms across his chest. "I am not going to sit here and let the stone crush me."

"Of course not," the king said. "We need only to collect a few things to enable our escape."

"And what do we need?" Blathen was still frowning, not convinced that his older brother had the answer.

"Just what Kestilan has asked for," the King Under Stone said, sitting back on his throne. "Just what our father wanted for us: brides.

"Beautiful brides who can walk in the sun."

Traveler

Petunia was knitting some fingerless gloves to match her new red velvet cloak when the Wolves of the Westfalian Woods attacked. She dropped one of her needles when she heard the first gunshot, and though she could clearly see the silver needle rolling on the floor of the coach, she didn't stoop to pick it up. The bandits had surrounded them so quickly and so silently that she froze at the sound of the coachman's rifle and the sudden halt.

"Put the gun down, my good man," called out one of the wolves. "All we ask is your coin and any jewels, and you can be on your way."

Sitting across from her, Petunia's maid, Maria, began to cry.

Petunia pushed back the hood of her cloak, intrigued. No one had ever told her that the Wolves of the Westfalian Woods were young . . . but the voice clearly belonged to someone near her own age. An educated someone near her own age, unless she was mistaken. She retrieved her knitting needle and then tucked all four needles and the yarn into the basket on the seat beside her, pulling out her pistol as she did so. She checked the bullets, then cocked the weapon.

"Oh, Your Highness!" Maria was scandalized, but she had the good sense to whisper, at least. "Put it away!"

"They aren't taking *my* jewelry," Petunia said.

She owned only a few pieces—as the youngest of twelve princesses, she was hardly dripping diamonds and pearls. But what little she had was in a cedar jewelry case under Maria's seat.

"They are not getting my mother's ruby earrings," she said. "Nor the necklace that Papa gave me for my sixteenth birthday. I've only gotten to wear it twice."

It had a small ruby in the center of a petunia-shaped pendant, and the chain was made to look like petunia leaves. She would shoot anyone who tried to take it. She might regret shooting them later, but she would still shoot.

Hearing a sound just outside one of the coach windows, Petunia trained her pistol on it and braced her wrist with her other hand. She could see figures outside the coach— masked figures in the trees on either side of the road—but none clear enough to shoot in the twilight.

Then a face, the upper half covered by a leather mask made to look like a wolf's head, poked through the coach window. Petunia carefully adjusted her aim so that the pistol was pointing at the bandit's left eye.

"Give us your— Here now! Put that thing away!"

It was the one with the young voice, who sounded as if he were in charge. Petunia didn't move.

"Now, Your Ladyship," the bandit began. "No one will get hurt if you just give me your jewels and your money."

"Correction," Petunia replied. "No one will get hurt if you crawl back to your filthy den and leave us be. If you try to take my jewels, however, you will be very, very dead."

"She means it," Maria said, and Petunia was decidedly irritated by the dismay in her maid's voice. "They can all shoot like men. A tragedy waiting to happen, I've always said."

"Who can all shoot like men?" The bandit peered into the coach to see if there was anyone else inside.

"The princesses," Maria said, before Petunia could shush her.

Petunia closed her eyes in despair, but only for a moment. She quickly refocused on the bandit, making sure that her aim was still true. She did not want the Wolves of the Westfalian Woods to know she was a princess. They would assume that she was loaded with gold and jewels, and they would not let her go until they had searched every inch of the coach.

"The princesses taught me how to shoot, when I was at court," Petunia said hastily. "Though I am only the daughter of a lowly earl."

"Only a lowly earl's daughter, is it?" the bandit snarled. "What a pity."

Petunia refused to be fazed by the bandit's sudden anger.

He was no doubt hoping for better quarry, but that was hardly her fault. She inched the pistol forward until it was almost touching his nose.

"I can hardly miss from this distance," she told him coldly. "Call off your men!"

The bandit had gray eyes, as gray as the dyed leather of his mask, which gave him a cold, wintry look. Petunia almost made a remark that wolves were supposed to have yellow eyes, but she didn't think he would find it particularly amusing. It was more something Poppy would do, anyway. She concentrated instead on her hands, which were about to start shaking from the strain of holding the pistol still for so long.

Finally the bandit stepped back. "Come now, lads, it seems that this young lady is only the daughter of a lowly earl," he called.

There were hoots of derision from the rest of the bandits.

"She can hardly have anything worth stealing, now can she?" their leader continued in his bitter, amused voice.

"Is she pretty?" asked one extremely large man, stepping into Petunia's line of sight.

She promptly transferred her aim to him.

"Not bad," countered the leader. "For an *earl's* daughter."

"Faugh!" There was the sound of spitting. "The only earl I've ever known was uglier than the backside of a donkey!"

The bandits seemed to find this the height of hilarity.

"Drive on, drive on," Petunia chanted under her breath. "Why won't you just drive on?"

None of the bandits that she could see were paying

attention to their coach anymore. Was the coachman having the vapors? Maria appeared to be doing so, but Petunia couldn't spare her much attention. Petunia released the hammer of her pistol and rapped on the roof of the coach with the butt, signaling for the driver to pick up the reins and *move*.

The coach moved. Not, however, in quite the way Petunia had in mind.

The noise of her pistol on the roof apparently scared the guard sitting on top of the coach, and he fired his rifle at one of the bandits. The bandit fired back, startling the horses. They bolted, dragging the coach behind them. There were shouts, and more shots fired, and the sudden lurching motion of the coach threw Maria off her seat and into Petunia's lap. Petunia dropped her pistol, and her knitting basket fell to the floor, the contents spilling out and entangling her and Maria in red wool.

There was a scream from the roof of the coach, and then a thud on the road as the guard fell off. Maria, still on the floor of the coach, was now praying loudly.

Petunia tried to stick her head out of the window to see what had become of the guard, but she was thrown sideways, landing on top of Maria. The horses screamed, the coachman cursed, and they came to a halt with the coach tilted so far to the right that Petunia would have fallen out the window had it not been filled with earth and grass from a roadside bank, upon which they had apparently stuck fast.

She extracted herself from Maria, braced herself against the sloping seats, and tried to get the door open. She was short, but surely not too short to reach up and just—

"Allow me, Your Highness," said the coachman, flinging open the door from the outside and making Petunia shriek in surprise. "Sorry," he said, abashed.

"It's all right," she told him, when she had taken a deep breath.

She grabbed his forearm and allowed herself to be pulled up and out of the door, to sit on the upward side of the coach. The coachman stretched back through the door to pull out Maria, who stopped having hysterics long enough to clamber out with much groaning and panting.

From her vantage point, Petunia could see exactly what had happened: the road curved sharply to the left on its way through the forest. The panicked horses, going much too fast with a heavy coach behind them, had failed to make the turn and smashed into the high bank.

The other outrider was with the horses, soothing them. Petunia could see that one horse was severely injured, and another looked to be favoring a foreleg. She looked back up the road but couldn't see any sign of the two-legged wolves or the injured man.

Petunia did not know what to do. She was not good with blood, preferring to spend her days gardening in the calm of her father's hothouses. And as the youngest, she rarely had to make any decisions, her father having very strong ideas about what his daughters could and could not do, and her eleven sisters nosing in on anything that their father didn't. The most drastic thing Petunia had done in recent memory was to have one of her oldest sister Rose's old gowns remade into this cloak.

But now what to do? She was supposed to be at the Grand Duchess Volenskaya's estate by nightfall, but the coach was broken, a man was hurt, and the horses were in no state to continue. Should she and Maria walk back to Bruch? Or should they wait for someone to find them? A shiver ran down her spine. The bandits had surely seen what had happened.

"Are there any estates close by?" she asked the coachman.

"None until we reach the grand duchess's, Your Highness," he said uneasily.

"What about an inn?"

"I'm afraid not, Your Highness."

He, too, was scanning the forest for the bandits. He climbed down from the coach and went to confer with a guard who was removing the harness of one of the horses. The men talked in low voices for a moment, and then the coachman ran back along the road to the injured man.

"Should I go and help him?" Petunia called to the guard with the horses.

"No, no, Your Highness!" The man took an anxious step toward her. "You stay right where you are!"

Uneasy, Petunia clung to the side of the coach and looked inside for her pistol. It was there at the bottom among the tangle of her knitting basket. She felt an itching between her shoulder blades and *knew* the bandits were watching her from the trees.

"Allow me, Your Highness."

One of the guards climbed inside and fetched the entire mess out, and Petunia distracted Maria from her fits by having the maid help her untangle the yarn and put everything neatly away, the pistol on top within easy reach.

"Now, just sit here and let the menfolk take care of matters," Maria chided her.

Petunia tried. But sitting still, she was confronted with a more urgent question than whether to walk on or wait for help. She tried to ignore it, but by the time the coachman had helped the half-fainting guard back to the coach, she could no longer sit still.

"If you'll excuse me," she said, sliding down off the coach.

"Princess Petunia! Where are you going?" Maria squawked.

"Into the bushes," Petunia said as casually as she could, while the coachman and the guards all opened their mouths to protest. "I'll be right back, and I'm armed," she assured them, tilting her basket to display the pistol resting atop her red wool, and then she climbed up the bank and into the underbrush before anyone could accompany her.

She did not need an audience to watch her relieve herself!

Kidnapper

Oliver sent his men back to the old hall by various routes, leaving only himself and his brother Simon to peer at the wreckage of the coach they had almost robbed. They took cover high up in one of the trees, on a platform concealed by branches and a few dead winter leaves.

"Does this happen a lot?" Simon leaned farther over the edge of the platform, and Oliver pulled him back before he fell.

"You mean, do we often cause people to crash their coaches?" Oliver couldn't keep the irritation out of his voice. "No, we don't!"

"I mean, one person points a gun at you and you back off," Simon said.

Oliver spluttered for a moment, insulted. "That crazy little girl had a pistol one inch from my right eye, Simon!"

"She was a little girl?" Simon looked like he was going to make a smart remark, but the expression on Oliver's face stopped him.

"I don't know how old she was," Oliver snapped. "But she wasn't very big, all right?"

"So was she small *young* or small *little*?" Simon pressed.

"Shush," Oliver said.

The truth was, Oliver really didn't know how old the girl was. Judging by the cut of her gown and her high-piled dark hair, she was in her late teens, but she was barely tall enough to look back at him through the high windows of the coach, and the hands holding the pistol had been just large enough to grip it. She also had the bluest eyes Oliver had ever seen, but that told him nothing.

Nor did he know why he had been so offended at her dismissing her father as being "a lowly earl." Earls often held a great deal of land and wealth and enjoyed prime places at court. There was no need for her to be insulting about it, and toward her own father.

But there'd been a flicker in her eyes when she'd said it. Perhaps she was downplaying her family's wealth and position in order to get away from him. The coach had been of good quality and so had the horses, before the crash, and she had a maid and three guards, plus the coachman. Of course, anyone traveling through the woods now had at least two guards with them, not that it stopped Oliver and his men from taking what they liked. Usually.

The combination of the pistol leveled at his eye and the girl's insistence that she was only an earl's daughter—though a friend of the royal court—had made Oliver hesitate. They

had enough for now; they didn't really need whatever the girl was hiding in her trunks. There was no harm in letting her go.

But then the horses had startled, and his men had barely had time to get out of the way of the stampede. A stray bullet had narrowly missed Simon, and then the idiot atop the coach had fallen onto the road. It rubbed Oliver's conscience raw not to help, but Oliver had to remember that he was the villain and it was not his place to assist someone he had almost robbed.

Simon, he was sure, had been hoping to see some grisly injuries, but Oliver had been praying that the girl and her maid wouldn't come to any harm. He would have stepped forward to help, then; he hadn't sunk so low as to refuse an injured woman aid.

Not yet, anyway.

"What's she doing?" Simon's voice was hushed.

"What now?"

Oliver leaned in close to his brother, peering over the edge of the platform. The girl had gotten off the coach and was saying something. Her people didn't look pleased, but she turned her back on them and went into the woods anyway.

"What is she doing?" Simon asked again. "Is she mad?"

As the girl stepped behind a large clump of juniper and flipped her heavy cloak up around her shoulders, Oliver felt the heat rise in his cheeks. He knew exactly what the girl was doing. He clapped a hand over Simon's eyes.

"Hey!"

"Shush, you," Oliver hissed.

"Get off!" Simon tried to pry off his brother's hand.

"You don't need to watch her...taking a..." He suddenly couldn't think of a polite way to say it.

Simon went still, but he started laughing, and not quietly. "Are you serious? I guess sometimes even the high and mighty have to pee in the bushes!"

"Simon, be quiet!"

Oliver had been trying not to watch, but now he checked to make sure that the girl couldn't hear them. He regretted taking Simon with them. The boy was barely fourteen and completely incapable of staying quiet for more than a pair of minutes. Oliver had started robbing coaches under the guidance of Karl and his father's other men when he was twelve, but their mother had coddled Simon.

The girl was looking around, but it wasn't stopping her from doing...what it was she needed to do. Oliver quickly looked away.

When he peeked again, she was gone. He let go of Simon's face.

"I'm not five; you don't have to cover my eyes like that," Simon griped.

Oliver couldn't see the girl anywhere. She hadn't gone back to the coach. The other guards were busy splinting the injured man's arm, but Oliver could see that the maid was watching the underbrush nervously, beginning to worry about her charge.

"Where did she go?" Simon strained the upper half of his

body over the edge of the platform. "Uh-oh," he began, and then he fell.

"Simon!"

Oliver grabbed the edge of the platform and leaned over to see where his brother had fallen. Simon had landed badly and was clutching one ankle and moaning. Standing over him, holding a pistol, was the girl. The gleaming blackness of her hair and pistol made a dramatic picture with her red cloak, Oliver noted. Then he drew his own weapon and leaped lightly down to her side.

"Give me the pistol, Your Ladyship," he said coolly, holding out his free hand.

"Why should I?"

She had courage, Oliver would give her that. Her voice didn't waver at all, and she barely flinched when he cocked his pistol in her ear.

"Because one of us is a dangerous criminal, and one of us is not," Oliver said, praying silently that she would give in. "And which do you think is more likely to shoot?"

With a sigh, the girl released the hammer of her pistol and handed it to Oliver, who stuck it in his belt. He tried not to show his relief, and heartily wished that he and Simon were still wearing their masks.

"I've faced worse than you," she announced.

"I'm sure you have," Oliver said, startled. She certainly didn't seem afraid of him, which he found flattering and insulting at the same time.

"Oliver, my ankle is broken," Simon whimpered.

"Your name is Oliver?" The princess raised her eyebrows. "Not a very wolfish name."

Oliver felt ice sliding through his gut. She had seen their faces and now she knew his name. He was holding a gun to her head, Simon was starting to cry from pain, and he could hear the voice of her coachman, who was starting to wonder where she had gone. This was not how his day was supposed to go.

"Move," he said. He pointed with the gun toward the deer path that led back to the old hall. "Now."

"I beg your pardon?"

It had clearly never occurred to her that he would abduct her. That made two of them. Three, actually: Simon had stopped crying and looked equally flabbergasted.

Oliver already regretted it, but he didn't know what else to do. Let her go? And then what? They couldn't move very fast, not if Simon's ankle really was broken. She would have ample time to summon her coachman and the uninjured guards. Oliver could not afford to be captured. Too many people were relying on him.

"Go," he snarled.

The girl went, stumbling a little over a tree root before she reached the path. When she was a few paces ahead, Oliver stooped down and grabbed Simon's elbow with his free hand, pulling his brother upright. He got Simon's arm around his shoulders, and they hobbled after the girl.

They were safely concealed by trees before the maid and the coachman started to look for their charge in earnest,

much to Oliver's relief. Oliver could hear them crashing around in the bushes behind them, but he had Simon and the girl well on their way. Once they got across the stream their tracks would be lost as well.

It was slowgoing with Simon injured and having to keep the pistol in one hand, threatening the girl. And with every step Oliver knew that he had done something terribly wrong. Robbing coaches that looked like they could spare the gold was vastly different from kidnapping. And how old *was* she? She seemed very confident, and he had to admit she was quick with her pistol, but the top of her head probably wouldn't reach to his collarbone.

"I'm going to hang," Oliver muttered under his breath.

"What?" Simon gasped. His face was gray and sweaty.

When they came to the stream, Oliver stepped down into the water so that Simon could use the bank to climb onto his brother's back. Now Oliver had both hands free, but Simon had his arms wrapped around Oliver's neck strangle-tight. Standing on the bank next to them, the girl gave Simon a concerned look.

"He doesn't look very good," she said.

"I know," Oliver snapped.

"Well, why don't you let me go so that you can find help for him faster?"

"No," Oliver said. He waved the gun at her. "Wade across. Go on."

"No, thank you," she said primly. "I don't want to get my shoes wet."

19

Oliver was about to argue with her, but she crossed the stream in one fantastic leap. On the far side, she adjusted her cloak and waited for him with arched brows as he trudged across through the water and up the other bank, panting already from Simon's weight on his back.

"That was amazing," Simon mumbled. "Not you, Oliver. Her."

"It wasn't that far," she said, dismissive. "Listen, I could still find my own way back to the road. I won't tell anyone your names."

"Don't know my name," Simon said. "It's Simon, though." He sounded like he was becoming feverish.

"It's nice to meet you, Simon," the girl said. "I'm Petunia."

"Petunia?" Oliver snorted. "Like the *flower*?"

The look she gave him made him wish he'd kept better control of his face, but really: *Petunia*? He'd thought she was going to say something simple, but pretty, like Anna or Emilia. Of course, Queen Maude and King Gregor had long ago set the fashion for flower names by giving all twelve of the princesses awful names like Campanula and Tulip.

He was starting to feel uneasy about how close her connections at court might be. If her father had the ear of the king, no matter how lowly an earl he was, Oliver was in very grave trouble. And that meant that his family and everyone under his care was in trouble as well.

"It's not much farther," Oliver grunted.

There was a birdcall, and then another, and Oliver knew that sentries had spotted them. He'd taken only a few more

paces when Karl came striding along the path. The big man gave Petunia only a cursory look before lifting Simon off Oliver's back. He pushed past Oliver and Petunia to hurry off with the injured boy.

The path twisted, and they were at the walls of the old hall. The gate was to the right, but it seemed like too much effort to Oliver, though he usually set an example by using it. Instead, he took the girl's elbow and steered her through one of the many large breaks in the wall, over the broken stones that had been purposefully left scattered about, half-covered by grass.

"Where are we?" Petunia asked. "Is this your . . . oh."

To their left was the hall, artfully propped up from the inside to preserve its derelict appearance. All around them were cooking fires and women carrying baskets of laundry or bread. The bellows were going in the smithy, and near the hall doors was a group of children reciting their lessons with a smiling teacher.

"What is this place?" Petunia's voice was hushed.

Oliver didn't answer. The less she knew, the safer his people would be . . . or was it naive to assume that they could go on living here, now that she had seen them? Part of him, however, wanted to boast, or make a sarcastic remark, welcoming her to his fine country estate.

He opened his mouth to do so, when his mother came out of the hall and headed toward them with an expression on her face that made Oliver feel all of six years old. He stepped a little behind Petunia and almost dropped his pistol trying to holster it.

His mother was brought up short when she got a good look at the girl. Her face went deadly white, and she swayed a little where she stood.

"Mother?" Oliver let go of Petunia's arm and hurried toward her.

"Maude?" His mother's voice was barely a whisper.

"No," the girl said. Her voice was quiet and her face looked strained. "I'm Petunia. But I understand that I look a great deal like my mother."

"Your mother's name is Maude?" Oliver felt like the ground had just dropped out from under his feet.

"Yes," Petunia said, throwing back her hood. "Queen Maude of Westfalin."

"Your Highness," Oliver's mother said respectfully, giving a small curtsy. "Welcome to our humble home. I am the Dowager Countess Emily Ellsworth-Saxony. I came from Breton with your mother when we were just girls." She gave Petunia a faint smile, but then her eyes hardened and she turned to Oliver.

"Now please explain what the princess is doing here, Oliver."

"She's here to visit our lowly earldom, Mother," Oliver said, and he knew with great certainty that if his mother didn't kill him, King Gregor would. His fate was sealed.

He started to laugh.

Kidnapped

Petunia promised herself that she would not panic. She would behave at all times in a manner befitting a princess. No matter how difficult it became.

At least she'd been left alone for a bit. Admittedly, it was in a room that belonged to that young man . . . who, it seemed, was an earl . . . who had kidnapped her. While the earl's mother scolded him for the kidnapping, a smiling woman in a patched but clean gown had taken Petunia into the hall to rest. As though she would curl up on a strange man's bed!

Instead she paced. The ornate bed filled most of the little room, but it still felt good to move. She had been frightened, when Oliver had first abducted her, that he was going to . . . er, ruin her, as Maria would say. She wasn't entirely sure what that meant, but she knew it was a terrible thing that was only talked about in whispers. But with his mother here, she thought she was fairly safe. Now she just had to convince them to let her go.

She checked the little watch pinned to her bodice and sighed. She should have arrived at the Volenskaya estate by now. The grand duchess would be concerned, and her grandson, the handsome Prince Grigori . . . Petunia suppressed a delicious little shiver. Prince Grigori would be beside himself with worry, she was sure. He had probably waited at the gates for her, and when she hadn't arrived . . . would he dare search for her in the darkness? He was a fearless huntsman—she was sure that he would.

She decided that she was in no real danger, now that she was under the protection of one of her mother's oldest friends. Not that she remembered Lady Emily. Maude had brought several ladies-in-waiting with her from Breton, most of whom had returned to Breton when Maude died. Petunia had been just two years old at the time. A few of the ladies had married Westfalian nobles and stayed behind, like this countess, and one had become the princesses' governess. Trapped in the bandit earl's bedchamber for the time being, Petunia had ample time to wonder just what had happened to this particular lady-in-waiting.

This hall, of a design that had not been in fashion for a good five hundred years, looked like a strong wind would blow it over from the outside, but within, the masonry was freshly repaired. The stairs to the upper gallery were only a few years old at most. The main doors were hanging askew, but from the inside she had seen that they were actually propped in place with thick beams. There was an entire village's worth of people outside, going about their business as if this was just an ordinary day. She supposed that it was, for them. But if Oliver was an earl, why was he robbing coaches as one of the notorious Wolves of the Westfalian Woods? And why were all his people hiding here in this carefully maintained squalor?

The room was a bit stuffy, so Petunia took off her cloak. She carefully smoothed its folds across the foot of the bed. Jonquil had been jealous when she'd seen it, especially after Petunia had embroidered the hood with silver bullion her godfather had given her. But the one perk of being the short-est was that Petunia never had to share her clothes. That was also how she had gotten a whole cloak out of Rose's old gown. Of course, that was also the drawback of being both the shortest and the youngest: she rarely got anything new. It was much more economical to just cut off the frayed hems of someone else's gowns.

Still, her height (or lack thereof) made her look more like her mother than any of the other girls did, and Iris griped that it had made her Father's favorite, which Petunia didn't mind at all. She was the only one of the sisters allowed to cut flowers from the special hothouses, and she was even working with her father and Reiner Orm, the head gardener, to develop a new strain of rose, which she planned on calling Maude's Sunrise. The flowers would have a blush pink center but be true yellow at the edges of their petals.

There was knock on the door.

"Enter," Petunia said, pushing at her hair to make sure all her pins were still in place.

"Hello, my dear," said the countess. Delicious smells wafted from a covered tray that she was carrying. "Are you hungry?"

"Oh, yes, thank you," Petunia said, trying to keep the eagerness out of her voice. She hoped that the countess wouldn't hear her stomach growling as her nose caught the aromas of chicken soup and fresh bread.

Petunia pulled over one of the room's two chairs and began to eat without hesitation. The countess sat in the other chair, hands neatly folded.

"I'm sure you've had quite the taxing day," the older woman said.

Petunia gave her a wry look rather than answering. The soup was excellent, and the little round loaf of bread was so fresh it steamed when she pulled it apart.

"I don't know why Oliver did what he did—" the countess began.

"Do you mean robbing my coach or abducting me?" Petunia did not bother to keep the tartness out of her voice. "The Wolves of the Westfalian Woods have been harassing travelers for several years now, growing bolder by the season. Surely this is not a fit pastime for an earl?"

"It isn't some hobby that my son has taken a fancy to," the countess replied, equally tart. "I'm afraid that we have had little choice."

"How do you not have a choice?" Petunia put down her spoon. "It's not like an earl has to steal to make his living. He should have farms to provide income, and . . ."

But the countess was shaking her head. "Do you know the name of this earldom?"

"Er. No," Petunia said after a moment's thought.

"Saxeborg-Rohlstein."

Petunia frowned. Their governess had insisted that the princesses memorize the names of all of the duchies and earldoms in Westfalin, yet Saxeborg-Rohlstein didn't sound at all familiar.

"I would be surprised if you knew it," the countess said, reading Petunia's baffled expression correctly. "It ceased to exist when you were . . . five? Six at the oldest."

"How does an earldom cease to exist?"

"We won the war with Analousia," the countess said, and now Petunia was even more confused. The countess sounded almost angry about the Westfalian victory.

The twelve-year-long war with Analousia had been one of the bloodiest episodes in Ionian history. Queen Maude had made her second pact with the King Under Stone in order to bring about the end of the war, which the sisters suspected had been engineered by the King Under Stone in order to bring Maude more securely into his power. And though the cost of the war had been awful, with great loss of life and wealth on both sides, Westfalin had prevailed in the end, which should have delighted the dowager countess.

But clearly it did not.

"When the boundary between Westfalin and Analousia was redrawn as part of the treaty," the dowager countess went

on, "my husband's earldom was cut in half, and the pieces were given away. Half stayed in Westfalin, the other half is now in Analousia." She took a piece of the bread, toying with it as she stared into the distance. "The earldom was small and almost entirely forest. And there was no one to remind Gregor that it even existed. My husband was killed in one of the final battles, when Oliver was only seven years old. We didn't even realize that the boundary had changed until some of our men were arrested for poaching in what had just become the King of Analousia's forest. I suppose he doesn't mind us living here in the old hall, as long as we don't kill any deer."

Petunia set down the cup of milk, slopping it over her hand. "We're in *Analousia*?"

"That's right," the dowager countess told her. "The highway is now the boundary of the two countries, whereas it used to be solidly in Westfalin. The estate that was my husband's seat is still in Westfalin but was given to a duke as a reward after the war. I assume that Gregor thought our entire family had been wiped out, and by the time I was able to take Oliver to Bruch to petition for its restoration, it was too late."

"I don't believe any of this," Petunia spluttered. "We *won* the war! Why would we give Analousia any of our land? And if you were really a friend of my mother's, then Father would have listened to you when you went to him for help!"

Petunia's face was burning hot, and there was a tight feeling in her chest. Her father would never take away someone's land and just give it to someone else! Preposterous!

"My dear," Lady Emily said quietly. "By the time Oliver

28

and I went to court, you and your sisters were caught up in whatever mischief it was that saw your dancing slippers worn through every night."

Petunia thought her head would burst, it felt so hot, but the dowager countess was moving on.

"We spent weeks trying to get an audience with Gregor, but he could not—or simply *would* not—see us. Then they arrested dear Anne Lewiston, your governess, on charges of witchcraft, and a friend advised me to flee before I, too, was charged. I had once been a confidant of your mother's, after all, and I was a foreigner. I brought my sons back to the forest to hide. We went to Analousia and tried petitioning King Philippe for help in regaining that part of the estate, but since my sons were Westfalian and I Bretoner, he would not listen to us either."

That was something that Petunia could believe. King Philippe's bitterness over losing the war ran deep, and she knew that her father's every message to Analousia had to be carefully worded so as to avoid the merest hint of gloating.

"The only good news," Lady Emily continued, "was that no one seemed to want this old hall. We'd taken refuge here during the war, when the fighting came too close to our estate, and here we have stayed. Eventually some of the men turned to crime to feed us. Stealing from farms, poaching deer and pheasant, surviving as best we could. We tried to send most of the people away. A few left, but many stayed to support Oliver in the only way they could." She smiled sadly. "It would have been easier if they had all gone, but we

hadn't the heart to refuse them. Karl, the large man you saw earlier, discovered that the easiest way to live was to rob the coaches that come along the highway, and then send people out with small amounts of money or jewels to various markets to purchase what we need. And you see how the old hall has been kept dilapidated? All to hide from the Analousians, though it is rare for anyone to wander into this part of the forest."

Petunia was completely aghast. She had never heard such . . . she had had no idea that there were people in her own country who lived this way! Well, in what had been her own country. She felt vaguely uneasy about having crossed into Analousia without knowing it. Shouldn't there have been some sort of fence or gate? Something guarded by soldiers?

"But I still don't understand why part of Westfalin is in Analousia now," Petunia said after a moment, though really that was the least of her questions.

"Because Gregor took a large portion of the Analousian plains to the north of here," the dowager countess explained, ever patient. "The vineyards there are unparalleled; even after the battles that were fought in them. As a small concession to Philippe, Gregor gave him this little piece of forest, which straightens the border between our two lands and makes the road easier to access for the Analousians."

Petunia's head was spinning. "Oh" was all she could say. She thought about asking why Oliver and his mother didn't go back to court and demand his rights as an earl now that he

was grown and the mystery of the worn-out dancing slippers had been solved (not that the reason behind it had been made public). But she knew how easy it was to get used to things, and how much simpler it was to just continue doing them the way they had always been done. After all, she had danced nearly every night of her life from the time she could walk until she was almost seven years old. And she had liked it, even though she and her sisters were under a curse, because it was all she had ever known.

And when she was eleven and her father sent her halfway around the world to Russaka as some sort of genteel hostage, she hadn't said a word, either. She had simply gone and smiled and pretended to understand what all the Russakan ladies were saying when they chucked her chin and patted her head as though she were a small dog. It was just too easy to do what you were accustomed to doing.

Not to mention the guilt she felt, knowing that it was at least partially her fault that Lady Emily hadn't been able to get an audience with King Gregor in the first place. If she and her sisters had found some way to fight back earlier, to defeat the King Under Stone before the rumors of witchcraft and murder, then the kingdom wouldn't have been in such a shambles after the war.

"Every year it grows harder and harder to stop," the dowager countess said softly, once again interpreting Petunia's thoughts. "We talk about it all the time. Or at least, I talk, and Oliver pretends to listen. I try to convince him to go to King Gregor and beg for clemency. But he could be

hanged a hundred times over, earl or no earl, for what he has done."

"If you let me go, I promise to talk to my father for you," Petunia said, attempting to soothe the older woman. "I'm sure once he hears your reasons it . . ."

But Lady Emily was shaking her head. "Please don't, Your Highness. It will only make matters worse if he hears it from you, after Oliver kidnapped you! No, I've told my son that this is the catalyst; he must come clean now. It would help if you would put in a good word for us when the time is right, but this is something that Oliver should do himself. After he delivers you safely home. Or wherever it was you were going," she added.

"Best go there first, yes," Petunia agreed. "The grand duchess must be frantic by now."

"The grand duchess?" The dowager countess's eyes widened. "The Grand Duchess Volenskaya? The Duke of Hrothenborg's widow?"

"Yes, do you know her too?" Petunia had been wondering if she should ask the dowager countess more about her mother. Petunia barely remembered her mother and knew her mostly through the beautiful gardens that her father had made for his bride.

"By reputation only," the dowager countess said. "But why, may I ask, are you traveling to her estate? Alone?"

"I met the grand duchess in Russaka a few years ago," Petunia said. "Now that she is in residence in her Westfalian estate, she asked for me to visit."

"I see," the dowager countess said, her voice chill.

Petunia didn't know what to do. The look on the older woman's face was frightening her. Still, if the dowager countess had been a friend of her mother's, and she was so kind to Petunia now, surely it would not hurt to ask.

"My lady? Why don't you like the grand duchess?"

"I don't know her one way or the other, so cannot like or dislike her," said Lady Emily stiffly. Then she softened a little. "It . . . simply . . . makes me nervous to see someone as young as you traveling alone."

Petunia was almost certain that that wasn't what the countess had been thinking.

Guide

Oliver was sitting on the cracked floor of the little chapel when his mother found him.

He often took refuge there. It was barely larger than an outhouse, having been built some seven centuries before to appease the handful of his ancestors' court who had converted to what must have seemed to be an odd and fleeting new religion, with its single god and its stiffly worded prayers. When the Church had taken a firmer hold on Westfalin, a larger chapel had been built behind the old hall, and the little cubby with its rough altar had been abandoned.

Oliver still liked it, though. It was made of thick stones left over from the outer wall and was very quiet.

"Oliver? Are you in there?"

Oliver hadn't bothered with a candle, so his mother couldn't see him sitting cross-legged within, his back to the altar. He sighed heavily in answer, and she came in, blocking the feeble morning light so that Oliver couldn't see her either.

"Did you spend the entire night here?"

He couldn't tell from her voice if she was still angry with him, but he assumed that she was. He was still angry with himself.

"No, I slept in Simon's room," he said. "But I woke up before dawn and I didn't want to bother him."

Simon's ankle was broken. By the time Karl had gotten Simon into bed and Karl's wife, Ilsa, had come to look at the injury, the boy's ankle was three times its normal size and livid with bruises. Ilsa had given him tincture of poppies to help with the pain before setting it, and he was sleeping like the dead still.

His little brother's injury was on top of botching the robbery, causing the royal coach to crash, and kidnapping the youngest princess. Not Oliver's finest hour.

If he were more religious, and if the little chapel was still a dedicated place for service, Oliver would have spent the entire night praying. But Oliver was sure that for his many crimes, God had long ago stopped listening to his prayers.

"Simon will be fine," Lady Emily said softly.

"He should never have been with us," Oliver replied. "I know you hated it. And now you have the perfect excuse to keep him here."

"Which he will hate," his mother said.

"I don't care if he hates it," Oliver said roughly. "When he's healed, we'll have to find some other excuse to keep him from coming. He was terrible at it, anyway. Maybe I should just tell him the truth. He can't shoot worth a damn, and he

won't keep his mouth shut." Oliver felt lower than ever, saying such things about his own brother, but they needed to be said. It was a savage feeling, like pressing a wound to feel the pain.

"Oliver, stop it," his mother chided. "When Simon is recovered, I am going to have Herr Ohmsford train him to be the next steward. Poor Herr Ohmsford is getting on in years, and I don't think he's keeping careful enough accounts of what you bring in and how it's distributed. I want to make sure everyone has enough, but just enough. There is no sense in getting yourself killed over gold we don't need."

"That would help," Oliver admitted.

He had been trying to do the accounts himself of late, but he never seemed to have enough time. And Simon was excellent with sums and very meticulous for someone his age. He'd long ago finished his schooling, having far outstripped the tutelage of Fraulein Ohmsford, the old steward's daughter, who was the nearest thing they had to a schoolteacher.

"At least one of us will be spared a life of villainy," Oliver said, and was surprised by the bitterness in his own voice.

"I'm sorry," his mother said. "I should have fought harder for you, but I didn't know how, and I . . . I was afraid. I was afraid that they would take you and Simon away from me, or that we would be driven out of even this poor shelter. I didn't know what to do then, and every day I see our chance to make things right slipping away."

"Don't blame yourself," Oliver said. He got to his feet,

lurching against the altar as he tried to maneuver in the tiny space. "You did the best you could."

"Did I?" She sounded more thoughtful than self-recriminating. "Perhaps. It will be for future generations to judge."

Oliver felt rather at sea. He wasn't entirely certain that Lady Emily was even talking to him, at this point. "It will be all right. . . ."

"Did you hear that poor child crying in the night?"

Oliver felt a fresh stab of guilt. "The princess? She was crying?" She hadn't seemed that frightened. . .

"Some terrible nightmare, I think," his mother said. "She was calling out strange names, arguing with them, I don't know what all. I tried to go to her, but she had barred the door from within."

Oliver shook his head, not sure what to make of this. "Do you think she and her sisters really are witches?"

"No," his mother said earnestly, not laughing off the idea the way he'd half hoped. "No, I don't think so. But something unnatural happened after the war. And Maude . . . poor Maude! She was prone to strange fancies. That's why I'm so surprised at where our little Petunia is headed."

"What do you mean?"

"She has no desire to bring you to justice, and she doesn't want to go home to Bruch," Lady Emily said. "She wants to continue on, to the estate of the Grand Duchess Volenskaya, the Duke of Hrothenborg's widow."

Oliver felt his mouth go dry, and a surge of emotions rose in his breast. He had escaped hanging for another day. The estate was closer than Bruch, which made his job of escorting the princess much easier, but . . .

"That's *our* estate," Oliver said, his voice coming out strangled. "Our home."

"It should be, yes," Lady Emily conceded. "In happier times, it was. But that's not the strange part: do you realize who the grand duchess is?"

"A reclusive old lady whose husband stole my estate?"

Oliver was surprised at how angry he felt. Maybe it was the way the princess had lied about being the daughter of an earl, as though earls had nothing to steal. Maybe it was the way she had looked at him when he'd seen her just before going to bed last night, staring at him so intently, like he was some rare animal in a menagerie. He'd known then that his mother had told her their history, and the princess would forever think of him as the earl without even enough land to keep a herd of sheep.

"Oliver," his mother said, a warning in her voice to shake him out of his self-pity. "The grand duchess is one of the Nine Daughters of Russaka! You know the story: about how they were placed in a tower by their father, because they were so beautiful and he wanted to discourage unworthy suitors?"

Oliver looked at his mother, incredulous. "That old fairy tale? About the nine sisters having nine sons by a sorcerer

who stole their babies away that same night?" He snorted. "I saw the puppet show once in a marketplace."

"Scoff if you will," his mother said, "but Queen Maude believed there was truth in that story. She spoke of it often.

"And something strange *did* happen in Russaka years ago," she went on. "I remember hearing reports of it—real reports, from the Russakan court, not just fairy stories!—when I was a girl. The Russakan emperor tore down the tower and all nine sisters married within the year. The grand duchess's husband wasn't even a duke at the time, but an earl like your father. The emperor gave him the title of grand duke as a wedding gift, and it was for valor during the Analousian war that he was elevated here—"

"And given my estate?"

"Yes," his mother said with a sigh. "The grand duke died shortly after that. But do you not find it odd that Princess Petunia, after having had the childhood she has had, is being sent to this woman's house? Alone? The grand duchess's life is shadowed by rumors of strange and violent magic. Surely Gregor would be more cautious!"

"Would he?" Oliver shook his head. "Didn't he farm the princesses out to any court who would take them? He might as well have offered to marry them to anyone who volunteered, just like the Russakan emperor!" Oliver had actually felt rather bad for the princesses when the news had come of the royal heir exchange a few years ago. To be traded around like an unlucky card at Devil's Corner must have been truly humiliating. "He was probably just angry that they didn't all come home betrothed, and now he's trying again."

"Now, Oliver, there is no need to be disrespectful! Gregor is your king, after all."

"We're on Analousian soil right now," he reminded his mother. "And I never swore fealty to him. He was too busy to bother with me, remember?"

"Oliver," said Lady Emily firmly. "I am sorry that this is your life. But we must make the best of it that we can. Petunia wants to go to the grand duchess's estate—" She held up one hand to stop him before he could correct her. "It *is* her estate, Oliver, no matter how it galls us. And you must take her there. But I want you to be careful. Not just to avoid capture, but I would also like you to be . . . sensitive to anything that seems untoward."

Oliver gave his mother a baffled look.

"If it seems like the princess is not safe there, I want you to bring her back," Lady Emily clarified.

"You want me to kidnap her all over again?"

Lady Emily gave a sigh of great suffering. "I want you to ask her to come with you," she explained. "Insist, in fact."

"What if insisting doesn't work?" Oliver was not about to throw Princess Petunia over one shoulder and run off with her into the forest. Not that it would be all that hard, she wasn't very big, but it was the principle of the thing.

"Just do your best, please," his mother said.

"All right," Oliver agreed, though he still felt like the conversation was slightly beyond his grasp.

He wasn't sure how he felt about his mother's believing in fairy tales, and that one of the Nine Daughters of Russaka was currently living on his estate. According to the stories, each of the Nine Daughters of Russaka had been visited in the night by the King Under Stone, had borne him a son, and then wept bitter tears when he took the children away to his invisible kingdom. What on earth would lead his mother to believe that one of the Nine Daughters would take up residence in the middle of the Westfalian Woods?

And how did his mother expect him to know if the princess was in trouble? He wasn't going to go into the manor house with her. He was going to leave her at the gates . . . just within sight of the gates, actually, and then run for it. It was his very fervent hope that he would never have to see Princess Petunia again, despite her thick, dark curls and blue, blue eyes. It could only lead to discovery or death for him, and either would be a disaster for his people.

But his mother seemed satisfied that he was going to look after the princess and so she left the little chapel after giving him a warm smile. Oliver wondered why she even cared. Being friends with the late Queen Maude hadn't helped their family one whit. Still, he gathered himself mentally and went out into the weak winter sunshine to find the princess and take her to the estate that should have been his home.

Guided

Looking at Oliver sidelong as they trudged through the woods, Petunia wondered if he was staring at her more than usual today. Was it because of her nightmares? Had he heard her? He was definitely watching her, but was that only so she wouldn't run away? They had been walking for an hour now, and Petunia could not have been more lost. The sun, which had been shining bravely through the trees as they set off, was now hiding behind gray clouds that threatened snow. Petunia pulled her cloak closer around her, but it caught on the basket and nearly made her stumble.

"All right, there?" Oliver tried to take hold of her arm, but she shook him off. "I'm just trying to help." He held up his hands in a placating gesture.

"I'm fine," Petunia said, not caring that she didn't sound fine, or very gracious, either.

"At least if it snows, no one can lose you," Oliver said, in what Petunia assumed was an attempt at humor. He indicated her red cloak.

She didn't bother to reply.

Petunia could not wait for her humiliation to end. If Poppy ever found out about this, she would never let Petunia live it down. First she had been kidnapped while relieving herself—or nearly so—despite having her pistol at hand, and then she had embarrassed herself further by raving in her sleep all night. She was sure that everyone in that crumbling old hall had heard her—how could they not? The walls were riddled with holes!

In the first few years after they had defeated the King Under Stone, Petunia had suffered only the occasional nightmare. And most of the time, these nightmares were about perfectly mundane things, like tripping and chipping her front teeth or finding a spider in her shoes. So when the dreams about the Kingdom Under Stone had started to come more regularly, she thought that it was just memories combining with other fears. But by last year they had become a nightly event and not just for Petunia, but for all twelve sisters.

Jonquil suffered the most. She had to take a potion that their oldest brother-in-law, Galen, prepared for her every night, otherwise she was too frightened to even close her eyes. Although the potion was supposed to bring dreamless sleep, she still woke more often than not, screaming and drenched in sweat. Always willowy, Jonquil was becoming gaunt, picking at her food and not paying half as much attention to her appearance as she once had, which worried them all.

Petunia heartlessly wished that Jonquil had been the one who had been kidnapped. *She* wouldn't have slept at all. Petunia had awakened herself shouting abuse at Kestilan, the youngest son of the King Under Stone, who came to her every night and told her that she belonged to him, and only him, forever. She was fairly certain that some of the words she used were of the sort that princesses weren't even supposed to know, let alone shout in their sleep. At least Oliver wouldn't be speaking to anyone who knew her, like the grand duchess, and couldn't carry tales about her behavior.

"If you would just tell me how to get to the grand duchess's estate," Petunia said after a long period in which their feet crunching the cold, dead leaves was the only sound, "I can get there by myself."

"I wish I believed that," Oliver began.

"Excuse me?" Petunia bristled. "I think I am perfectly capable of finding a large estate that is only a stone's throw from the main road, thank you!"

She hated being condescended to. Her older sisters still treated her like a child because she was the youngest, and her father was little better. In his eyes, she was perpetually six and needed to be led by the hand all the time. Yet he trusted her to work in his hothouses. Perhaps he didn't think flowers required much maturity, just intuition. Reiner Orm, the gardener, certainly didn't think that she belonged there, now or ever. But then, Herr Orm would never forgive her for once using a rosebush as kindling for a campfire nearly eight years before.

"I'm sorry," Oliver said, surprised at her reaction. "I didn't mean anything like that. I just meant that it's easy to get lost in the forest. We're cutting straight across the thickest part, using the deer paths. We won't reach the road until we're nearly there, and then you can go it alone if you like. But there's wolves in the forest—"

"I'm well aware of that," Petunia said. He had his gray leather wolf mask dangling from the hood of the cloak he wore over his more practical coat, in case he needed to disguise himself, she supposed.

"I meant real wolves," he said, his cheeks red. He brandished the rifle he was carrying.

Petunia didn't answer that, either. He was right, though. When her father had first heard the reports about the wolves in the woods a few years ago, he had sent out hunters to find them, assuming that the first garbled report of a coach being attacked had meant that four-legged wolves were growing bolder with the coming winter. The clarification that it was men in wolf masks attacking the coaches had meant only that a different kind of hunter was sent out. Their lack of success, Petunia realized, was probably in part due to Oliver and his men making their home in what was now Analousia.

She supposed she should be grateful that he was willing to guard her all the way to the grand duchess's. He could have

45

simply turned her loose in the forest to make her own way. But she was too tired to be grateful, or gracious, and merely trudged alongside him.

She didn't remember being tired all the time as a child, though her sisters spoke with horror of the long days and even longer nights that they had endured at the Midnight Balls. Petunia did remember being sick toward the end, so sick that it hurt to move, but having to dance with Kestilan all the same. Jonquil, in particular, grew hysterical at any mention of the balls, and she, Hyacinth, and Iris still refused to dance no matter the occasion.

Petunia, however, had been delighted when Poppy had come home from Breton three years before with a renewed fondness for dancing. Petunia had missed dancing, and she had been hopeful that her time at the Russakan court would allow her plenty of opportunities to do so. But the letter of introduction that her father had sent with her to the Emperor of Russaka had excused her from dancing, saying that she was incapable of such strenuous activity.

She knew that her father had meant well, had been trying to save her from something that he assumed she held in disgust, but it had made Petunia's stay in Russaka dreadfully awkward. Not only was she forced to spend every ball sitting with the chaperones, but the letter gave the impression that she was an invalid. The Russakan people were very vigorous, enjoying all sorts of outdoor events as well as dances and parlor games that involved running through the sprawling Imperial palace, hiding in wardrobes and under beds.

Petunia, just twelve at the time and only allowed to put her hair up and wear ball gowns because she was on a "state visit," had been anxious to join in, but it was not to be. Instead she sat beside great ladies like the Grand Duchess Volenskaya and judged the games, trying to smile bravely as she handed out boxes of sweets or bottles of scent to other girls who had ridden their ponies over elaborate steeplechase courses or hidden longer than any other guest or danced particularly well.

Her hero had been the grand duchess's grandson, Prince Grigori. Though older than she, he had gone out of his way to make Petunia feel welcome, sitting beside her through many of the games and dances so that she wasn't lonely, with all the chaperones' talk of "grandchildren and poor health" as he had put it. He also spoke impeccable Westfalian, thanks to his Westfalian grandfather, and was able to teach her a great deal of Russakan during her year at the court.

Which led to her being here, in the middle of the forest with a cold nose and dead leaves catching at the hem of her beautiful new cloak. When the grand duchess had invited Petunia to keep her company at her Westfalian estate, she had mentioned specifically that her favorite grandson would be there.

"I must have all my favorites about me," the elderly lady's letter had said. "And that includes my most dashing grandson as well as my most beautiful flower princess."

"We're almost there," Oliver said.

Once again Petunia was so startled that she tripped and

would have fallen if Oliver hadn't caught her around the waist and pulled her upright.

"You must have been far away," he said, laughing. He was so close that his breath stirred her hair.

"I'm right here," she said, shrugging him off.

"I meant in your head," he said.

Petunia straightened her cloak with as much dignity as she could manage. "I suppose I was," she conceded. "Not that *your* conversation isn't riveting."

She was pleased to see him turn red again, but then she felt ashamed. It was the kind of comment that Jonquil could carry off but Petunia never could. Jonquil would say such things to her suitors, and they would fall over themselves trying to please her. Oliver just looked hurt.

"I'm sorry," she said. "Did you say that we're almost there?"

"Yes. The road is just through those trees. Once we reach it, we'll only be a few minutes from the estate."

"Oh," she said, hardly showing a sparkling wit herself.

They walked in silence until they were standing atop a low bank that looked down on the road. Petunia hopped down the bank, glad for the hard-packed dirt of the road to walk on. Struggling over hidden rocks and tree roots had mostly ruined her low boots, which were for riding in a comfortable coach and not foot travel.

"It's to the right," Oliver instructed, sliding down the bank to stand beside her on the road. He started to lead the way.

"Is it far?" She did a little skip to catch up to his longer legs.

"Not far," he said. He pointed at the other side of the road, which was just as dark with forest. "If you go just past the first line of trees, there's a wall that surrounds the estate's grounds."

"Really?" Petunia peered through the thick trunks but couldn't make out a wall.

"It's made of a brownish gray stone," Oliver said. "It's fairly hard to see from here."

"Are the grounds quite large?"

"Very," Oliver said, and his voice was strained.

Petunia gave him a quick look. She was hit, suddenly, with how hard this must be for him. He had been disinherited through no fault of his own; he had lived most of his life in the forest, responsible for the survival of dozens of people; and now, because of her, he had to see his old home again, the home that had been given to someone else.

"If it's only a few minutes walk, I can go alone," Petunia said. She gave him a quick smile. "I'm not trying to be rude, but won't it be better for you if you're not seen? I can tell them that I got lost and made my own way here."

"That *would* be better," Oliver admitted. "But are you sure that you can find the way?"

She raised one eyebrow.

"Yes, all right," he said with a laugh. "I'm sure that you're capable of following a road! Well then, just follow it around this bend; the wall comes right up alongside the road. The gates are perhaps a mile along, you can't miss them." He swept a low bow. "And so, princess, this lowly earl will bid you farewell!"

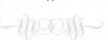

Petunia felt another stab of pity for Oliver, and guilt over her own behavior. She gave him a proper curtsy, as befit an earl.

"Thank you for all your help," she told him.

"The pleasure, I assure you, was mine," he said, and bowed again. This time Petunia couldn't detect any irony in the gesture.

"Please give my best to your mother," she said. "And convey my wishes for a speedy recovery to your brother." She gave him a small smile, and then turned, feeling self-conscious, and continued on up the road.

After a moment, she looked over her shoulder, pretending to fuss with the way her basket hung over her elbow. Oliver was gone, and the road was empty.

Hidden

Oliver faded back into the forest, putting on his mask out of habit. He kept to the side opposite the estate wall, staring at Petunia. If the princess couldn't find the gates to the estate from that point, she really was more helpless than a babe, but still he watched. Oliver knew that if he didn't report back to his mother that he had seen her safely through the gates, he would never be forgiven.

Besides which, his mother wasn't the only person who wanted to make sure she was safe.

He could feel the knot of tension between his shoulder blades beginning to unravel. She was almost there. Now he could relax and just go back to the old hall and be what he was: a disgraced earl with nothing more pressing on his mind than whether to rob the very next traveler on the main road or wait a few days.

Oliver sidled through the trees. There was a crash and a roar of sound from the direction of the still-hidden gates. Oliver saw Petunia freeze in the middle of the road, her right hand reaching into her basket for her pistol. Why didn't she move? Oliver knew exactly what that sound was, but she just stood there with her head cocked in curiosity.

Oliver didn't hesitate for another second. He ran for the princess. She still hadn't moved when he reached her, dragging her to the opposite side of the road. They tripped over each other's feet and fell against the leaf-strewn bank. She screamed, but Oliver wasn't sure if it was because of him or because of the pack of hunters who were bearing down on them. Had he not hauled her out of the way, the superb black stallion at the front would have run her down.

"Out of the way," the black horse's rider shouted, brandishing his whip. It snapped out and nearly struck Oliver's cheek, which was fortunately still covered by his mask.

"Watch yourself!" Oliver shouted back.

Oliver could feel Petunia trembling with shock. He scrambled to his feet and helped her up. Her cloak was covered with leaf mold, and the hood had fallen back to show all her masses of curls. Her eyes were extremely wide, and her face was very white. Oliver could see that she realized now just how close she had come to dying under the hooves of that horse.

Knowing that the sight of his wolf mask was only adding to her fright, Oliver reached up to unfasten it, but Petunia put out a hand to stop him. She darted a look over her shoulder at the rider, who was now bringing the black horse around, whip still raised.

"Gypsies, are you? Stay out of the road," the rider said in faintly accented Westfalian. He was very tall and had dark hair beneath a black hat. Petunia was staring up at him.

"Run," she said, her voice soft.

"What?" Oliver leaned in closer.

Petunia turned and pushed his chest, nearly sending him onto his rump with surprise. "Run!"

"You there!" The rider was standing in his stirrups, his whip coming down to point at Oliver. "Why are you wearing that mask?"

"Your Highness," called out one of the other men. "It's the princess! The Wolves have kidnapped the princess!"

"Run, you fool," snapped Petunia, and then she lunged forward and caught the black horse's reins just as its rider spurred it toward Oliver.

Oliver didn't want to run, but he was no fool, regardless of what Petunia thought. He spun and ran through the forest as though all the hounds of hell were after him. Which, to a certain extent, they were.

"Prince Grigori," Petunia called out. "Stop!"

Oliver felt sick. This was Prince Grigori, the beloved grandson of the Grand Duchess Volenskaya? He and his black horse were no strangers to Oliver, though he had never known the man's name. This man was the leader of the hunters who had been tracking Oliver and his men for months, hounding them at every turn.

If the Russakan prince was hunting for human wolves in Westfalin, then Oliver had no doubt that Grigori had the

blessing of King Gregor and probably King Phillippe of Analousia as well. Oliver and his men crossed the border with impunity and had robbed travelers from many lands. But even knowing his own crimes, Oliver had hoped that the men hunting them were vigilantes who had simply lost a purse or two to the bandits. That way Oliver had no qualms about evading them or taking stronger action if the hunters came too close to the old hall. But if they had royal support, any retaliation would be treason as well as murder.

Oliver was on the wrong side of the road now, with the wall of the estate preventing him from fading into the forest, and the hunters were almost outpacing him. He would have to take to the trees or go over the wall and hide on the grounds for a time.

When he thought the trees were thick enough to conceal him, he stopped and listened until he heard the horses go past. Oliver located a sturdy elm that had branches that hung over the wall of the estate and swung himself up. He sat in the crook of one of the larger branches and listened some more, pushing back his hood so that he could hear better. They were definitely on foot now; the underbrush was too thick for a mounted search.

Oliver leaned along the branch as far as he could, looking through the dry, rattling leaves that still clung to the winter branches. There was no snow on the yellowed lawns of the estate, and the bareness of the bushes and trees provided little concealment. It had been a terrible winter: bitter cold yet with little snow.

Still, if he made a break back through the trees he would have to cross the road at some point, and he felt certain that Grigori would catch him. So instead Oliver quickly shed his mask and cloak and bundled it into another crook of the tree's branches. It looked rather like a large, mossy nest. Then he slithered out to the end of the branch, which bent under his weight and dropped him down on the grounds of the estate, hidden from Grigori and his men by the high wall.

Straightening his leather jerkin, he did his best to look like a gardener off on some serious task, and strode along one of the winding gravel paths where he had played as a small child. If memory served, there were several outbuildings on the grounds. One of them was bound to be empty, and he could hide for a time before slipping back over the fence and on his way.

He came around a large juniper bush and nearly bumped into two men with a wheelbarrow full of dead branches. Oliver froze for a moment, but the men just nodded and continued on. Oliver managed to fight down the urge to flee, and nodded back. As he passed them, forcing himself to walk with purpose, he heard one of the men say, "Another new one. I wonder which of us got the ax this time."

To Oliver's immense relief, another turn of the path brought him to the hothouses. In his childhood the last one in the row had been a treasure trove of old potting tables and other discarded paraphernalia. Peering through the old, dingy glass he saw that it was not being put to any better use now. He unlatched the door and hurried inside.

Nothing had changed. Oliver could have navigated the rickety tables and cracked urns with his eyes closed. The floor at the front was remarkably clean, but that was the only improvement. He found the old bench just where he had left it. It was stone, badly chipped, and covered in a thick layer of old burlap sacks. Oliver shoved them to the floor, coughing at the resulting cloud of dust, and settled himself on the bench. He braced his feet on the edge of one of the tables and tried to rest. It would be far easier to leave in the dark. The hunters were rarely out then, afraid of running into four-legged wolves or having a horse put a foot wrong.

It was late afternoon, and the sky was already beginning to darken, so he knew he wouldn't have long to wait. But as the purple-gray twilight took over the weak winter day, Oliver fell asleep.

∽

When he awoke it was completely dark. The darkness was strange and thick, and Oliver thought he heard someone whispering. He sat up very slowly and peered into the blackness. The door opened, and Oliver made himself as still as possible. Every urn in the hothouse rattled, as though there was an earthquake, but Oliver felt nothing. There was a howl of laughter and the hothouse door slammed shut, leaving Oliver feeling distinctly alone. But if he was alone now, what had been in the hothouse with him a moment before?

Cursing, he stumbled through the darkness. Once he reached the door, he slipped through, pausing only for a moment to listen for someone outside. Shadows seemed to wind through the hedges, shadows that had nothing to do with the moonlight and the pattern of darkness cast by the trees and shrubs. Oliver followed in the wake of the weird shadows, across the lawns, to the great estate house itself.

It was very late, and all the windows were dark. Oliver found himself praying silently that someone would light a lamp or a candle, even if the light exposed him. What were those things crawling across the lawn? With a mounting sense of horror, he saw the dark shapes reach the house.

With a terrible laugh, the shadow creatures pulled themselves up the wall to a window on the second floor that was open despite the cold. Oliver hid behind a fountain. The room they had just entered had been his childhood bedroom. Whose was it now? He prayed again, this time that the room had not been given to Petunia.

His question was answered a few moments later when a young woman's voice cried out, the sound carrying clearly through the open window. She screamed out denials, she screamed out insults, and over and over again she reviled someone called "Kestilan."

"Oh, ye gods, Petunia," Oliver whispered from his concealment. "What is all this?"

Oliver didn't know what to do. There were . . . things crawling up the wall of the manor house. He was armed, but what would he be shooting at? Shadows moving on the wall? And what if he fired through the window and hit Petunia?

Something rushed by him, cackling, and Oliver swung at

it. His arm went cold where it passed through the shadow, but there was nothing of substance to meet his fist. The attempted punch did not go unnoticed, however, and the shadow creature turned and hovered in front of Oliver.

"Stay away from her," Oliver said, trying to sound dangerous and not terrified.

Another cackling laugh. The shadow reached out and put its hand into Oliver's chest. A sheath of ice instantly covered his heart, and then the shadow squeezed. Oliver gasped as intense pain flared in his chest, streaking through his entire body. He tried to step back but found that he couldn't move so much as an eyelid.

"She is not for you," the shadow said in a low, harsh voice. "She is for *us*. All of them are for us."

"No," Oliver gasped out.

"Yes," the shadow snarled.

Then it pulled its hand back. Oliver fell to his knees, choking for air.

"What are you?"

But the shadow was gone.

Oliver struggled back to his feet, clutching his chest in one hand. He looked around, but he was alone in the garden now. Through Petunia's window he could still hear faint cries.

No one in the house seemed to have been roused at all. How was it possible that these creatures could have attacked the house and he was the only witness? Hadn't even her maid heard her screaming and come to see if she was all right?

Oliver crept closer to the house, stopping behind a large

azalea. Squinting at the darkness of her window, he saw a figure in white. It was Petunia. She pushed the curtains aside and stood there for a few heartbeats, then closed them with a jerk.

"There," Oliver muttered to himself. "She's fine. Whatever those things were, they're gone. And there's nothing I can do to help her, anyway."

But that was a lie, and Oliver knew it. He had to help her, somehow. Something or someone had set out to harm Petunia. Someone far more wicked than himself, with his coach robbing and his botched abduction of the princess.

And yet, what could he do to help? The first step would be getting out of the garden and back to the old hall. His mother might know more and be able to help him decide what to do from there. But in the back of his head, Oliver was already entertaining a terrible thought.

It was time for him to go to Bruch. And King Gregor.

Guest

Dearest Papa,

I have arrived safe and sound at the grand duchess's manor. Did you know that the estate used to be the seat of an earldom? There appears to be hard feelings among the local folk over this incident, and I wondered if you were aware.

Petunia stopped and looked over the beginning of her letter. Should she start out that bluntly? Perhaps she should wait and add a little postscript about the earldom. Jumping in like that was something Poppy would do, but Petunia was normally more circumspect.

She left the lines there anyway.

As you have no doubt heard, I disappeared shortly after the coach was smashed. I can assure you that I am quite safe. I wandered too far into the woods and got lost. A kindly woodcutter and his family took me in for the night, and then delivered me to the

*gates of the estate today. The grand duchess, dear soul, was quite
beside herself, thinking that I had come to harm. I was quick to
reassure her, and all is well here. How do you and my sisters get on?*

With love, your daughter,
Petunia

There. She had wanted to write her father yesterday when
she'd first arrived at the estate, but her arrival at the estate
had been so inauspicious that it had taken the whole day to
get settled.

And then the nightmares had been so real and so terrible
that she had woken up at the open window, screaming into
the night. She had dreamed that there were shadowy figures in the garden calling her name, and even now she wasn't
sure that it had been a dream. She could remember the last
time that Kestilan and his brothers had ventured out of
the Kingdom Under Stone, taking on shadowy forms in the
night. Petunia had studied the gardens carefully from her
window, but she had seen only moonlight on the winter-
dead lawns.

Petunia had slept late and then found herself being fluttered about by maids attempting to find clothes for her from
the wardrobes at the estate. Her own trunks had gone back to
Bruch with the damaged coach, and so gowns left behind by
the grand duchess's granddaughters were brought in and tried
on Petunia. Before she knew it, it was time to bathe for her
first formal dinner with the grand duchess, and she still
hadn't written to her father. After she had done so, leaving

the remarks about Oliver's earldom as they were, she decided to write her brother-in-law Galen in the morning.

She wondered what Galen would think of Oliver's situation. Galen was nothing if not practical, and he had a keen understanding of politics, having seen it from both sides. Born a commoner and having served as a foot soldier in the war, he gave King Gregor unique advice, but it was always "worth its weight in gold" as her father was quick to tell anyone who doubted.

But for now Petunia stretched and cast an eye over her shoulder. There was rustling from her dressing room, where a maid was preparing a bath for her. Tonight she would be having dinner with the grand duchess and Prince Grigori, and she was surprised at how nervous she felt. It was not just because of Prince Grigori, though the prince was even more handsome than she remembered. Petunia had forgotten how imposing the grand duchess was. That lady, still beautiful despite her years, was more regal than many a queen, and Petunia found herself quite tongue-tied by the duchess's gracious ways.

"Are you ready, Your Highness?" The maid, Olga, popped out of the dressing room, startling Petunia.

"What? Oh, yes." Petunia folded up her letter and put it in an envelope, hastily pressing her seal to the wax and smearing it badly. She sighed as she handed it to the maid. "Please send this immediately."

"Of course, Your Highness." Olga took the letter and scurried out.

Petunia struggled out of her gown. Her own maid, Maria, had apparently insisted on walking back toward Bruch with the coachman to get help.

One of Petunia's guards had gone to the grand duchess to tell her what had happened, but the others had headed back to Bruch with the limping horses and ruined coach. The grand duchess had sent out servants to search when Petunia did not arrive on schedule, and it was a miracle, Petunia thought, that she and Oliver had not run into them. But then, Oliver was very good at eluding people in the forest.

Petunia was down to her petticoats and stockings when Olga came back. The maid simply walked into the room, nearly causing Petunia to fall over as she rolled down one of her stockings. At the palace in Bruch, maids always knocked, but Olga seemed to think nothing of flitting in and out without a sound. Petunia had been startled by her at least three times since she had arrived, and for a moment she contemplated making the girl wear a bell.

"Oh, Your Highness! Allow me!" Olga scurried over and started to roll down Petunia's stockings.

This was the sort of thing that Petunia had always done herself, and she knew she was blushing. Olga set her stockings aside and unfastened Petunia's petticoats, then her corset. She was reaching for the hem of Petunia's camisole when Petunia caught Olga's hands.

"Thank you, I'll take care of that," Petunia said firmly.

"But, Your Highness—" Olga began, and Petunia interrupted her.

"I prefer to do this myself. Also, I bathe alone," she said. "There are towels and soap laid out?"

Olga nodded, looking distressed.

"Thank you. I'll ring when I need you to help me dress," Petunia said, though she privately resolved to see how far she could get without any assistance. There was something so annoyingly obsequious about Olga. "I will be fine," Petunia assured her.

Once the door closed behind Olga, Petunia fled to the bath. She was convinced that the maid would come creeping back without being summoned, and she hated the thought of having her back forcibly scrubbed.

Petunia took a very short bath and was into her underthings and trying to get her corset on straight when Olga suddenly appeared at her elbow. The maid, who was barely taller than Petunia and probably no more than a pair of years older, frowned and started to scold in her accented Westfalian.

"I knew it! I knew you would not ring for me! And now you are all in a muddle!"

Her movements brisk, Olga got Petunia's corset sorted out, then her petticoats. She helped Petunia into an evening gown that the grand duchess's granddaughter, Princess Nastasya, had left behind after her last visit. Nastasya's gowns fit Petunia the best, and there was the added benefit that she was very vain and only wore a gown once, which meant that the wardrobes were full of Nastasya's gowns.

She was also taller than Petunia, though slightly smaller in the bust. Olga did the best she could to adjust the gown,

which was apricot satin with straw-colored lace, but Petunia would have to keep the skirts lifted as she walked and be very careful about bending or reaching for anything. Not that she was complaining about the way the bodice fitted, exactly. It wasn't unflattering . . . and her father wasn't here to object.

"I'll start fixing the hem of a gown for tomorrow immediately," Olga said as she fixed Petunia's hair. "There's a blue silk with only two flounces that should be easy to alter."

"Thank you," Petunia said with genuine relief. She didn't particularly enjoy feeling like a midget, as Jonquil always called her.

As Petunia left her room to go to dinner, she was still preoccupied with wondering whether Nastasya would care if Petunia took some of her gowns. So much so that she didn't see Prince Grigori until she stepped on a trailing hem and fell down the last four steps into his arms.

"Goodness, Princess Petunia!" The prince held her for a moment before setting her on her feet. "Must we keep meeting in these dire circumstances?" He smiled down at her.

Petunia laughed uneasily and disentangled herself. She did her best to make the apricot satin pool around her feet in a becoming way. She wished that the prince hadn't reminded her of how he'd nearly run her down on his horse the day before, and then hustled her rather roughly onto the estate while his men looked for Oliver, despite her protests that he was just a shepherd who had helped her. In the dazzle of Prince Grigori's smile it was easy to forget all that, but less so when he brought it up.

To her relief he began to talk of pleasantries like the sort of dishes she could expect from his grandmother's celebrated Russakan chef. Grigori led her into the dining room, where the Grand Duchess Volenskaya kissed Petunia on the cheek and told her that the apricot gown was so ravishing that she should keep it, making Petunia feel even better.

And once dinner was served, Petunia was in heaven. Not only was the food divine—the very best dishes that she remembered from Russaka, served exquisitely on gold-edged plates—but the only diners were herself, Prince Grigori, and the grand duchess. She had been worried that the grand duchess might have invited other young people and that Petunia would have to vie for the attention of the duchess and her grandson. But it was only the three of them, so she basked in their compliments and listened with fascination as the grand duchess talked of her youth in the dark forests of Russaka.

The only awkward moment came when Prince Grigori asked what Petunia had been doing in the company of one of the two-legged wolves he was hunting for her father.

"I beg your pardon?" Petunia tilted her head to one side, affecting confusion. "A wolf? That man who pushed me out of the way? I thought you said he was a gypsy."

"A gypsy?" Prince Grigori frowned. "You said he was a shepherd. And did you not see the mask he wore?"

"Actually, no," Petunia said. "He came and went so quickly that I never got a proper look at him at all."

"But you were held at gunpoint by those men just the day

66

before," Prince Grigori said. "Did you not even glimpse the horrible snout of that mask coming over your shoulder?"

Petunia feigned a shudder and hoped that it looked real. "I didn't . . . I suppose I was just so frightened. It was all happening so fast, and I—" She stopped herself just in time from saying that she was afraid that the prince was going to slash her face with his hunting whip. Looking back, she was embarrassed that she could have ever thought such a thing of Grigori. "I suppose I just wasn't expecting one of *them* to leap out of nowhere and save me. At first I thought it was the kindly woodcutter who had taken me most of the way to your estate, ma'am." She nodded at the grand duchess, who was watching the exchange with an expression of displeasure.

"And why did this helpful woodcutter not bring you all the way to my gates?" The grand duchess raised one eyebrow, still dark despite her age, though Petunia rather wondered if that was cosmetic rather than natural.

"I begged him not to," Petunia replied promptly, glad to be able to use some of the truth. "He had taken me so far already, I felt guilty making him go all the way to the gates with me, as though I were a child. He . . . he was Analousian, you see," she invented. "So once we could see the walls, and he told me that the gates were just around the bend, I urged him to return to his family. He had been gone only a few minutes, which is why at first I thought it was he who had pushed me off the road. But when you said gypsies, Your Highness"— and now a nod at Prince Grigori, who was still looking skeptical—"I was quite panic-stricken and wanted nothing more than to get away, so I didn't look behind me at all."

"I see," Prince Grigori said, looking only slightly mollified.

Petunia relaxed and enjoyed the rest of the meal. She also enjoyed having Prince Grigori walk her to the door of her bedchamber afterward and kiss her hand as he bade her good night. Really, it was hard to believe that he was the same person on the black horse she had been afraid of the day before. He was all easy smiles and gallant words, just as he had been in Russaka. And now that she was sixteen, the age difference between them seemed hardly to matter.

Giving a happy sigh, she went in to be undressed by Olga and tucked into bed, where she hoped to dream of dancing in the arms of Prince Grigori. The one disappointment in being the grand duchess's only guest was that there would be no excuse to hold a ball.

She drifted off with a smile that was soon chased from her lips. Rather than dreaming of Grigori, she dreamed that Kestilan and his surviving brothers crawled up the wall to her bedroom window again. They filled her dreams with whispers, whispers of how she and her sisters would be their brides before the moon was full.

Witness

When Oliver arrived home the next morning, Lady Emily was standing in the doorway of the old hall, looking pale and drawn. Her eyes searched her son for any sign of injury.

"I'm fine, but I wanted to make certain that Petunia was all right," he said in a low voice.

His mother saw several people sidling closer with curious faces, so she smiled and threw up her hands theatrically. "Never worry me like that again," she scolded. She took Oliver's arm. "Come have something to eat; you must be famished."

Oliver let his mother lead him into the room on the upper gallery of the old hall, where they dined. He slumped in one of the chairs while she sent for food and waited until someone had brought him roasted chicken and potatoes. When they were alone once more, and after Oliver had bitten into the largest potato and burnt his tongue in the process, he began to speak. He told his mother everything that had happened from Petunia's nearly being run down by Prince Grigori's horse to the realization that it was the grand duchess's grand-son who was tracking him and his men to hiding in the old hothouse.

As he related each part of the story, his mother's face grew whiter and whiter until he feared she might faint. He reached out a hand to her.

"It's all right, Mother. But . . . what does this all mean?"

"I don't know," Lady Emily admitted. "But I've told you how those poor girls were accused of witchcraft. Their governess was nearly put to death for teaching it to them."

"Do you think they were guilty?"

"I knew Anne," his mother said, shaking her head. "She is no more a witch than I am. But *something* was causing all that horror at the palace: the worn-out dancing slippers and the dead princes, you've heard about that as well."

"Of course." Oliver drummed on the table and stopped himself with an effort, forcing down a bite of the cooled potatoes.

Of course. The situation with the worn-out dancing slippers was what had prevented his mother from getting him his rights as an earl after the death of his father in the war. Not that he blamed her. He blamed King Gregor. He supposed he could blame Petunia, too, but she would only have been five or six years old, so the very idea was ludicrous. And it was very hard to blame Petunia for anything after hearing her crying out in the night and seeing her menaced by creatures made of shadow.

"There's something to all this," his mother went on.

"There's some connection between the grand duchess and the earlier tragedies. I would stake my life on it."

"But what?" Oliver shook his head, tearing off a hunk of bread to sop up the gravy. "Because the grand duchess is one of the Nine Daughters of Russaka? What would that have to do with worn-out dancing slippers?" He tried not to sound derisive. He really did want his mother's opinions on the matter, but if she started talking about fairy stories again . . .

"The Nine Daughters of Russaka bore the sons of the King Under Stone," his mother said primly. "But no one has ever said whether the Nine Daughters had any further contact with the King Under Stone, or the babies. Did they ever see their sons again?" His mother looked at him archly.

Oliver began to think. His mother believed that this had really happened. And heaven knew that he had seen some strange sights, even before last night. The forest was full of odd creatures, mysterious lights—and Karl's wife claimed to have found a dragon's lair while gathering mushrooms one day. What if the King Under Stone *was* real? What if he had fathered nine sons with the Russakan princesses, and one of those princesses was now the Grand Duchess Volenskaya? *Was* she allowed to visit her son? Did the King Under Stone have a hold over her?

"Let's say that the grand duchess did have a child of the King Under Stone's," Oliver said. "Where is the child now? Is it human?"

"Exactly," his mother said, looking uneasy. "No one knows. And what all this has to do with Petunia and her sisters, I

don't know, either. But I do know that something strange is happening around those girls again."

"He fathered nine sons with nine sisters in Russaka," Oliver said, convulsively swallowing the last bite of chicken with a dry throat. "But who's to say he doesn't have more? And if the king of Westfalin has twelve daughters . . . whose suitors kept being killed . . ." He shook his head, dismissing the idea. "It's all too strange, and we just don't know enough," he said.

His mother put both hands to her mouth, face chalky white. "I just hope the King Under Stone doesn't see *you* as a potential suitor," she said in a strangled voice.

Oliver laughed bitterly. "Please, Mother, I'm not even a real earl."

Chilled

"Must this window be open? It's freezing!"

Petunia slammed her window shut yet again, wincing at the chill wind that bit into her borrowed nightgown. It seemed that the Princess Nastasya cared more about the draping of fine muslin and cobweb lace than catching her death of cold—and the matching dressing gown was hardly any warmer. It also appeared that Olga was attempting to kill Petunia by keeping her window open all night.

When Petunia had awakened from her nightmare, there had been cold air and mist pouring into the room through the open window. But no sooner had she shut it than Olga had peeped into the room to see if she was all right, and immediately bustled over to open the window again, saying that the "brisk" air was good for the complexion. Petunia's demands that the maid leave the window shut fell on deaf ears, so between skirmishes in the window war she had snatched little sleep.

And now she wanted very much to write to Rose and Galen about her latest nightmares, but Olga insisted on dressing her for breakfast at once. Petunia was still not certain that she was only dreaming the shadowy figures in the garden and needed to tell her sisters. The shadowy figures looked different, older, and those princes who had died when she and her sisters had escaped the Kingdom Under Stone did not appear, which made all too convincing an argument that what she was seeing, both in the gardens and in her dreams, was real.

But she couldn't write the letter with Olga fussing over her, pulling up Petunia's stockings, chivvying her into a freshly altered gown. Though Petunia had to admit that Olga had done a wonderful job—the gown fit as though it had been made for Petunia, and she determined at once to keep it. Then there was her hair to be done up and her face to be powdered and rouged, even though King Gregor did not approve of such things. But her father was not here, Petunia reasoned, studying the effect in the mirror.

"Very nice," she complimented Olga, who glowed at the praise. "Now if you'll excuse me, I really must write a letter to my sister."

"Oh, no, Your Highness!" Olga hustled her off the dressing-table stool and toward the door. "You must go downstairs at once! They'll be waiting for you in the breakfast room! I'll show you myself."

"No, really I'm sure that I can find it in just a moment," said Petunia helplessly.

She was already out the door of her bedchamber and going down the corridor now, with Olga pushing gently on the small of her back. Really, Petunia was starting to think that the maid didn't want her to write a letter at all, and why would Olga care about such a thing? Perhaps Olga was worried that she would be blamed if Petunia was late for breakfast, so Petunia let herself be pushed down the stairs and into the breakfast room.

The breakfast room was empty save for a footman laying out silverware. He bowed to Petunia and hastily set down the rest of the forks before bowing his way out. Petunia raised her eyebrows at Olga.

"Oh, good, you are early," Olga said. "I am sure that Her Grace and His Highness will join you shortly." Then she curtsied and left, leaving Petunia gaping at her.

"She's completely mad," Petunia grumbled to herself. "But very good with a needle."

With nothing better to do, Petunia took a plate and helped herself to rolls and soft cheese, preserves, and toast. The grand duchess did not care for coffee but preferred the strong, dark Russakan tea, which Petunia also loved, so she poured herself a cup.

She had had a roll and was spreading marmalade on toast when Prince Grigori and his grandmother entered the room. Petunia dropped her toast and leaped to her feet to curtsy to the old lady, who looked her over with an approving eye.

"That gown suits you. You should keep it." The grand

duchess sank down into the chair that Prince Grigori held for her.

"Thank you, ma'am, I would love to," Petunia said with gratitude. She sat at her own place, self-conscious about the crumbs on the white tablecloth that made it look as though she had eaten at least a half-dozen rolls instead of just one. "If Princess Nastasya doesn't mind, that is."

"She will never notice." Prince Grigori laughed. "My cousin has more clothes than any three young ladies put together!"

He filled a plate for his grandmother and himself and sat down opposite Petunia. He smiled at her and gave a subtle wink. To her embarrassment, Petunia felt the color rising in her cheeks. She took a sip of tea, which was too hot and nearly choked her, and managed to recover without gasping or spitting the dark liquid onto the table.

"We cannot have you languishing here in that beautiful gown," the grand duchess declared, fortunately not noticing Petunia's moment of distress. She gave Prince Grigori a meaningful look, and Petunia thought he dipped his chin in a subtle nod. "After breakfast, Grigori must take you around the gardens. It is winter, but your work in your father's gardens is well known, and I'm sure mine will hold some small interest for you."

Did everyone here want her to catch her death of cold? Petunia wondered.

"That sounds lovely," she said.

"My Grigori, I know you feel you must go about your

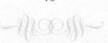

duties, but please be a gallant and keep dear Petunia entertained during her visit." The grand duchess's voice sounded very *studied*, as though she were trying to sound spontaneous but had rehearsed her words in advance. "I charge you with keeping her from boredom, Grigori. It is your new calling in life."

"It would be my pleasure," Prince Grigori said. He didn't sound quite as rehearsed, but he was obviously not at all surprised by the request. "However, the small matter of my duty to the king will still remain," he added, making a face.

Petunia tried her best not to feel snubbed or to read too much into the strange playacting of both grandmother and grandson. She picked up her toast and continued to spread marmalade on it as calmly as she could.

"What duty to the king?"

"I have promised your royal father that I would hunt down these two-legged wolves," Prince Grigori said. "And as yet I have had no luck." He shook his head in self-deprecation.

Petunia felt a little sick. Had her father really ordered Grigori to hunt Oliver and his people, as though they were deer or foxes or . . . actual wolves? And if Grigori caught them, what then? Was he supposed to bring them to Bruch, or had her father given Grigori the authority to mete out punishment on the spot?

"How long have you been hunting them?" she finally asked.

"Since King Philippe of Analousia's brother was accosted in the autumn," Prince Grigori replied. "They took everything: gold, jewels, even his wife's fur cloak. The only things

of value they left the poor lady were her wedding ring and a mourning brooch containing a lock of hair. Things of sentimental value, of no worth to the bandits."

"How kind," Petunia murmured.

Prince Grigori snorted his agreement, thinking that she was being facetious.

"Your men may continue the hunt," the grand duchess said. "But I would like Petunia to not sit here all day, bored as a brick, dancing attendance on an old lady like me."

"I don't mind," Petunia protested.

"Don't be silly," the grand duchess said, not taking her gaze from her grandson. Her face was hard. "Grigori can spare some time for you."

Petunia busied herself with her breakfast, and so did the prince. Petunia didn't know what to say. Prince Grigori clearly did not want to argue with his grandmother, and Petunia could hardly blame him. The grand duchess was so very *sharp*, both in wits and speech, and there was an air about her as if she could not tolerate the weakness of those around her.

If there was any truth to the legend of the Nine Daughters of Russaka, Petunia thought suddenly, this is precisely what one of them would look like now. Beautiful and hard and full of secrets.

Once breakfast was finished, Petunia walked to the entrance hall with Prince Grigori, where they found Olga waiting with Petunia's cloak and some white mittens. Petunia wondered if her maid had been eavesdropping on the breakfast room conversation, or if she was such a good lady's maid that she simply knew these things through some sixth sense. Grigori's valet appeared mere seconds later with his overcoat, hat, and gloves.

As Petunia put on the mittens, she thought with a pang of the fingerless gloves she hadn't finished knitting. They would not be as warm, but they would look less childish. And she was accustomed to wearing knitwear with considerably more embellishment than this.

"Are you ready?" Grigori sounded impatient, but like he was trying to hold it in check.

"Of course," Petunia said, pulling away from Olga, who was attempting to retie her cloak with a more flattering bow.

Petunia gave the bow a tweak of her own, no doubt only making it crooked, but not really caring. The cloak was so glorious that it could hardly be marred by having a crooked bow. Even Grigori's hard eyes softened as he got a good look at Petunia with her black hair framed by the scarlet hood with its scrolls of silver embroidery. He held out his arm to her, and she took it, wishing that there were not quite such a discrepancy in their heights. He had to hold his arm down low and she had to reach up a bit more than was comfortable. Still, by the time they had gone out to the path to the gardens, they had fallen into a kind of rhythm with their steps that felt quite natural.

But it soon became apparent that Prince Grigori knew

next to nothing about gardens. Petunia had to stifle her giggles as he waved his free arm vaguely at "Some sort of trees. The hedges. A statue."

Petunia finally couldn't conceal her laughter. "That was a rosebush," she said when he looked at her questioningly.

"I beg your pardon?" He stopped and looked back at the rose, which had been trimmed into a small ornamental tree. "It is a very stunted tree, I believe."

"Forgive me, Your Highness, but I can assure you that it is a rosebush. It has been pruned into that shape."

She gently touched the bare branches with her mitten, wondering what color the rose was. If it was yellow, she might take a slip home, but she guessed that most of the roses in this garden would be white, pink, or red. They always were, in gardens where nobody truly cared about such matters. This garden was very clean: everything neatly pruned or wrapped for the winter, the grass short, the paths swept, but it was . . . well, boring. She could almost predict the hedge maze that was sure to appear on their left, just past the large fountain shaped like a nymph pouring water.

"It's true," Prince Grigori admitted with a laugh. "I don't know much about these gardens. Well, can you forgive me? They are all your Westfalian trees and flowers!"

Petunia had to laugh too. But when she looked around to point out some of the better features of the common Westfalian garden in winter—such as they were—she realized that he was wrong. These weren't Westfalian trees and flowers; they were Bretoner.

Her laugh died on her lips as she realized that this was Lady Emily's garden. Oliver's father must have planted it for his new Bretoner bride just the way her father had planted the garden for Maude in Bruch. It was on a less grand scale, true, but all the signs were there that someone, here in the middle of the Westfalian Woods, had tried to make a small corner of Breton.

"What's the matter, princess?" Prince Grigori stopped, looking at her with concern. "Are you homesick already? Or tired from walking? Let me take you back to the house to rest."

"Oh, no, it's . . ." She realized that she could hardly tell him what was the matter. She hesitated. "Well, perhaps I am still a little rattled by the accident with the coach."

She looked down at the ground so that he couldn't detect the lie in her eyes. No one but her sisters could ever understand that the possibility of Rionin and his brothers crawling into her bedroom was far more terrifying than being in a runaway carriage.

As she stared at the lawn around them, however, avoiding the prince's piercing eyes, she got another shock. This one nearly made her reel, and as she swayed just a little, Prince Grigori held her even closer.

"Are you faint? Are you ill?"

"No. Yes. Please take me inside," Petunia said, her voice shaking.

His black brows drawn together in concern, Prince Grigori put one arm around her waist and guided her swiftly back to the manor. He must have thought Petunia was nearly

swooning because she could not seem to raise her head, she was so busy staring at the lawn.

The winter-dead grass, still lightly dusted with frost despite the weak sunlight, bore the tracks of a half-dozen men. The trail of footprints led directly from the far end of the gardens to the flowerbed beneath her bedroom window. Any doubt in her mind fled, and she knew that Kestilan and his brothers had slipped out of the Kingdom Under Stone and come after her.

Supplicant

"You're going to be executed; you know that, don't you?" Having said this, Simon lay back on Oliver's bed and watched him pack, not appearing all that concerned.

"Well, I have robbed a great many coaches," Oliver said philosophically. "I suppose that it's only fair that I pay the price for that. Since I cannot give back the money now."

"And Mother approves of this scheme?"

"I am the earl, and the head of this household," Oliver said, all attempt at humor gone.

Oliver was the earl. It was time that he started acting like one.

He finished packing. He didn't own that much: a few changes of clothing, including a suit that had been his father's and that his mother had tailored to fit him. He would save that for his audience with the king, of course. He had some books and a few other effects, but there was no sense in taking them. Simon could have them if Oliver didn't return.

"Karl says you're doing this for the princess," Simon said.

"I'm doing this for a lot of reasons," Oliver said. "And that's really all I'll say about it right now, if you don't mind."

"Fine," Simon retorted, and he rolled off Oliver's bed.

He grabbed his crutches and hobbled out the door in as high a dudgeon as he could manage. Oliver watched without saying a word. He knew that his brother was worried and didn't know how to express it. Oliver also suspected that Lady Emily had sent Simon to see how firmly Oliver was resolved to going to Bruch.

The answer was that Oliver had never been so committed to anything in his life. He had sat for an entire day and night in his room, thinking, and could not see any other path to take. It was partly to do with Petunia, it was true, but Petunia was merely the final straw, if anything. He wanted to tell King Gregor about the shadow creatures in the garden that night at the manor because he did not know who else could help her.

But in wondering how to help Petunia, Oliver had come to the realization that he could not be the one to help her because he could not even help himself. He was trapped. He could not continue thieving to support his people; he would be killed eventually, either by Prince Grigori or some traveler's guard. But beyond that, he and Simon would never be able to marry, would never be able to further their educations or travel, but would spend their lives doling out stolen gold to their people, who dwindled with every season.

The older folk, who followed Oliver for his father's sake,

were dying off. And the young people were slipping away to find better lives. Oliver wished them nothing but luck, yet others spoke of them as traitors. So far as they could tell, no one had ever revealed a thing about the old hall or Oliver, though. Oliver used to entertain dreams of going too. Sneaking off in the night, making his way to Bruch or the Analousian capital of Amide, and finding work as . . . And here his imagination would fail him. Oliver knew how to do only one thing: rob coaches.

It had to stop. He was going to beg an audience with King Gregor, confess all, and seek help for his people as well as for Petunia. He was certain that he would not escape life in prison, that is, if the king didn't order him executed. But he hoped that by turning himself in, his men might earn clemency, though he had warned them to prepare to flee with their families, just in case. And he hoped that by going directly to the king and confessing his connection to Petunia, strange as it was, the king would see immediately to his youngest daughter's protection.

But Oliver was not planning on returning from this trip.

Karl appeared in the doorway of Oliver's room and found the young earl slumped on the bed. His bag was beside him, and the sun was already rising. Oliver had meant to start an hour earlier. And, he thought, eyeing the pack on Karl's back, alone.

"Where are you going? Taking your family away?" Oliver said halfheartedly. Karl's wolf mask was hanging from its strap at his shoulder.

Karl just grunted.

Knowing that it was useless to argue, and that Karl would only grunt in reply anyway, Oliver took up his bag and followed the big man downstairs. Outside the hall he found the rest of his Wolves waiting, all with packs, cloaks, and masks.

"You do understand that I'm going to give myself up?" Oliver looked each man carefully in the eyes. None of them seemed any more nervous than they did before a raid, which was either great folly or great courage on their part. He hoped for the latter.

"We're just as guilty. More so, since we're older and should know better," said Johan, a grizzled man who had been Oliver's father's captain of arms.

"I was hoping that if I turned myself in, I could plead for mercy for the rest of you," Oliver said.

"Lad, it's foolish to assume that the king will punish you and not us," Johan said. "Better if we all go. Besides which, it's a two-day walk, and you've no food in that little bundle." He shrugged the straps of his own pack, which was twice the size of Oliver's and had a large cast-iron frying pan tied to one side.

He knew if he ordered them to stay, they would just disobey.

"It would be nice to have a decent meal or two before I turn myself over to Gregor," Oliver admitted.

His mother was waiting at the outer gate. She kissed his cheek, her eyes bright but her face resolute and calm. He took her hands and squeezed them.

"I shall do my best," he said to her.

"You always have," she replied. She kissed his cheek again. "One piece of advice, my son. If you fail to get an audience, try to go into the gardens."

"Queen Maude's gardens?" He gave her a surprised look.

"Yes. There's a man who works there, an old man, named Walter Vogel. Tell him what's happening to the princess."

"How could he . . . ? Why?"

"If you cannot find him, simply asking after him should direct you to someone who can help."

"Very well," Oliver promised, though he was still confused.

His confusion took his mind off what he would face in Bruch, though. While his mother and his people watched, Oliver led his men into the forest.

∽

They were in Bruch and standing at the gates of the palace. The guards were watching them curiously, and Oliver knew that it was time. Their masks were hidden in their packs, they had stopped at a bathhouse to wash and put on their best suits, and Oliver had run out of excuses. He thought of Petunia, whom he had left three days before in that house with those creatures haunting her.

He gave one of the guards a cold look, pretending that he had not been gawping at the palace for the past few minutes.

"We wish to see King Gregor," Oliver said.

"Do you have an invitation?" The guard on the left looked past Oliver as though he already knew the answer.

"We . . . do not have an invitation," Oliver said, doing his

best not to sound sheepish. "But we will wait until the king can see us."

"You might be waiting a long time," said the guard. His face softened a little. "Send a servant with a letter stating your business. The king's secretary will arrange an audience."

"How long with that take?" Oliver felt like his heart was in his shoes. His people could wait, but he had a feeling that Petunia could not.

"No more than a month," said the guard.

"A month?" Oliver gaped at the guard.

What if he had urgent news for the king? No wonder Oliver's mother had given up trying to get an audience all those years ago. Save for the upcoming double wedding of two of Petunia's sisters, all was relatively quiet in Westfalin . . . and it might still take a month to speak to the king!

"I don't think you understand, we have very important—" Oliver began.

There was a clatter of hooves on the cobbles of the square, and the guard's face became stern. He put out an arm as though to brush Oliver aside.

"Make way," the man said in a strident voice. "Make way!"

Oliver looked around and then hurried to step aside. Four horses with elegantly dressed riders—two young women and two young men—were coming toward them. The couple in front were laughing, and Oliver could see that they were at ease in the saddle. Behind them, the other couple's horses were considerably slower and older, something that their riders appeared grateful for.

"You see," the young man at the front was saying to his companion, "she's got a perfect gait, even here in the city."

"I suppose," said the young woman, looking lofty. "If I cannot have a cavalry horse, this mare is quite fine."

The young woman behind her started to shrill something about cavalry horses being unsuitable and dangerous, but Oliver had stopped paying attention. He was trying to get the attention of the young woman in front, bowing to her and trying to make his expression pleading.

He was sure that the young women were two of Petunia's sisters. They were enough like her to give him a little pang, particularly the one in front. She wore a plum-colored riding habit with a daring little hat pinned atop her black hair.

"Your Highness, I'm here on a very important matter," Oliver blurted out.

"Don't bother the princesses," the guard snapped, stepping forward to take hold of Oliver's arm. Behind him, Oliver heard Karl and one of the others moving closer.

"What's the matter?"

The princess in the plum-colored gown had reined in her horse and was looking at him curiously. The other riders all reined in as well, and the young man at the front moved his horse around so that he was closer to Oliver, looking wary. The other princess, in blue, leaned forward and whispered loudly, "Poppy, don't!"

"I need to speak with your father, Your Highness," Oliver said. "It's very urgent. It concerns Princess Petunia."

Poppy's black brows shot toward her rakish hat.

"You'd better come with us, then," she said.

She signaled to the guards, who hurried to open the gates. Oliver and his men followed the four horses into the courtyard. The riders gave their mounts to the grooms, and then Poppy took the arm of her betrothed, a tall, blond young man who Oliver vaguely thought might be Norsker or possibly a Dane. A prince, either way, Oliver thought with a little bitterness. Not just a mere earl.

The other sister must be her twin, Daisy, he decided. She had slightly lighter hair and eyes, but their faces were very much alike (save for her suspicious expression), and her partner was a young man with black hair and swarthy skin. The heir to some southern principality, Oliver remembered. Venenzia? That seemed right. Even in the forest, they were able to glean a little royal gossip.

Poppy sashayed into the palace without looking back, taking off her gloves as she went. In the front hall, she asked the butler if her father was still in the council room, leading them all up a broad oak staircase without waiting for a reply.

"Your Highness," the butler called out weakly. "His Majesty is with his ministers of state."

"This young man has news of Petunia; they will surely want to hear it," Poppy said airily.

But at the gallery at the top of the stairs, she turned to Oliver.

"Will they?" Her dark brows were drawn level, and her look could have skewered a braver man than Oliver.

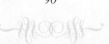

"I don't know," Oliver said. "It may be a . . . matter for the family only."

"We shall see what Father thinks," she said, continuing up the stairs. "He becomes irate when he is left out of things." Then she stopped again. "Is Petunia all right?"

"I hope so," he replied.

She nodded as though that were the correct answer, and led them all to a broad wooden door at the end of the gallery. She knocked twice but then swung open the door without waiting, sailing into a room that contained a long table, several tall chairs, some very startled gentlemen, and the king.

"Poppy!" The king's face turned red in an instant, and he rose to his feet. "Who are these people?"

"I'm terribly sorry, Papa," Poppy said, not sounding even slightly remorseful. "But this young man has an urgent message concerning Petunia."

Oliver bowed to the king. Then he waited. He wasn't sure what to do. He was fairly certain that he wasn't supposed to speak first, but the king didn't say anything. He was also afraid to rise without permission.

"Well?" The king's roar made Oliver jerk upright out of his bow. "What is this message?"

"I— It's— I—"

"Spit it out, boy!"

"You see, sire, my name is Oliver, and I—"

"Am I supposed to know you? What are you yammering about?"

Oliver panicked.

"I abducted Princess Petunia last week. I didn't harm her; I delivered her to the Grand Duchess Volenskaya, but now she is in terrible danger," he said.

Dreamer

Sometimes when Petunia slept, she was afraid that she was actually awake. If she was awake, that would mean that this was real life, and not a dream. She said as much to Lily, as they crossed hands and turned within the circle of the gentlemen, dancing a raucous Bretoner gigue, surrounded by their pale sisters and the sneering courtiers of the Kingdom Under Stone.

"No, it's still a dream," Lily said, her voice hardly more than a whisper. Even in the dream she was shockingly white, and her hands shook in Petunia's grasp.

"Lilykins, are you all right?"

Petunia tried to stop the dance, but Lily's partner snarled at her. He wasn't one of the princes, but a courtier with a face like a fox and nasty ginger hair that wanted barbering. Petunia renewed her grip on Lily's hands and kept spinning.

"You're right; it's just a dream," she told her sister. "Just a dream, after all. Don't listen to my silly talk."

"It has to be a dream," Lily said. "I can't bear to think that it isn't."

"What?" Petunia did stop dancing, and when Lily's partner snarled again, Petunia snapped her fingers at her own partner. "Kestilan, he's bothering me," she said.

Prince Kestilan grabbed Lily's partner by the collar and hauled the unfortunate fox-faced man away. Petunia took Lily's arm and led her to the side of the dance floor. Lily was staring at her in astonishment.

"Oh," Petunia said, waving an airy hand as they sat in a pair of gilt chairs, "I've decided to start treating Kestilan like any other unwanted suitor. He behaves better that way.

"But I was just being silly about it being real life," Petunia continued. "It must be a dream, it's not like before: I didn't walk here through the silver wood; I just went to sleep and *whoosh*." She frowned down at the flimsy blue silk gown that she wore. "And I certainly never would have picked this gown myself; it looks like some sort of racy Analousian negligee."

Lily tugged self-consciously at her own gown, which was lavender and trimmed with black velvet ribbons that made it look, if possible, even more tawdry than Petunia's gown.

"I'm not sure I should tell you, Pet," said Lily in her most evasive big-sister voice.

She looked around, seeking out the others, but none of the rest of their sisters could get free of the dance to help her explain. On the dais, the King Under Stone was sitting on his crumbling throne, watching them through hooded eyes.

Somehow knowing he had once been a prince like his brothers made what he was now all the more frightening.

"I'm not six years old anymore, Lily," Petunia said with impatience when she realized that her sister did not mean to continue. "It's time you all stop treating me like I didn't know what was happening. I knew. And I remember too."

"Do you?" Lily looked startled. "Oh, Pet, I'm so sorry! We all thought that . . . well, we hoped that you were so young you wouldn't—"

"Remember coming here every night? Remember Rionin leading an attack on the palace to force us to come, even though we were all so ill we could hardly walk? Things like that will stay with a person," Petunia said, a bit more sharply than she meant to. "I'm sorry." She put a hand on Lily's, contrite. "But I'm sixteen now, and it's all starting to happen again, isn't it?"

Lily nodded her head, her face grief-stricken.

"We thought we had spared you, at least," Lily murmured. "But you're as old as Hya was back then." Her gaze was drawn to Hyacinth, who danced on the far side of the room with her prince. Though normally quite graceful, Hyacinth looked like a dressmaker's dummy, twirling woodenly in the arms of her sullen prince. Dancing next to her, Jonquil appeared to be held up entirely by her partner, a grim man with the manners of a much-abused schoolmaster.

"What would happen if we all left the country?" Petunia asked.

"Galen says it wouldn't matter," Lily said. "And Poppy's and Daisy's weddings will be in a month. There's no time to go very far."

"What else is happening at home? I haven't gotten a single letter since I arrived at the grand duchess's," Petunia said. This was the first time in years she and her sisters had been together in the Kingdom Under Stone, and even though it was a dream, she would still remember Lily's words upon waking.

But all the while her eyes were on the dais. In the past they had been allowed to sit out only a dance or maybe two, even when ill, and now Kestilan was back and conversing with his brother the king. Both their gazes were on Petunia and Lily.

"You haven't?" Lily was startled. "But someone's written every day! It's you who hasn't written to us!"

"I've written," Petunia protested, "when stupid Olga will let me!" Lily just gave her a confused look, so Petunia hurried to tell her what had been happening, running her words together as Kestilan started back around the edge of the dance floor toward her. "Rionin and the others have been sneaking through the gardens as shadows at night. They're close to coming right into my room. Have they been after you all?"

"No," Lily said, her eyes wide. "We've only had the nightmares. And none as real as tonight's dancing."

Poppy, coming over with a glass of punch, started shaking her head. "I think you need to come home, Pet. The Grand Duchess Volenskaya's estate is not a safe place for someone who is plagued by the King Under Stone."

"What on earth do you mean, Poppy?" Petunia looked

from her to Lily, but it was clear that Lily didn't know what their sister meant either.

"I've been reading some of Galen's books," Poppy said. "Did you know that the grand duchess is one of the Nine Daughters of Russaka?"

"Oh, nonsense," Petunia said. She started to laugh, but then she saw Poppy's and Lily's faces. "That story isn't real, is it?"

"Of course it is," Lily said. "I remember Dr. Kelling talking about it with Anne once. It was the greatest scandal in Ionia, until our suitors started dying."

"But if the grand duchess ... if she really is ... and it's not just a story ...," Petunia sputtered.

"Then she was once the lover of the first King Under Stone," Poppy finished for her. "Which is why I think you're not safe there, Pet."

"If we had known," Lily said, stricken. "We never would have sent you."

"Ask Galen when you wake up," Petunia said with authority, ignoring the way Poppy raised her eyebrows at Petunia's tone. "I want you to be sure before you start causing problems with the grand duchess, Poppy. And I still want to know what's been happening with the lot of you since I've been gone."

"Clearly nothing as exciting as what you've been up to," Poppy said.

"What excitement has Petunia been up to?" Kestilan demanded, stalking over to dance with Petunia again.

But before she could think of a cutting reply, they all froze.

The King Under Stone had left his throne and was walking toward them, the dancers parting to make way for the gaunt ruler. Petunia could see that Jonquil had actually stepped behind her partner, visibly shaking. Rionin had once been Jonquil's partner at the Midnight Balls, but he had not danced in any of the dreams Petunia had had. His father had never danced either but had drawn power from the life and energy of the princesses as they danced with his sons and his court night after night.

"I have come to a decision," said the king, his voice light but carrying across the entire room like a piercing winter wind. "My father never chose a queen, preferring instead the freedom of bachelorhood."

The court all laughed, but Lily gave a small moan, pressing back against the chipped silver-and-ebony chair in which she sat. Petunia looked around, distressed, until she saw Rose sidling toward them. Their oldest sister was wearing a dark purple gown, and her partner kept trying to take hold of her arm again, but Rose simply ignored him. Like Lily, Violet, and Orchid, Rose's original dancing partner had been killed during the battle to free them from the Kingdom Under Stone, and now she danced with some nameless courtier night after night.

"But I would like a queen to sit by my side," the King Under Stone announced. "A helpmeet, as they say in the sunlight world. To share the joys and pains of this life with me, and to provide me with heirs, who, in turn, I hope will give me grandchildren. Beautiful, sunlight-dwelling grandchildren."

The court greeted this pronouncement with applause and cheers.

And a scream.

Petunia, who had gone numb at this horrible revelation, felt the scream run through her like a jolt of lightning. She looked at Poppy and Lily, who were closest to her, but it was neither of them.

"It's Jonquil," someone called over the continued sound of screaming.

That sounded like Iris, but Petunia couldn't be sure in the tumult. Where were the rest of the younger set? Pansy? Orchid? All she could see were the cruel faces of Under Stone's court.

Rose shoved Kestilan hard in the chest to get by and ran to Jonquil. Petunia followed in her wake but stopped when the King Under Stone brushed past her, going in the opposite direction. He wasn't going toward Jonquil after all but advancing on Lily, who was now prevented from going to their sister by the king's tall, spare form.

"Never! Never! Never! I would sooner die!" Jonquil was screaming in a voice like splinters. *"Never! Never! Never!"*

"Rose," Petunia said, her throat so dry that there was no way even Kestilan, standing just beside her, could have heard. "Rose. Rose. Rose. *Rose.*" She managed to shout the name at last, shaking off Kestilan's attempt to grab her elbow and taking the last few steps to reach her sister Lily.

The King Under Stone had his arm around Lily's waist, pulling her close to his side. His mouth was stretched wide in

a smile that showed distinctly pointed canines. Lily was staring down at the toes of her dancing slippers, just peeping from beneath her gown, and her pale skin had grayish undertones now.

Someone took hold of Petunia's arm again, and she almost elbowed the person in the ribs before she realized that it was Lilac. Violet came up on Petunia's other side.

"What's he doing?" Lilac's whisper was hardly more than a fevered breath.

"We're not going to like what he says next," Orchid said flatly, coming up behind Petunia.

Petunia glanced over her shoulder and got a little jolt from seeing Orchid without the spectacles she had had to wear since she was twelve. But, after all, this was just a dream.

No, it was a nightmare. A nightmare that went on and on.

"Rose," Petunia shouted again. "It's not Jonquil!"

There was no way that Rose could hear her. Jonquil was now simply sobbing, wordless, and Petunia's heart shuddered at the depth of her older sister's pain.

"'Never' is quite right," the King Under Stone said, his voice drowning out Jonquil, though it was not all that loud.

His lips twisted in derision, and even from across the ballroom, his eyes took in Jonquil's wasted frame, her lank hair and extreme pallor. Petunia wanted to claw out his eyes for looking at Jonquil like that—Jonquil, who had once been the great beauty of Westfalin, who had been courted by princes from across Ionia. It was the King Under Stone's fault that her looks were spoiled now, and now that they were, he mocked her and tossed her aside.

"Such as you would be wholly unsuited to being my queen," he went on. "An accident of birth made us partners during my father's reign, but it seems silly for me not to have a choice, when there are more princesses than princes."

He laughed, but none of the courtiers did this time. Looking at them, Petunia thought some of the gentlemen seemed almost sulky. She wondered if they had petitioned to be partnered with one of her sisters and been denied. Served them right, she thought. Nasty things.

"At first I thought to marry the eldest and make myself king of Westfalin as well," Rionin continued in a smooth, amused voice. "But the taint of that common gardener and his dribs and drabs of magic has become offensive to me," the King Under Stone said to Rose, who was now holding a silent, semiconscious Jonquil in her arms.

"I'm married too," Lily murmured. She rubbed her ring finger, but in this nightmare, there were no rings there.

"What's that, my beloved?" The King Under Stone looked down at Lily with a smirk.

"*I am married,*" Lily said in a louder voice. She slammed her elbow into the king's ribs and twisted out of his arm in the same motion.

"We do not recognize the mumblings of your quaint little religion down here," the King Under Stone sneered, straightening his jacket as though Lily's strike had been

nothing. His smile grew even wider than before. "And," he added, "it's not as if you have any children to tie him to you. I may not have my father's temperament, but I do have all his powers." He threw back his head, his black-and-silver hair rippling down his back, and laughed.

Petunia's heart turned to ice. Lily sank to her knees.

"You bastard," someone screamed. To Petunia's shock, it was Hyacinth. "I will see your head mounted on the front gate!"

Hyacinth made a run at the king but was caught by Pansy and Daisy, who had gathered near to help Rose with Jonquil. Jonquil now appeared to have fallen unconscious, and Rose sagged beneath Jonquil's weight, her face bleak. Poppy stood by Rose's side, watching the king with calculating eyes, and Petunia wondered if there was some way that Poppy could bring her beloved pistols into this nightmare.

"Let her go, Daise," Poppy said. "I, for one, would like to see him torn apart. And if Hyacinth is willing . . ."

"You can't do a thing," the King Under Stone said lightly. He raised Lily to her feet and kissed her on the cheek. She shuddered and tried to pull away, but he held her all the more tightly, both arms winding around her. "After all, it's just a dream."

Petunia woke in her bed, sweating even though the window was open.

She got up, closed the window, and lit the candle on her

bedside table. She took a moment to look at the flame as it grew and steadied; fire always soothed her. Then, holding her candle before her like a weapon, she marched across the corridor in nothing but her nightgown.

Petunia entered Prince Grigori's room without knocking. She yanked the bed curtains aside and looked down at the sleeping prince. He was terribly handsome, but Petunia didn't stop to stare, just grabbed his shoulder and shook.

"Wake up," she said. "Wake up, Grigori!"

"Hmm? What is it?" He blinked around sleepily, but then his eyes widened when he took in Petunia in her nightgown, her candle held just over his head. "My petal, what has happened?"

"I need to go home," Petunia said tersely. "Now."

"What time is it?"

"I don't care," Petunia said. "I need to go home."

Dodging out from under her candle, Prince Grigori struggled upright. "Have you had a bad dream?"

Petunia started to laugh. She laughed so hard that the prince had to take the candle out of her hand before she dropped it on the bedclothes. She laughed until she was crying, sobbing, in a heap on the floor by his bed.

The prince set the candle aside and climbed out of bed. He scooped Petunia up in his long arms and carried her back to her own room, where he tucked her into her high bed and summoned Olga to sit with her. Then he sent for his grandmother's physician, who brought extract of poppies to help her sleep.

"No," Petunia gasped as the physician held the cup to her lips. He tipped a little down her throat. "No! Not poppies!" He forced her to drink a little more. "No! Not unless Poppy can take her pistol! And where's mine? I don't want to sleep without my pistol!"

"She's delirious," Petunia heard the physician say as she slipped into the grayness. "You'd better send a letter to her father."

And then she heard the sound of a valse being played, shrill and just slightly out of tune.

$\mathscr{P}$risoner

Things had not gone as Oliver had hoped, but they had certainly gone as he had expected.

He was being held in a tiny attic room at the palace while Karl and the others had been taken to the Bruch jail. King Gregor didn't believe Oliver was an earl, but apparently being the leader of the bandits, the abductor of Princess Petunia, *and* the claimant to a divided earldom made him too interesting for the regular jail.

But not interesting enough for immediate questioning. Oliver sat in the little room until evening, when the door was unlocked and a dinner tray shoved inside. An hour later the door opened and a hand groped around for the tray. Oliver obligingly pushed it closer to the door with his foot.

"Every compliment to the royal chef," Oliver called as the door closed.

The guard only grunted.

He grunted, too, when Oliver thanked him for the breakfast tray. And Oliver thanked him for lunch as well.

And that was all Oliver did. Sit in the room. Sleep. Eat. And try to get the burly guard to do more than grunt.

In the late afternoon, he heard voices outside his room, and the door swung all the way open. The guard stood in the doorway, his rifle held crosswise, and behind him Oliver saw skirts of red-sprigged muslin.

"Hello," Oliver said cautiously.

"Hello," said a voice, and Poppy peeped around one of the guard's large arms. "Are you well?"

"A little bored," Oliver said. "But otherwise unharmed."

A spark of amusement lit her eyes. "I'll send up some books. You can read, can't you?"

"All the Wolves of the Westfalian Woods can read," Oliver said grandly.

"Even the ones with four legs?"

"Poppy," someone whispered loudly from a hiding place a little way down the passage. "What are you *doing*?"

Oliver guessed that it was Daisy, who seemed a good deal more timid than her twin. He gave Poppy a wink over the guard's arm and raised his voice a little. "I have endeavored to teach them myself," he said. "And they are coming along nicely."

"So tell me," Poppy said, "what is an educated young man with courtly manners, who even teaches wolves to read, doing robbing coaches in the middle of the forest?"

"Poppppyyyy," moaned her sister.

"Hush, Pan," said Poppy without taking her eyes off Oliver.

Not Daisy then, but Pansy, who was less than a year older than Petunia. Oliver considered his answer for a long time. It was possible that Poppy and Pansy were here out of mere curiosity, without their father's permission. But it was also possible that King Gregor wanted Oliver to reveal some dastardly intent while flirting with Gregor's beautiful daughters.

"Well, Your Highness," Oliver replied at last, "I needed to feed my people. And after the depredations of the war, and with our homes and farms gone, we had no other recourse."

"Your people?"

Poppy asked it at the same time Pansy asked, "What happened to the farms?"

"When the border was redrawn, some of the farms in my earldom ended up in Analousia," Oliver explained. "They were given to Analousian families who had lost their lands in the war. Some of them were near the manor, however, and that was given to the Grand Duke Volenskaya, who became the Duke of Hrothenborg."

"That's where Pet is staying," Pansy said, and Oliver heard a rustling as she came closer.

"That's right," Oliver said.

"So you really are an earl," Poppy mused.

The guard snorted at this, but Oliver and Poppy ignored him.

"Yes, I am," Oliver said simply.

"Then why didn't you come to Bruch and explain to Father what had happened?" Poppy studied him for a moment. "Or, your father would have, I guess."

"My father died in the war," Oliver said. "I became the earl when I was seven. My mother's family did not approve of the marriage; I doubt anyone even knew that I existed. My mother tried to have me confirmed in my title and to petition for the return of our lands, but that was during the uproar over the worn-out slippers and the dying suitors. Since my mother is Bretoner, she was afraid to bring attention to herself."

"Bretoner?" Pansy had crept even closer. Oliver could see the edge of a pink muslin gown just peeping around the edge of the door. "Did she know Mother?"

"Indeed," Oliver said. He felt like he was holding out bread-crumbs for birds, and any sudden movement would make them take flight. Or, in Poppy's case, peck him. "She was one of your mother's ladies-in-waiting. But her family wanted her to return home to marry a Bretoner lord, and my father's family had a second cousin handpicked to marry him."

"No wonder she didn't dare come to the palace," Poppy said. "Bishop Angiers would have had her on trial for witchcraft in a heartbeat. But don't worry, the Church has long since made things right, and he got what he deserved."

"That's good," Oliver said. The way that Poppy kept looking over her shoulder made Oliver think that they would leave soon. It was time to ask his own questions.

"Are my men all right?"

"For now," Poppy said. "Until Father decides what to do with *you*."

"That's good," Oliver said again, not sure what else to say. He wanted them released, but he supposed that they were just as guilty. "And Petunia? Have you heard from your sister?"

"Not since the first day," Pansy said.

She pushed in next to Poppy so that she could see him around the guard's elbow. She was as tall as Poppy, with shining dark-brown hair and blue eyes. An utterly lovely girl, as all the princesses were, yet Oliver thought Petunia was far more beautiful.

"We got one letter explaining that she'd gotten lost and had to find her own way to the manor, but nothing since. Did you really kidnap her?"

"It was an accident, but yes," Oliver said. "She saw me and my brother with our masks off, so we snatched her before she could raise the alarm. She stayed with us one night, and then I took her to the manor. Quite unharmed, I assure you."

"And things at the estate, they seemed . . . all right . . . to you?" Pansy pressed.

Oliver started to say that they had been fine, but then he stopped. "I don't know." He leaned forward a little, conscious more than ever of the guard. "Your Highnesses, I saw . . . creatures in the garden of the manor. People . . . made of shadow. I think they were trying to get to Petunia." Oliver moved back a little, waiting for Poppy to scoff or Pansy to squeak in fright.

But both the princesses surprised him.

Poppy shrank back, and her hands twisted in her skirts. It was Pansy who stood up straighter and looked him in the eye.

"Shadowy creatures?" Pansy's voice was shrill despite her stern posture. "What nonsense! Come, Poppy, we're going." She tugged Poppy's arm to make her move.

Oliver stared after them. They'd believed him—he knew they had. But why were they pretending they hadn't?

The guard glared at Oliver. "If you're lying, there's a special place in hell for you." He slammed the door in Oliver's face, locking it with a scraping of metal that made Oliver's teeth ache.

He hadn't been dreaming the shadows in the garden. One look at Poppy's face told him that much, and Pansy's and the guard's reactions had confirmed it.

"But what are they?" Oliver asked his empty room.

∾

After another night and morning spent pacing the tiny room, Oliver was frantic. His mother and Simon would be beside themselves with anxiety, he wanted reassurance that his men were all right, and he couldn't stop wondering if the shadow creatures had gone after Petunia again.

Poppy had sent books to him with his dinner tray, but he couldn't concentrate for more than a pair of minutes. Besides his personal distractions, the books were both rather dry histories of Westfalin. Oliver wasn't sure whether Poppy was joking or she really thought such things riveting reading for the imprisoned. A scrap of paper fell from one as he leafed through it, but if it had been marking a particular page, he couldn't find it now.

And then, just when he was expecting his lunch tray, King Gregor sent for him.

Oliver was taken to the same room where he had first met the king, with its long, dark table and the high-backed chairs full of scowling men. The king was at the head of the table, a broad-shouldered man with wiry gray hair and wild eyebrows at his left, a gentle-faced priest at his right. The men along each side of the table were all uniformly older, grim, and dressed in black. This made the pair sitting at the end of the table all the more striking.

Opposite King Gregor at the foot of the table was a young man with unfashionably short hair and a pair of silver knitting needles in his hands. By his side in a cushioned chair sat the only woman in the room. She was gravely beautiful, with golden brown hair held up with garnet-studded combs, a gleaming gold watch pinned to the bosom of her green gown. She was untangling a skein of gray yarn with her slender fingers, and Oliver thought that together the two of them looked remarkably like a woodcut he had seen of the Destinies. If the older man seated on the woman's other side had been holding a knife, with which the Destinies sever the thread of a man's life, it would have completed the picture. He was toying with a pen, to Oliver's relief.

Oliver bowed to the king. "Your Majesty," he murmured. Then he turned and bowed to the pair at the other end of the table. "Crown Prince Galen, Crown Princess Rose."

"Smart lad," grunted the man with the eyebrows at the king's side. "I'll give him that."

"If you're that smart, why did you turn yourself in, hey?" King Gregor barked.

"Because it was time," Oliver said.

"Time to stop stealing from the innocent . . . time to stop stealing the innocent themselves?" King Gregor's face was red. "If you did indeed abduct my youngest daughter—and why you would boast about it if you hadn't, I don't know—she hasn't said a word about it, nor has the Grand Duchess Volenskaya von Hrothenborg, who is hosting Petunia at her estate!"

"*My* estate, if it please Your Majesty," Oliver said, cutting across the bluster. He could see how his mother had quailed at the thought of facing the king.

Gregor thumped the table with his fist. "Still pretending to be an earl?"

"I *am* an earl," Oliver said. "The Earl of Saxeborg-Rohlstein. My father was Caspar Gerhard Saxony, the twenty-fifth earl of Saxeborg-Rohlstein. My mother is the Dowager Countess Emily Ellsworth Saxony, once lady-in-waiting to Queen Maude, may her soul rest in peace. My father died in service to the crown, leading a regiment in the war with Analousia. When my mother brought me to Bruch to be confirmed in my title, she found that my earldom had been divided up and given to others, and Bretoners like herself were being accused of witchcraft."

This statement was followed by the sharpest silence Oliver had ever experienced.

"Your Majesty, I believe that Heinrich might be some help in this matter," said Prince Galen after the longest minute of Oliver's life.

"Heinrich? What would he know about it?" King Gregor looked at his oldest son-in-law in distraction, rubbing at his chin as though trying to scrub the clean-shaven skin right off.

"The captain of Heinrich's regiment was the Earl Caspar Saxony," Galen said. He took the neatly wound yarn from Rose's hands with a smile and began wrapping it around one of his knitting needles.

"My father was the captain of the Eagle regiment," said Oliver. His mother had told him that often and with great pride.

The king raised one eyebrow, and Oliver saw a sudden similarity to Poppy in the expression and the set of his jaw. "Fetch the boy," the king snapped at one of the guards.

What boy? Oliver wondered.

"To the victor go the spoils, they say," King Gregor went on after one of the guards had left. "I drew up the border to take whatever spoils I could when the war ended. Which is why I can't believe I would give Analousia half an earldom."

"I'm afraid you did, Your Majesty," said one of the ministers.

Everyone in the room turned to stare at the man, who shuffled through some papers on the table in front of him. He absently stuck a pen behind his ear, leaving streak of black ink on his gray hair.

"Here it is," he announced. "The earldom of Saxeborg-Rohlstein was declared defunct, according to this. There are

no heirs listed. All dwellings within its borders were declared empty. 'Estate abandoned, land to be divided,' it says in your own handwriting, sire. And here is your signature." He held up the paper for the king's inspection.

King Gregor snatched it from his hands and studied it. "That's my hand, all right," he said after a moment. "But I don't remember writing this. Why would I say it was abandoned?" He looked around the room, but no one answered. "I'd been to that estate, with Maude, just before the war. It was a fine place!"

Oliver wanted to snatch the paper from the king's hands and throw it on the fire, as though that would do any good. He caught the crown prince looking at him and glared. The crown prince raised his eyebrows and the fingers of one hand, as though urging Oliver to be calm.

The old minister had more papers to hand to the king. "And here is a copy of the deed giving the estate and surrounding farms to the grand duke as a reward for his service during the war, along with the title of Duke of Hrothenborg."

"Blustering fool," the king said, almost to himself. "Made a terrible duke. Does anyone remember what Hrothenborg did to deserve that?" He looked around. "Anyone?"

It seemed that no one did.

"This is highly irregular," the king remarked, striding around the room. "I'm starting to suspect that it falls into your area of expertise, Galen," he said to the crown prince.

Oliver wondered what the crown prince's area of expertise

was, and saw he wasn't the only one. He saw one of the ministers mouth, *"Knitting?"* to his fellow, who smirked.

The man with the impressive eyebrows did not look puzzled but was looking over the papers with great concern. "This isn't good, Gregor," he said in a gravelly voice.

"No, it isn't, Hans," the king retorted. "I would like to—"

"Prince Heinrich," announced the guard at the door, and Oliver's question was answered as the "boy" King Gregor had sent for entered the room.

He was actually a man in his late twenties who walked with a pronounced limp. He looked a great deal like Galen but slightly shorter and more weather-beaten. And, Oliver supposed, to someone like King Gregor, just a boy.

Oliver himself must appear to be a squalling infant, then.

Heinrich bowed and nodded all around, and then his gaze fixed on Oliver. "Yes, Your Majesty?" he said to his father-in-law without moving his eyes from Oliver.

He was married to Lily, the second oldest princess, Oliver remembered. Also, Oliver thought that Heinrich was Galen's cousin or some other relation, and looking at them made that obvious. He wondered that the two oldest princesses had been allowed to marry commoners—Galen would be the future king! What had they done to deserve such rewards?

"Heinrich," King Gregor said. "What was the name of your captain in the war?"

"The Earl of Saxeborg-Rohlstein, Caspar Saxony, sire," Heinrich said promptly.

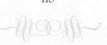

"Ever talk about his family?" The man was all but shouting at Heinrich, who looked as though it were nothing out of the ordinary.

"Oh, yes. His wife was foreign, I believe." Heinrich tilted his head, studying the ceiling as he thought. "I don't remember her name," he went on after a moment. "But he always spoke of her with great affection. He had a young son, and then a daughter? Perhaps the youngest was another son . . ." Heinrich shook his head. "I'm sorry, I just don't remember much."

"Does this young man bear any resemblance?" King Gregor asked gruffly.

Heinrich stared intently at Oliver, then nodded. "I marked it as soon as I entered, yes."

"Very well," King Gregor said. "You can stay or go."

"I believe I will go," Heinrich said deferentially. "Lily is not feeling well."

"Still?" A cloud passed over the king's face. "Hans," he said to the man with the eyebrows. "You could do more good with Lily than here, I'll wager."

"Most likely," said the other man. He handed the papers to Crown Princess Rose before following Heinrich out of the room.

"So," King Gregor barked at Oliver when the door had closed behind them. "You're an earl. Now I have to find out if I can hang an earl for banditry, or just keep you in prison for the rest of your life."

$\mathcal{F}$ugitive

Two days passed in silence. Oliver wondered if this was to be his punishment: to spend the rest of his life in the attic of the palace, alone, reading the same two books over and over.

The books were mildly interesting, but he still could not figure out why Princess Poppy had sent them. There were surely plenty of novels and books of poetry in the palace library, so Oliver was convinced that the princess had sent him these particular books for a reason, and he was determined to find it.

And really, what else was there for him to do?

One book was a history of Westfalin, beginning before it *was* Westfalin. Prior to the late fourth century, it had been nothing but a collection of walled cities. Then Ranulf, ruler of the largest city, had united them to fight the Rhwamanes in the south. After the Rhwamanes were defeated, he had declared himself king.

Oliver felt his eyes glazing over, then something jolted him, and he read one of the passages over again. Ranulf the Second, grandson of the first king, had been closely tied to a sorcerer named Wolfram von Aue. Later, Wolfram von Aue became known as the King Under Stone. The author of the book noted this with some distaste, as though reporting the rumors of magic and evildoing made him less of a historian.

Tossing that book onto the bed, Oliver scrabbled for the other. This was a slightly more whimsical work on the legends of Westfalin; there was sure to be more about the King Under Stone.

At last he found what he was looking for. This author not only believed that Under Stone had really done all that the rumors claimed, but was quite obviously afraid of the sorcerer king. The book asserted, as Oliver's mother had, that the Nine Daughters of Russaka had borne the king's sons, and it listed three other noblewomen who had done the same.

"He has at least twelve sons?" Oliver whistled. "And where do they all live? That is a lot of mouths to feed, assuming they eat and . . ."

Petunia. Poppy and Daisy. Rose. Lily, Lilac, Orchid, Violet, Hyacinth, Jonquil, Pansy, Iris. Twelve princesses, and the King Under Stone had twelve sons. Would these sons want brides to keep them company in their father's prison? The author didn't know much about the prison, saying only that it was all too appropriate that Wolfram von Aue was called the King Under Stone, which wasn't much help.

Oliver went to the door and banged on it until the guard opened up.

"I need to speak to Princess Poppy at once," Oliver said.

"No," the man said and started to close the door again.

"It's very important," Oliver protested.

The guard shook his head. "You couldn't even if it was allowed," he said. "Her Highness has gone visiting."

"When will she be back? Could I speak to Crown Princess Rose? Or Crown Prince Galen? Princess Pansy?" Oliver tried to wedge himself through the half-closed door.

"They've all gone," the man said, pushing him back into the room. "They're visiting the youngest princess in the south."

"At the Grand Duchess Volenskaya's?" Oliver felt the color drain from his face.

"Yes," the man said, and closed the door.

"Bloody hell," Oliver whispered, and slumped onto his narrow bed.

It was a trap. The Grand Duchess Volenskaya was one of the Nine Daughters of Russaka, and she was part of some plot against the princesses, Oliver was sure of it. A plot that had originated with the King Under Stone.

Oliver put his hands over his face. What was he thinking? If the King Under Stone was real, then he was long dead. Perhaps the grand duchess and her sisters had had some secret lover who braved the walls of their tower, but that hardly meant the old woman was evil.

Oliver lay back on the bed, his hands still over his face. He needed to stop worrying about Petunia and start worrying about himself and his people. Particularly if his thoughts

of Petunia were going to turn increasingly fantastical. If she was in any danger, she could take care of herself, and she was soon to be surrounded by her eleven sisters and her brothers-in-law. He'd known the princess for less than twenty-four hours; it was not his place to rescue her.

What he needed to know, much more urgently, was if his men were all right. Oliver had known that he wouldn't be coming back from Bruch, but at the time it had seemed like the right thing to do. It had filled him with a righteous sense of courage. Now that courage was fading, and he wanted to get out of here, to take his men home to their families and see his mother and brother.

And he wanted to make certain that Petunia was all right.

He leaped to his feet and started pacing. Thoughts of Petunia clearly could not be brushed aside. She was not all right, and the legends were true. He knew it. He'd seen it in the garden that night. Poppy had tried to give him clues. But there was nothing he could do, trapped in this room.

He went to the door again and pounded.

"What?" The guard looked irritated.

"I need to speak to the king at once."

"The king's done with you now, my lad," the guard told Oliver, then snapped his mouth shut as if he'd said too much.

Oliver felt like cold water had been poured over his head. "He's *done* with me?"

"You're to be sentenced in the morning," the guard muttered, and he patted Oliver on the shoulder, which was more unsettling than his words. "It's to be execution. But not hanging," he hastened to add. "Firing squad, as befits an earl." He seemed to think this would comfort Oliver.

"And my men?" Oliver could barely choke out the question.

"Hanging," the guard said, his eyes full of sympathy.

"When?"

"Soon. The king will want to do it while the princesses are gone. It would upset them."

"Yes," said Oliver. "I suppose it would."

He went to lie down again. What else was there to do?

"Do you . . . want anything?" the guard asked. "Something to eat? Or . . . to see a priest, maybe?" Having told Oliver that he would be dead before the end of the week seemed to have made the guard uncomfortable.

"No, thank you," Oliver said. Then he sat up again. "Wait! Could I speak to one of the gardeners?"

"One of the gardeners?" The guard stared.

"Yes, a gardener named Walter Vogel."

The guard shook his head. "I'm sorry, Walter's been gone for years."

"Oh." There went his mother's last piece of advice, Oliver thought. And just as well: what could a gardener do to change the mind of a king?

"Well, if you think of anything else—" the guard began.

A commotion at the end of the passage caught the man's attention. "Sorry," he said to Oliver, before closing the door.

"It's all right," Oliver said to the empty room.

"Is it really?" The voice came from near the window.

Oliver was on his feet in an instant, groping at his waist

121

for a pistol, a knife . . . But there was nothing on his belt and nothing by the window, either. Who, or what, had spoken?

"What are you?" he demanded.

"Just a man," said the voice quietly.

And then Prince Heinrich was standing in front of the window, one hand holding the collar of a dull purple cavalry cape that looked incongruous with his blue suit.

"I want to help you," he said.

"How . . . how did you do that?" Oliver stammered.

"It's this," Heinrich said.

Oliver flinched as the commoner-turned-prince reached up and fastened the cape, disappearing from view. He reappeared again, opening the cape with a wry smile.

"It's not mine," he said, sounding apologetic. "Galen let me borrow it."

"Oh," was all Oliver could think to say.

"I want to help you," Heinrich said again. "Help you escape, that is."

Oliver stared at him in astonishment. "You want to help me? But the king is about to sentence me to death! The king—your father-in-law!" Oliver made an effort to keep his voice down. "And what about my men? They have families who need them."

"They're being freed right now," Heinrich said, looking more embarrassed . . . then Oliver realized it wasn't embarrassment: the prince looked guilty.

"They are? But why? Why are you doing this?"

Oliver wondered if this was some sort of test. If he stayed

in his room with the door unlocked and the guard gone, would the king reward his honesty?

"Your father saved my life," Heinrich said, and in that instant the guilt was gone, replaced by a ferocity that caused Oliver to take a small step back. "He was one of the greatest men I have ever known. He died for me, for all of us in the Eagle Regiment. I will not let his son die for something he could not control."

"I could have—" Oliver began.

Heinrich was shaking his head. "It's not your fault that your estate was taken from you. Or that you had to turn to banditry to support your people."

"But it was still banditry," Oliver said, though he wasn't really sure why he was arguing with someone who wanted to help him.

Heinrich's gaze was far away now, seeing other rooms or perhaps a battlefield.

"My father-in-law is not a cruel man," Heinrich said. "Though he is sometimes too hasty. In a few days he will regret executing you and then it will be too late. But if you are not here to be executed . . ."

"Won't that just make him even angrier?"

"At first, but once Galen and I have had a chance to talk to him, and once his ire has cooled . . ." Heinrich shrugged. "All I know is, I will not see you face a firing squad. Something can, and will, be done to make things right for you and your people. Even the king suspects that other powers were at play when he divided up your earldom. We just need to buy a

little time while we figure this all out." His face tightened, and he looked down at his knuckles, which bore small white scars. "Fortunately, my wife and her sisters are providing a distraction."

"What's happening? Is Petunia all right?"

Heinrich looked at him for a moment. "I don't know," he said finally. "But as soon as you leave, I'll be riding after them."

"How do I leave?"

"Wearing this," Heinrich said, and swept off the cape. He offered it to Oliver, who put his hands behind his back. "Climb down the ivy outside the window," Heinrich instructed, "go to the back of the gardens. Over the wall and you're free. Your men will meet you outside of Bruch, on the road to the forest."

"How will you get out of here?" Oliver still hadn't taken the cape.

"I'll climb down to the window below yours. It's Rose and Galen's sitting room, no one will notice."

"Very clever," Oliver grudgingly admitted. "How does this work?" He finally reached out a hand for the cape.

"Put it on and fasten it, and not even your shadow can be seen," Heinrich told him.

"Where did Prince Galen get such a thing?" Oliver wondered aloud as he put on the cape and clipped the little chain. His body disappeared, giving him a strangely disconnected feeling.

"From an old woman he met on the road," Heinrich said

as though such things happened every day. "We are all very careful to be kind to every traveler we meet."

Oliver grinned, then he realized that the prince was not joking. Oliver made a mental note to also be kind to unknown travelers.

"All right," he said. "Out I go." He threw his leg over the windowsill.

"I promise you," Heinrich said sincerely, "once we get a few family matters squared away, Galen and I will work on getting amnesty for you and your men."

Oliver hesitated. "These family matters ... do you mean the shadows? In the garden at my—at the grand duchess's estate?"

Heinrich whirled around, reaching out with one hand until he connected with Oliver's shoulder. Oliver pulled his leg in and undid the cape so that Heinrich could see him. The prince's face was intense, and Oliver saw that there were fine lines around his eyes.

"You saw them?" Heinrich's voice was tight. "What did you see?"

"It— They looked like shadows, people made of shadow," Oliver stammered. "They were running across the lawn toward the manor. I followed them; they climbed the ivy to Petunia's window. I don't think that any of them got inside, though."

"They can't come inside; that's the one consolation we have," Heinrich said, looking even grimmer.

"One of them saw me," Oliver went on. "It put its hand in my chest."

"Did he speak to you? What did he say?" Heinrich asked urgently.

"His hand went into my chest and was squeezing my heart." He put a hand there, the memory causing a pang of remembered pain. "Then he said that she wasn't for me."

Oliver grimaced, suddenly embarrassed that Petunia's brother-in-law might think he was trying to woo her himself. Of course, Heinrich had been born a commoner, but at least he wasn't a wanted criminal.

"It was probably Kestilan, then," Heinrich said, his face twisted. "What else?"

"They just, they turned and went away," Oliver said. Who *was* this Kestilan? One of the King Under Stone's sons? "Back to the hothouse."

"What hothouse?"

Heinrich's gaze sharpened on Oliver again.

"The . . . shadow people . . . or whatever they were. They came out of the hothouse, the one that isn't used anymore. I mean, they store old pots and tools in it, but no plants. They came out of there."

Oliver realized that he was babbling. His greatest fear in coming to Bruch was that he would risk his life and the lives of his men, and the court would laugh at him. Shadows in the garden threatening the princess? It sounded ludicrous. But Heinrich was not laughing. The more Oliver told him, the more intense the prince's expression became.

"Are you certain?"

"Yes," Oliver said. "I was in the hothouse, sleeping." He felt himself turning red. "I was hiding from Prince Grigori," he added, so that Heinrich would not think he was living in the hothouse like a vagrant. "I dozed, and when I woke, the creatures were coming out of the floor. I followed them through the gardens to the manor."

"Excellent," Heinrich said. He clapped Oliver on the shoulder. "Thank you. Now get out of here."

Oliver put his foot on the windowsill again but stopped before he fastened the cloak.

"How will I know . . . how will you find me if you, if the king . . ." He couldn't even finish the sentence.

Heinrich, whose thoughts had clearly been miles away, focused sharply on Oliver again. "Do you remember where the royal coach crashed? That bank, where the road curves?"

"Yes," Oliver said, wondering if he would ever not remember the place where he had watched, sick, to see whether Petunia had been hurt. And where, just through the trees, he had kidnapped her.

"We'll leave a message there." Heinrich's smile turned into a grimace again. "It would help if you did not rob any more coaches."

"I'll see what I can do," Oliver said, thinking about what stores they had and how much they had taken on their last raid. "But I have people who need to eat."

"I understand," Heinrich said. "We'll work as quickly as we can to help you."

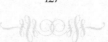

"Thank you," Oliver said. He fastened the cloak, then he stopped again. "But first . . . make sure Petunia and her sisters are safe."

"Don't worry," Heinrich said. "We will."

Oliver climbed down the ivy to freedom.

Youngest

Petunia embarrassed herself by bursting into tears when her sisters arrived.

Rose swept Petunia into her arms and held her tightly, and the others crowded in to hug or pat what part of her they could reach, even Poppy. When Rose set Petunia back on her feet and offered her a handkerchief, Petunia looked at Lily's pale, haggard face, and burst into tears all over again.

"Lilykins, what will we do?" Petunia sobbed. "It's happening all over again!"

Lily nodded soberly, opening her mouth to speak, but was interrupted.

"Now, now, my beautiful princesses," cried the grand duchess. "Into the parlor with you! You are tired from your journey, and dear Petunia has not had the rest that she needs, she has pined so for you. So first a nice cold supper in the parlor, and then early to bed, or there will only be more tears tomorrow!"

The grand dame spread her lace-gowned arms wide and ushered them all into the parlor while anxious maids tried to get the last of the cloaks, gloves, and muffs from the princesses before they entered. Petunia let the crowd of familiar faces and gowns carry her into the parlor and took the place of honor on the sofa between Rose and Lily without a murmur.

She had not returned to the Kingdom Under Stone in her sleep for three nights, not since Rionin had declared his intention to marry Lily. But now her sleep was even more restless, plagued with nightmares not sent by the King Under Stone, but by her own mind: nightmares of being trapped in the sunless kingdom forever, of fox-faced men laughing and taunting her, of marrying Kestilan in some arcane ceremony.

When the courier had arrived the next day, to announce that all the princesses would be coming to visit their sister, Petunia had nearly collapsed with relief. She had been begging the grand duchess to let her go home, but the older woman was convinced that Petunia's nighttime hysteria was a symptom of impending illness and would not let her travel.

But the sisters needed to talk. Rionin was proving to be as great a threat as his father had been, and it would only be a matter of time until a new gateway was created and they were pulled once more into the Kingdom Under Stone.

As the footmen laid out trays of tiny sandwiches, hothouse fruits, cheeses, and pastries on the side tables, Petunia looked around at her sisters. They were all uniformly pale and tired, much as they had been when they had actually danced at the Midnight Balls. Jonquil looked especially ill.

Petunia had thought (rather uncharitably) that Jonquil would have perked up when she found that Rionin didn't want her anymore, but that did not seem to be the case. Her hands shook as she accepted a cup of tea from a young footman, who seemed concerned that Jonquil would spill it down the skirts of her fine golden wool carriage dress.

"Is Jonquil still—" Petunia started to say to Rose in a low voice, but Rose shook her head. Her eyes went to the grand duchess, seated in her usual high-backed chair with its many small pillows to cushion the elderly woman's back.

"You all look so worn out, my dears," said the grand duchess, whose ears had not been dimmed by her age, something Petunia always forgot. "Is it the preparations for the double wedding that keep you so busy?" She smiled at Poppy and Daisy.

"I wish," muttered Poppy.

At the same time, from her seat on a pouf in front of Petunia's, Iris said, "Yes, but it's the wrong royal wedding." Lily gave her a light poke between the shoulder blades before she could say anything else.

"How is that, my dear Iris?"

The grand duchess had remembered their names instantly upon meeting them, which impressed Petunia. She'd spent years being called Pansy or Poppy, sometimes even by her own father. And most people seemed to have trouble telling Orchid and Iris apart, despite Orchid's wearing spectacles.

"I just . . . it was nothing," Iris said, and from behind her, Petunia could see her ears turn pink.

"I think that perhaps Iris is a touch jealous," Rose said in a confidential voice, leaning over the arm of the sofa a bit, as though sharing a secret with the grand duchess. "She is only a year younger than the twins, you know."

"I'm not—" began Iris, but both Petunia and Lily poked her and she subsided.

"It has been most trying," Poppy said in a posh voice that Petunia suspected was modeled after that of Lady Margaret, their mother's cousin, a famous Bretoner society lady with whom Poppy had lived for a year. "One wedding takes quite enough planning, but two?" She threw up her hands dramatically.

Petunia had to admire Poppy's skill at deflecting the grand duchess. Poppy, who as a child had been known for her sharp tongue and hoydenish ways, had been greatly improved by her time in Breton. Yet Petunia often got the impression that Poppy was merely playing a part, impersonating Lady Margaret, and was relieved that Poppy's personality had not gone through a permanent transformation. She could tell that Prince Christian loved Poppy just as she was, too.

"A difficult task, indeed," the grand duchess agreed. "I recall my own wedding, so many years ago. Russaka has always held itself aloof from the rest of Ionia, and our customs are very different. I thought my betrothed's mother would faint from shock when she saw my wedding headdress and heard the mandolins and flutes playing instead of the church organ."

"Did you marry here in Westfalin?" Pansy looked dreamy

at the thought. If anyone was feeling a bit jealous of the twins' upcoming marriages, reflected Petunia, it was probably Pan.

"Yes," the grand duchess said, nodding. "My betrothed was already an earl, and I was only one of nine daughters. It was easier to send me here with my mother and two of my sisters as attendants than to bring every Westfalian noble who wished to attend to Russaka!" She laughed at the memory.

Pansy looked as though she was going to press for more details, but Hyacinth, seated on the chair just beside Petunia's sofa, spoke up first.

"Nine daughters?" Her eyes were narrowed.

"Yes, it was considered a lot, until your mother went three further than mine!" The old lady cackled good-naturedly.

Hyacinth muttered under her breath, "I wonder who her mother bargained with to get nine daughters."

"My *mother* didn't make any bargains," the grand duchess said coolly, and Hyacinth looked nonplussed at being heard.

Petunia wondered if any of her sisters caught the emphasis on the word "mother." Did she, then, know someone who had made a bargain with a supernatural being? Who? The grand duchess herself? If she had in fact borne a son to the King Under Stone . . . no, Petunia couldn't even think it of her.

"Now, we must get you rested before your husbands join us tomorrow!" The grand duchess got to her feet, moving to the door of the parlor. "Though I find it most strange that none of them came with you," she added.

"Galen and Heinrich had business in Bruch," Rose said. There was a small line between her brows, and Petunia

wondered just what the cousins were doing. "And Poppy and Daisy's husbands-to-be had to return to the Danelaw and Venenzia to make their own preparations for the wedding."

"But lucky Violet's husband is coming tomorrow," Daisy said.

"Ah, the Archduke von Schwabian's son," the grand duchess said, and Petunia thought she detected a slight curl to the older woman's lip. "The musical one."

"He's picking up a new cello from the luthier," Violet said, as though it was a matter of grave political importance.

"And yours? Where is your husband?" The grand duchess looked at Hyacinth.

"He's going to Venenzia with Ricard, actually," Hyacinth said, a blush staining her cheeks. "He wished to consult with a physician there."

They were all poised to follow the grand duchess into the hall, but she stood unmoving in the doorway. "None of you have children, correct?" The question was shockingly blunt.

Lily swayed and Lilac put her arm around her older sister. Petunia glanced up at Rose and saw Rose's jaw clench. Someone gave a little gasp, and Petunia looked at Hyacinth, but Hyacinth's expression was cool, her blush gone. It was Orchid whose mouth was open in shock, her eyes flashing behind her spectacles.

"No," Rose said finally. "None of the four of us who are married have children." Her voice was steady, but deeper than normal.

"What a shame," the grand duchess said. "It's children that really tie a man and woman together."

"If I may be shown to my room," Lily said. "This has all quite worn me out."

"And I as well," Jonquil said, moving to stand beside Lily. The two of them together looked like they might simply break in half if a strong draft blew through the room.

"Of course," said the grand duchess. "Come into the front hall, and I'll have the maids show you up. I'm afraid that the stairs have become too much for me." The grand duchess's private apartments were on the main floor overlooking the gardens. In fact, they were directly below Petunia's room, and Petunia wondered if she'd seen Kestilan and his shadowy brethren coming across the lawns at night.

After the sisters had been shown to their rooms and thanked the maids for working so swiftly to unpack the princesses' luggage, they all gathered in Rose's sitting room. The maids tried to crowd in as well, but Rose sent them off with a few firm words and a quick close of the door.

"What's happening?" Petunia asked as soon as she was sure the maids were out of earshot.

"Galen and Heinrich are setting your young man free," Rose said. "That's why they won't be joining us until tomorrow. They wanted to make sure that we were out of the way, and so was Father. Dr. Kelling is taking him to the fortress for a few days, to clear his head."

"My young man? Setting him free?" Petunia stared at her.

"I have no idea what you're talking about, Rosie. What young man?"

"The handsome bandit earl," Poppy supplied.

Petunia felt her mouth slip open. *"Oliver?"*

"Yes," Rose said, and gave Poppy a quelling look before she could say anything else. "He came to Bruch last week and confessed to leading the bandits, and to abducting you."

"He did? Why would he do that?"

Petunia felt like the floor had just dropped out from under her feet. She sank down onto the very edge of a sofa, and Lilac, grumbling, made room for her. Having the leader of the Wolves of the Westfalian Woods turn himself in after all attempts to capture him had failed was likely to have put her father in a very dangerous mood.

Especially if the bandit also confessed to kidnapping one of his daughters.

Petunia could picture Oliver in the Bruch jail . . . well, what her imagination conjured for the Bruch jail, anyway. She imagined a small, dank cell with a barred door, and Oliver sitting forlorn in one corner with a rat by his feet and his curly hair lank over his smudged forehead. What purpose could turning himself in serve? She knew that he hated banditry, but his people still depended on him!

Shaking herself, Petunia looked around. Several of her sisters had been talking to her, but she hadn't heard them.

"And that answers our questions about why he gave himself up," Poppy was saying, a smile turning up one corner of her mouth as she looked at Petunia. "Now if everyone could

please avoid saying his name, so that Petunia doesn't drift off again . . . ?"

"I didn't drift off," Petunia said hotly. "I was just wondering what would make him throw it all away. . . ."

"Throw all what away?" Poppy asked. "He made it sound like he'd been living in squalor out in the forest, despite all the gold he's stolen."

"He doesn't keep it," Petunia said, defensive. "There are people who depend on him. They use the gold to buy food."

"That's what bothers me," Lily said, before Poppy could think of a retort. "If he has so many people depending on him, why didn't he tell Papa before?"

"Didn't he explain?" Petunia was eager to defend Oliver, despite Poppy's teasing. "His mother brought him to court to try to have his estate returned to him." She pointed at the floor. "This estate. It's the center of his earldom. But after the war, half of the earldom was in Analousia, and the other half was given to the grand duchess's husband." She lowered her voice on the last part. "But when they got to Bruch, we were being accused of witchcraft, and Anne was imprisoned for supposedly teaching it to us. Oliver's mother is Bretoner, and she was afraid that she would be accused too."

"That's what he told Father and the ministers," Rose said, nodding.

"But it's just silly," Orchid protested. "Why would they think she was a witch just because she was Bretoner? Papa isn't completely unreasonable!"

"But Bishop Angiers was," Petunia said. "And he was the

one doing the accusing. I remember that horrible man trying to question me, as though I were a murderer." She shuddered.

"Oliver's mother, Lady Emily, was one of Mama's closest friends," Rose said. "I remember her, though the rest of you are probably too young. Anyone who knew Mama would have recognized Lady Emily."

"She was there when Mama thought she couldn't have any children?" Poppy asked.

"And when she suddenly started to have us, one after the other," Rose said with a nod. "Witchcraft."

"I still say that's a silly way to think," Orchid protested, but they ignored her.

"I wonder," Daisy said slowly. "I wonder if Lady Emily wasn't already scared because their estate had been given away. That would certainly make me wonder if the king was angry with me. And when they arrived in Bruch, she heard the rumors and thought that she had already been accused, and that was why the earldom had been divided up?"

"Oh, pooh!" Lilac fluttered her hand. "Like Petunia said, Papa wasn't the one doing the accusing! I agree with Orchid: this whole thing seems very odd."

"Indeed it is," Rose said. "More than odd. Galen and I are certain that there was witchcraft involved—but it wasn't Lady Emily who was responsible."

"Then who *is* responsible?" Petunia asked.

"We don't know yet, although now that we know the grand duchess is one of the Nine Daughters," Rose began, but Petunia interrupted her.

"The grand duchess couldn't possibly be a witch! You'll never meet a more respectable lady!"

"At any rate," Rose said, "something is highly suspicious about Oliver's situation. Once we've . . . taken care of . . . our own problem with the King Under Stone and his brothers, Galen has promised to sort out Oliver's missing earldom."

"That's wonderful," Petunia said.

"If it works," Lilac said ominously, and then, at the expression on Petunia's face, she took out her knitting and fiddled with the needles.

"It will be well," Rose said firmly. "Galen and Heinrich took care of it; that's why they aren't joining us until tomorrow."

"What did they take care of?" Petunia felt faint, and the question was barely a whisper.

"They let Oliver go," Rose said complacently. She took out her own knitting. "And the men that came with him to confess."

"It was Heinrich's idea," Lily said with pride. "Papa was determined to execute the poor boy at the end of the week! But the old earl, Oliver's father, was Heinrich's commander in the Eagle Regiment. He saved Heinrich's life, twice, and Heinrich said he couldn't possibly let his son die. Dr. Kelling had already convinced father to go to the fortress for a few days, to take some time to think. Once they left, Galen was going to set Oliver's men free while Heinrich helped Oliver escape."

"Do you think they succeeded?" Pansy's hands were twisted together.

But Petunia didn't doubt it. She felt as if a great weight had been lifted from her chest. Galen and Heinrich had set Oliver and his men free. They could return to the forest and hide. They would be all right—*he* would be all right!

"If Galen can defeat the King Under Stone, I'm sure he can let a few prisoners out of the Bruch jail," Poppy said staunchly, and Rose smiled at her.

"But Galen didn't defeat the King Under Stone," Hyacinth said, gazing out the window at the barren winter gardens. "Not yet, anyway."

Worried

When Oliver and his men walked through the gates of the old hall, everyone within froze. Sentries had seen them, of course, and sounded no alarm, since there was no sign of any Westfalian soldiers. But they did not have the look of men returning triumphant, either. A few of the children sent up a ragged cheer, but their mothers quickly hurried them away, as though they knew that Oliver's news was nothing to celebrate.

"What happened?" Simon couldn't wait for Oliver to start talking. He leaned forward on his crutches, his face eager. "Did you see the king? Will he make you a real earl?"

"We went to Bruch," Oliver said, and to his own ears his voice sounded ten years older. Lady Emily put a hand on her younger son's arm. "And we saw the king."

"What did the king do?" Lady Emily asked gently, when Oliver did not continue.

"I was put in the palace attic," Oliver said, "and the others were put in the city jail."

Karl's wife, Ilsa, who had followed them into the old hall, clucked a bit at this, but Karl put a comforting arm around her.

"The room was small, and the windows were barred, but we had clean bedding and there was plenty of food to eat," he said. "Not that it was as good as yours," he added.

"I was in much the same situation," Oliver told his mother and brother. "A small room, but clean, good food. I even had books to read. I told the king everything—about Father, about us. I told him about meeting Petunia, and ... accidentally abducting her. He brought in one of his sons-in-law, Heinrich, who had been in Father's regiment. He confirmed that Father had died, that he had had a son, and that I looked like him," Oliver finished.

"And then what did you do, Lord Oliver?" Karl's eight-year-old daughter gazed up at him in awe, as though this were the best story she had ever heard.

"And then I went back to my room," Oliver said, wishing he had a better story to tell her. "Two of the princesses came to see me, and I told them everything as well. One of them brought me two books she thought would interest me. I read them, trying to find out why. Both of them had stories of the King Under Stone in them." He looked at his mother. "One talked of the King Under Stone being the father of the sons of the Nine Daughters of Russaka," he said meaningfully. "And other children."

"What does that have to do with us?" Simon's face was screwed up with confusion.

The men, who had not heard this part before, also looked confused, but Oliver ignored them for the moment. He could see that his mother was starting to understand some of the implications in the King Under Stone having a whole pack of strange half-human sons, and what it might mean for the beautiful daughters of King Gregor.

"But then Prince Heinrich came to my room." Oliver reached under his jacket and pulled out the dull purple cape he had stuffed there for safekeeping. "Wearing this. It makes you invisible." Karl's daughter clapped her hands in delight, and Simon looked like he would have done the same if not for his crutches. "King Gregor had decided to execute us." This did not make Karl's daughter clap. "But Heinrich owed Father his life. He claims that once the king has had time to think, he will go easier on us. He and Crown Prince Galen will argue with the king on our behalf."

"It was the crown prince himself who set us free," Johan said. "He marched right into the jail, and all the guards went to sleep like new lambs. He opened our cell, told us where to meet young Oliver, and then saw us out the door like we had been guests in his home."

"So, it's good news," Ilsa said doubtfully.

"We're wanted men," Karl told her.

"You have been for years," she scoffed.

"But now we're wanted men who've escaped jail," Karl

clarified. "And who are to wait and see if two princes can argue their father-in-law to amnesty."

"Princes can be rather flighty," Ilsa said sagely. She had been born and raised in the forest, and Oliver's parents were the closest she had ever come to nobility, let alone royalty.

"So, now what?" Simon looked disgusted. "We all just sit here and wait to see if the king forgives you?"

"More or less," Oliver said. "They'll send someone with the new verdict to the place where Petunia's coach got smashed." He turned to Karl. "We'll have to keep a watch on it. But not for a few days. The king is hunting, and the princes will be at the grand duchess's estate with their wives."

Karl grunted. "We watch that spot anyway," he said with a shrug. "It's not far from where we wait for likely coaches."

Oliver shook his head. "Just have the sentries watch that one spot. We won't need to know about any other coaches."

"What do you mean?" Simon looked from Oliver to Karl. "Did they give you money?"

"Think, Simon," Oliver said. "We're trying to convince the king to forgive us for robbing all those coaches for all those years. In order to show him that we're penitent, we need to *stop* robbing coaches."

"But what will we live on?" Simon wanted to know.

Oliver rubbed his face, wondering if he had lines etched at the corners of his mouth the way Johan did. He felt like it. He felt like he was a hundred years old. He took a breath and let it out.

"Well, you tell me," he said to his little brother. "Haven't

you begun taking over the steward's duties? What have we got? How long will it last?"

Simon thought for a moment. "We've got potatoes," he said. "Lots of dried things. You'll still let us poach game, I hope? And there's some money in the strongbox. . . ."

"We'll be fine," Lady Emily said.

And abruptly Oliver was done. He was tired. He wanted to lie in his own bed, in his own room, and never come back out. He spun on his heel and made his way up the creaking staircase, not looking back at the circle of faces below, watching him.

When he got to the top of the stairs, however, Karl's little daughter called out, "Nighty-night, Earl Oliver!"

He leaned over the banister and waved to the child, not meeting her or anyone else's eyes, and then went into his room and shut the door.

Fingering the invisibility cloak, Oliver sat down on his bed. Then he lay down, boots and all, and went to sleep. When he woke up it was dark in the room except for a single lamp near the one chair. His mother was sitting in the chair, darning a stocking.

"Are you ready to talk?" Lady Emily asked as he blinked at her.

"I hate the king," Oliver said. It surprised him.

It did not, however, appear to surprise his mother.

"He changed when Maude died," she said. She bit off the thread and rolled up the stocking, putting it in her sewing basket and taking out another. "But then, you've always hated Gregor."

"I didn't meet him until four days ago," Oliver protested weakly.

"Don't think that I don't know why you and your men have gone after every coach with a crest on the doors," she said in a reproving voice. "It was only a matter of time until you robbed one of the princesses, or Gregor himself. You've been trying to get the king's attention."

"And now I've succeeded," Oliver said bitterly. "And I didn't even have to let that fool of a Russakan prince hunt me down."

"For which I will always be grateful," Lady Emily said.

The real fervor in her voice made Oliver look at her more carefully. The golden lamplight couldn't hide her pallor or the strain around her eyes.

"I don't like the sound of this Prince Grigori," she said, and Oliver nearly laughed. "And if the King Under Stone is the father of the Nine Daughters's children, then Prince Grigori is the nephew of Under Stone's sons."

"Which means what for us?" Oliver asked.

He shifted uneasily on the bed, sitting up and fussing with the pillow behind his back. Oliver pictured Grigori roaring through the forest on his black horse, sitting impossibly tall, dark-haired, white-skinned—he didn't look human. But he was, wasn't he?

"I don't know what it means," Lady Emily said, "except that we must be cautious."

"I am," Oliver began.

"You are not," his mother countered. "Now, you

cannot just lie here until the princes send word. And you did not just throw in that link between the grand duchess and the King Under Stone as a point of minor interest to your story. What is happening?"

"You're too clever," Oliver told his mother.

"It's why your father married me," she said with a small smile. "Now talk, boy."

Oliver did smile now, but it soon faded as he related the rest of the story to her. How he had told Heinrich about the shadows in the garden, and how Heinrich had taken the matter very seriously. He told her about meeting Rose and Galen, and how they, too, had seemed haunted by something.

"The King Under Stone wants them for his sons, if not for himself," Oliver finished. "I know it. He wants Petunia."

"I can hardly blame him," Lady Emily said. "Beautiful girls—beautiful women, I should say—all of them." She eyed him. "If you were a properly landed and titled earl, you would make a fine match for Petunia."

Oliver opened his mouth and closed it again. He wasn't thinking such things. He only wanted to help.

Didn't he?

"Thank heavens you still have the crown prince's invisibility cloak," Lady Emily said with a heavy sigh. She finished darning the second stocking and put it away. Getting to her feet, she shook her head. "Just try to be careful, sneaking onto the estate. Prince Grigori, as we've said, is not to be trifled with."

Oliver opened his mouth and closed it yet again, feeling like a fish gasping on the bank.

"I—I'm not—" he finally managed.

"Of course not," his mother said drily. She bent over and kissed his forehead on her way out of the room. "I'm just glad that Simon's injury keeps him from following you."

Assassin

That night, for the first time since Rionin had declared he would marry Lily, Petunia dreamed she was back in the Palace Under Stone. She didn't know why they weren't returning there every night, but knowing Rionin, it was probably just another way to toy with them.

In this dream she was not in the ballroom, however, but in a room that contained furniture made from worn ebony, upholstered with faded violet silk. It was a bedroom, but not one she had been in before. Before, when she and her sisters had been trapped there overnight, they had all slept in one long room furnished with six narrow beds.

She looked around, almost idly, glad that she wasn't being forced to dance in her dreams, or being pestered by the princes and court of the Kingdom Under Stone. The dressing table had an onyx box of face powder and a set of silver-backed brushes, the silver tarnished black. She fiddled with one of the brushes, wondering whose room it was. One of the strange court ladies? It didn't seem much used.

"Do you like it?"

Petunia dropped the brush with a clatter and wheeled around, nearly falling over the stool as well. Kestilan stood in the doorway, his face so blank that if she hadn't recognized his voice, Petunia wouldn't have known who had spoken.

"It's the same as every other room here," she said, desperately seeking for her composure. "Black, purple, blue, silver, black, purple, blue, silver. An entire palace of bruises and darkness and nothingness, night after night, always the same."

Kestilan looked at her, one eyebrow just slightly arched. "Why would my father have wanted to be reminded of what he had lost?"

"What he had lost?" She gave him a baffled look. "What *had* he lost?"

"The sun," Kestilan said.

There was silence for a moment.

Then Kestilan went on, "Even I, who have never seen it, feel diminished when you come to us, reeking of upper world as you do, clad in colors that hurt our eyes with envy."

Petunia blinked. Rose had once accused the princes of being fools, but they weren't, she had later said. They had played at being dull because their father had wanted no rivals, and he saw his sons as easily replaced as well. What Kestilan had said made terrible sense. Gold, brocade, bright colors all belonged to the sun, to flowers and things that could not be replicated here below, where even the trees were made of silver and bore no fruit.

"I don't remember everything being so tatty," Petunia said, and now she was covering up the sudden pang of sympathy she had just felt for the late and previously unlamented King Under Stone. She fingered the silver inlay on the edge of the dressing table. It was tarnished, and there was a bit missing at the corner.

"My brother's power is not as great as our father's," Kestilan said. "But that is easily remedied."

"Is it?" She tried not to look too interested, but rubbed her fingers on her skirt as though the table had dirtied them.

"Yes," Kestilan said with the same rather studied indifference that Petunia was trying for. "He will give Jonquil and some of your other sisters to members of the court, since we are lessened in numbers. That will elevate the courtiers, and bring more power to Rionin when we dance."

"If we let you," Petunia said.

Kestilan laughed. "I have always loved how you all pretend to have any choice in the matter." He came toward her, and she did her best not to back away. He was tall, as tall as Prince Grigori, and he loomed over her, making her bend back over the dressing table a little. She put her hands behind her. "As if you were not born for this very purpose," he hissed in her ear. "To marry us, and bear our sons."

Petunia struck Kestilan across the face as hard as she could with the grimy silver hairbrush. When he howled and

grabbed his cheek, she skipped around him and out the door of the room, though she did not know where she was going. She ran down the hall with him in pursuit, dark blood—darker than human blood—coming from his nose.

"This will be our room, Petunia," he shouted after her. "When we are wed."

Petunia ignored him, running even faster as ahead she saw the front hall of the palace. The front doors were open wide, and she ran out and down the steps to the black lake. There was no way across: the water of the lake burned the skin and the boats were gone. Across the water, she could see the silver trees moving in a breeze that no one could feel.

The trees had grown from a blessed silver cross their mother had once dropped on her way to the Midnight Ball, and their wood had proved to be deadly to Under Stone and his sons. Now Petunia wished she could get to the little wood, not to escape, but so she could gather some of the branches of those trees. She imagined whittling daggers or arrows from them, weapons that could be used to attack Rionin and Kestilan and the others.

She felt in her pockets for the little scissors she carried to snip yarn with, and remembered that this was just a dream. And even if she could get across the water and break off some of the branches, she wouldn't wake up in the morning with the silver in her hands.

"Come here," Kestilan ordered, crunching across the coarse black sand of the shore.

The sand, too, was more than it appeared: Galen had

brought a handful out with him during their escape from the first King Under Stone, and it had turned out to be tiny black diamonds. Galen later had them set into a bracelet for Rose. Petunia bent and gathered up a handful, rubbing the sharp little jewels between her palms.

"What are you doing?" Kestilan's nose still bled, and he was flushed to an almost normal human ruddiness with his anger.

"This is just a dream," Petunia said. "So this won't hurt."

She cast the diamonds into his eyes.

As he howled and clawed at his face. Petunia reached into the sash of her gown. It was just a dream, so the rules of the real world didn't apply. She normally didn't walk around with a pistol stuck into her sash like a pirate in a romance, but in a dream she could do as she liked. She drew the pistol she found there, cocked it, and fired, shooting the ground an inch from Kestilan's right boot.

"Don't worry, it's just a dream," she told him, her voice sounding strange and faraway.

"Have you gone mad?"

Servants and courtiers came running at the sound of the shot, and Petunia brandished the pistol at them, causing them to draw back. Among the crowd she saw Blathen and Telinros, and she aimed at the latter. He was Pansy's partner at the Midnight Balls.

"If you can do what you like to us in our dreams, then we should have the same freedom," she said as she drew back the hammer and heard the bullet click into place. Telinros put his hands up in a gesture of surrender. "Coward," she muttered.

"Petunia," said the King Under Stone, arriving at last, the servant who had summoned him cringing at his heels. "Let us not be foolish."

"I am not being foolish," Petunia said, and now she aimed at the king. The pistol shook only slightly. "I am merely taking my cue from you, Your Majesty, and doing what I like with these dreams. A pity this isn't a real pistol, and that I am not really here. You are not immune to bullets, as I recall from the last time we met in the flesh."

"That has changed now that I am king," Rionin said with cold pride. "Though my brothers have not that advantage."

"Good to know," Petunia said. She readied her finger on the trigger.

"But Petunia," Rionin said with a smile. "When next we meet in the flesh, and that moment is rapidly approaching, you will not have a pistol. You will have nothing but what we give you."

"How enticing," Petunia said, her voice just as cold and distant as his. "I can hardly wait."

She squeezed the trigger and shot the King Under Stone. And woke up, in a sweat, in the bed she shared with Pansy at the grand duchess's estate.

"Are you all right?" Pansy's voice came in a mumble, her face half buried in her pillow.

"I just shot Rionin," Petunia gasped, sitting up.

"You did what?" Pansy pushed herself up on her elbows. "You shot Rionin?"

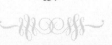

"In my dream," Petunia said.

"I wasn't there," Pansy said. "I was sleeping, just sleeping."

"I dreamed that I was there with Kestilan," Petunia told her, "and I got so angry that I hit him. I threw the diamond sand in his eyes, and then I thought of having a pistol and it appeared. The others came out of the palace and I shot Rionin," Petunia said, panting. "He made me look at the room he said would be our room—his and mine—when we are wed. Kestilan, not Rionin. Rionin wants to marry Lily. Still. I think. But Kestilan said that Rionin is going to give Jonquil and those of us whose partners are dead to some of the courtiers, to increase his power."

"What are we going to do?" Pansy asked, her face white.

~

"Did he say when you would wed?" Rose asked when Petunia had awakened her to tell her about the dream. "Do you have any idea when this will happen?"

"No," Petunia said, and tried not to feel guilty that she hadn't thought to find out.

She and Pansy had gone to Rose's room, which she was sharing with Jonquil for the night, to tell them what had happened. Jonquil was sitting up, and Lily was trying to coax her to drink some chamomile tea and try to sleep, when the two youngest sisters entered. Soon they were all huddled on the wide bed, with Petunia describing her dream in detail.

Maybe she should have asked more questions of Kestilan,

she thought, and done less hitting. And shooting. But she didn't particularly enjoy these dreams, and attacking Kestilan and Rionin had been deeply satisfying.

"Galen thinks ... he thinks Rionin will make his move soon," Rose said with a little catch to her voice. "I just wondered if they'd hinted at how soon."

"Now, Rose," Lily said comfortingly. "It was three years ago when Blathen went after Poppy in Breton. We thought then that Rionin would try to do something, but there was nothing except the dreams."

"Yes, I know," Rose sighed. "But now the dreams are coming nearly every night. And they're more than just dreams ... the line between dreaming of the balls and being there physically is blurring somehow. Their father couldn't do such things."

"And they're trying to come into the house, through the garden, like they did that time at home," Petunia said, then rather wished she hadn't when Jonquil made a small sobbing noise.

But Rose just nodded. "Keep whatever charms you've got on at all times," she said.

Petunia self-consciously checked for hers. She had both a knitted bracelet and a charmed garter on, even though she was in her nightgown and not wearing any stockings.

"I gave you those sachets to put under your pillows, though it doesn't seem to have worked for Petunia tonight," Rose went on. "Also, keep your pistols handy, and plenty of bullets. The silver daggers that Bishop Schelker blessed for us too."

"I feel strange carrying weapons around," Pansy admitted.

"We're at war," Petunia told her. "A soldier needs his weapons close during a war." It was something both Galen and Heinrich had always told them.

"I don't want to be a soldier," Pansy whined.

"I don't think we have a choice, Pan," Lily said gently.

Petunia's pistol and dagger were hidden under her mattress. She hadn't been carrying them at all, here at the estate, even though she knew it was foolish. But it wasn't as if she could wear a leather belt and holsters over a morning gown. She'd tried cutting slits in her skirts so that she could wear her weapons underneath them, but Olga kept sewing them up again. She supposed she'd just have to settle for hiking up her skirts, flashing her legs at Kestilan, and then shooting him, if it came to that.

"I keep thinking about the silver wood," Petunia said. "Galen and Lily shot four of the princes. But if they become king, they have to be killed with blessed silver and their true name. Do we know Rionin's true name? Is it Rionin?"

"We can hardly ask to look in the family bible," Pansy grumbled.

"But . . . maybe it's foolish, but I just keep thinking of how the wood was Mother's . . . it sprouted from her brooch," Petunia said. "I wonder if it has extra power. I wish we could get a few branches, and make arrows or bullets or knives out of it."

"To do that," Jonquil said in a faint voice. "You'd have to go back *there*."

"It would be worth it, to get some of their silver branches," Petunia said stubbornly.

Rose just shook her head. "There's simply no way to sneak into the Kingdom Under Stone," she said. "For one thing, we don't know how to get there anymore. And once you got there, you'd have to unlock the gate . . . and goodness knows that Galen's chain is barely holding it closed as it is. I think that's the only thing that's keeping Rionin and his brothers from coming to take us away."

Jonquil gave a small moan, but the others ignored her.

"And Galen's working on a way to seal them in permanently?" Lily asked.

Rose nodded.

This made Petunia want some of the silver branches more, before they lost that piece of their mother forever. Their father had created the gardens around the palace for Maude, but the silver wood had been truly Maude's, and only hers, in a way.

"He is working on a spell to close the gate for good," Rose told them. "If he can't find a way to destroy the Kingdom Under Stone completely."

Spy

In the end, Oliver arrived at the estate at the same time as the princesses' husbands, though they arrived in coaches, and Oliver was on foot. And, while the princes were welcomed at the front gates, Oliver went to the back wall and climbed over.

Of course, Oliver could have walked through the front gate with the princes. He had been wearing the dull purple invisibility cloak since he'd left the old hall.

Being invisible made Oliver feel very strange. Animals sensed him coming, heard him, smelled him, but panicked when they could not see him. He walked openly along the road, and other travelers passed him without pausing, as though he didn't exist. He wasn't sure he liked the feeling, and invisibility was dangerous besides. He thought constantly of all things that could happen to someone who could not be seen: coaches could run him down, stray bullets from hunters might hit him, and who would find his body? Even if he fell, broke his leg, bumped his head...if he were unconscious, there would be no way to receive help.

It was with a profound relief that he made his way to the unused hothouse and went inside. He left the cloak in place, but at least he knew he wouldn't be shot, trampled, or otherwise injured inside the little building. He would be able to investigate the floor at his leisure, in good light, without worrying about one of the gardeners seeing him moving about and coming to look. Which, he supposed, made the invisibility cloak worth the other problems it might cause.

Oliver tried to remember where the shadows had come from. It had been toward the front of the hothouse, he thought. There was a large worktable there, covered with pots and rusty spades with chipped blades. He wondered why they didn't throw such things away: the pots were cracked, the tools broken, and it wasn't as if they were using the hothouse to start new plants. It had clearly become a dumping ground for junk, even more so than in his family's time.

"And now here's a thing," said Oliver aloud.

Bending down, he could see that there was no dust on the tiled floor under the table. Not like it had been disturbed by the shadow creatures, but like it had been carefully cleaned. The red clay tiles looked almost polished. Oliver squatted to look at the floor more closely.

Nothing about the tiles under the table and leading to the door looked any different than the tiles on the rest of the floor. They were just...cleaner. But how often were they cleaned? He could see the scuffed footprints he had made both times he had come into the hothouse, but no others. So if anyone had come in to sweep in the nearly two weeks since he had last been here, they hadn't stepped beyond this front area. And how often did someone sweep? It was as clean as if it had been done this morning, and yet the latch on the door had been grimy and hard to lift.

And who swept the way for the shadow creatures, anyway? One of the gardeners? Or Prince Grigori himself?

More baffled than ever, Oliver put one hand down to help lever himself up and felt something on the tiles. Knees creaking, he crouched down farther and rubbed his fingers across the floor. There was definitely something on the tiles, but he still couldn't see anything. He scraped it with a fingernail and came up with a little skiff of clear wax.

Leaning over until his nose nearly touched the tiles; he saw that someone had drawn on the floor with wax. He could feel the marks and lines with his fingers. They had sketched or written something on the tiles under the table and leading to the door.

But once again he thought: who had done this? If this was how the shadows gained access to the gardens and to Petunia, then surely someone else must have done the wax writing, in order to summon them here.

No matter who it was, the princes would need to know. Oliver had told Heinrich which hothouse he had seen the shadow creatures come from, but would he find the wax writing? With their status as honored guests, and without the invisibility cloak, it would be hard for the princes to slip

away long enough to thoroughly investigate the place. Oliver wondered if he dared to leave them a message, but he didn't have anything to write with.

His heart thudding, Oliver realized that there was nothing for it: he would have to sneak into the manor and tell someone in person. And the only person he knew he could find easily was Petunia.

At first he wondered how to occupy himself until nightfall, but he remembered that there was no need to wait. No one would see him climbing up to her window, and everyone would be downstairs with the newly arrived princes. Oliver would be able to find himself a comfortable spot to hide until Petunia returned to her chamber.

He almost whistled as he strode across the lawns.

The ivy that grew up the back wall of the manor was just as thick as at the palace in Bruch and easily bore Oliver's weight. He made it to the window ledge without incident, which was a relief. Even though he was invisible, he had still felt exposed scaling the wall of the manor in broad daylight. He couldn't imagine what would have happened if the clasp of the cloak had broken or if a gardener had investigated the strange way the ivy was shaking on a windless day.

He latched the window and searched the room for a hiding spot. He was worried that if he sat in one of the chairs to wait, someone would come in and sit on him before he could move.

The wardrobe? It was so full of gowns that he didn't think he could cram himself inside. Besides, it would be awkward if

the maid came in to lay out a gown for dinner and grabbed Oliver instead of the blue silk with the lace sleeves.

He finally settled on the space under the bed. It was high enough that he could lie on his back comfortably, and the maids were very diligent; there was not a speck of dust to irritate his nose. He crawled under on his elbows and settled himself to wait.

Once again Oliver found himself falling asleep. He pinched his thigh, embarrassed, but it was no good. He had trouble sleeping at night, worrying about everything from Simon's ankle to Petunia's safety. But apparently he could drop off to sleep in places far less comfortable and far more dangerous than his own bed. Still, he was a light sleeper, and he knew he would awaken when someone came into the room, so at last he let himself drift.

"—not going to work," came Petunia's voice. "It's already been remade to fit me."

"Why must you be so short," grumbled another voice. Groggily, Oliver placed it as Princess Pansy as she continued to talk. "I mean, honestly, are you *trying* to grow?"

"Do you think I enjoy being short?" Petunia shot back. Then she laughed, taking the sting out of her words. "Cousin Edgar keeps calling me Pocket-size! It's disgusting!"

Through a bubble of laughter, Pansy replied, "I thought you were just doing it so you wouldn't have to share your clothes."

Continuing their good-natured bickering, they went over to the wardrobe. Oliver was about to slide out from under

the bed when he noticed a third pair of feet had followed them into the room. From the plain gray hem of her gown Oliver knew that it was a maid, and one of the grand duchess's household. If she had been wearing the black gown of the royal household he might have risked it, but one of the grand duchess's maids was sure to sound the alarm. He stifled a sigh and prepared to wait some more.

There was no fear he would doze off again, as he saw the day gowns of first one sister, then the other, hit the floor. Stocking feet walked all around the bed, and then the stockings were rolled off as well. Oliver tried not to look, but he couldn't help himself. Petunia's feet were just as delicate as the rest of her, he noticed, and she had a habit of spinning on her toes when she turned, as though she were dancing.

New silk stockings were pulled on. Ruffled petticoats. Corsets were tightened—judging from the grunting—and satin slippers tied onto narrow little feet. And then came the gowns. Petunia was indeed wearing the blue silk with lace sleeves that Oliver had noticed before, and Pansy wore something pink. Oliver hoped to catch them on their way out of the room, and hoped that the maid would not stay behind to straighten up.

But the princesses' evening toilette was not yet finished. They each had their hair taken down and redone by the maid, and then there were jewels to put on, and gloves and fans to be gathered. Oliver really began to wonder if he shouldn't just roll out of his hiding spot and try to overpower the maid. This was interminable!

"Olga," Petunia said, just as Oliver had decided to risk it. "Would you please go see if Maria needs any help? She's supposed to be dressing Rose, Lily, and Jonquil, and Jonquil is very particular."

"Yes, Your Highness."

The door closed behind the maid, and Petunia stuck her head under the edge of the bed.

"Oliver, is that you?"

"Petunia! What are you doing?" Pansy sounded startled.

"I can hear you breathing under there," Petunia announced. "And I smelled evergreen sap."

She frowned, her blue eyes searching in the darkness under the bed, and Oliver remembered that he was still wearing the cloak.

"Yes, it's me," he said.

Pansy let out a small scream, and Petunia shushed her.

"I'll come out, I've got Prince Galen's cloak on."

Petunia stepped back as Oliver crawled out from under the bed. Once he was on his feet, he took off the cloak and folded it over his arm. Pansy gasped again as he became visible but didn't scream.

"What are you doing here?" Petunia demanded.

Pansy had a more pressing question, however. "Did you watch us undress?"

Oliver felt himself turning red. "Just . . . just your feet," he stammered. "I mean, I only saw your feet. I wasn't trying to look, I swear!"

Pansy looked scandalized, and she actually bent her knees

165

a little so that the hem of her gown concealed her feet even more. He must have been born under an unlucky moon, he thought ruefully.

Petunia smacked his upper arm. "So what are you doing here, other than spying on us in our underthings?"

"I came to warn you," he said, trying to stand up straight and appear trustworthy.

Both princesses immediately looked wary, exchanging glances. "Warn us of what?" Petunia asked. She studied him with those blue, blue eyes and Oliver wondered all over again what he was doing here.

"The Nine Daughters of Russaka," he blurted out at last, before he lost his nerve.

Petunia blinked, but she didn't say anything.

"The grand duchess is one of the Nine Daughters of Russaka," he continued. "And they . . . their sons that they had in the tower . . . were the sons of the King Under Stone."

"We know about the grand duchess," Petunia said. "Though I still don't believe it entirely. And who told *you* about the King Under Stone?" There was a crease between Petunia's brows.

"Princess Poppy," he replied. "It was in a book that she gave me, while I was in Bruch. So I guessed that . . . that you and your sisters, you were entrapped by the King Under Stone all those years ago, and that's why your dancing shoes wore out every night. Now that you're here as *her* guests, I thought you should know about the connection between them. Also, I found something in the hothouse where I saw the shadows coming up out of the floor, and I wondered if Crown Prince Galen had had a chance to look at the floor there."

The princesses seemed slightly stunned by all the words that had come out of Oliver's mouth, and neither of them said anything for minute. Then Pansy took a tentative step toward the door, and Petunia stopped her with a hand on her older sister's arm.

"Are you accusing the grand duchess of being in league with the King Under Stone?" Petunia didn't look shocked, but her face had gone hard, and Oliver's heart sank a little.

"Yes?" He wished that it didn't sound like a question. "I mean, I don't know. But I do know . . . or, er, I believe that she did have one of the King Under Stone's sons. Did you know he had twelve? All with noblewomen?"

"Yes," Petunia said, and now her voice was wintry. "I knew."

"Oh," Oliver said. He suddenly felt extremely foolish. "So, I just, was worried that you might not be safe," he said lamely.

Oliver could feel his ears burning. Why had he come? They probably knew much more than he did. Princess Poppy had probably just given him the books because he was bored and she had them at hand, and not in some roundabout plea for help.

"You saw shadows in the garden?" Petunia asked.

"Yes," Oliver said. "The first night that you were here. They looked like men, or the shadows of men, and they ran through the garden toward your window," he told her, hoping that at least this bit of information would be useful.

Petunia looked toward the window, thoughtful. "You say they came out of one of the hothouses? And you found something there? What?"

Before he could answer, though, Pansy spoke up. "If you won't let me get Rose and Galen," she complained, "at least let me lock the door, Pet."

Petunia let go of her sister, who hurried to lock the door.

"Keep one ear to the door, please," Petunia told her. "Olga never lets me out of her sight for very long. And she has her own key." She sighed heavily.

"I found wax, clear wax all over the floor leading to the door of the hothouse," Oliver said, before he put his boot in his mouth by saying that Olga sounded more like a jailer than a maid. "It looks like someone has written something in the wax, but I can't make it out."

Petunia rose up on her toes, seemingly excited. "So you've seen Kestilan and his brothers, and you think you know how they get into the gardens here?"

"Kestilan?" There was that name again. Oliver fought down an irrational surge of jealousy for this mysterious being who took up so much of Petunia's attention.

"That's the name of the youngest prince," Petunia clarified.

"Yes, then, I suppose I did see him," Oliver told her. "I didn't really know what he—they—were."

"They are the sons of the King Under Stone," Petunia said. "But they aren't supposed to be here, in this world. They're supposed to be shut up in the prison that was created to hold their father."

"Someone's coming," Pansy whispered.

Oliver slung the cloak over his shoulders and fastened the clasp.

"Get back under the bed," Petunia murmured. "And listen."

"All right." Oliver crawled back under the bed and lay still, trying to keep his breathing as quiet as possible.

"We all took a tour of the gardens this afternoon at Galen's insistence," Petunia said, speaking in a quick, low voice. "Grigori led us around, though, and I guess he just thought that Galen was interested because he used to be a gardener. But Grigori said the hothouses were boring, and we didn't go anywhere near them. So we'll have to try tomorrow—"

The doorknob rattled.

"My princesses, it is time for dinner," called the maid through the door. "Why have you locked the door? Open, please."

Oliver bit back a laugh as Petunia said something under her breath that was not fit language for either a princess or indeed a young lady of any rank. He settled in for another nap, and wished he'd asked her to bring him something from dinner. It was going to be a very long night.

Prayer

At dinner, Petunia could not stop thinking about how much Prince Grigori looked like the princes Under Stone. She had never thought about it before, but with his pale skin and black hair, he could easily be one of them. But did that mean that he was part of some larger plot? Was he helping the princes? How could she find out? She caught herself staring at him, eyes narrowed, and tried to concentrate on the food instead.

"Pet is always a bit out of sorts in the winter," Pansy suddenly said, in a lighthearted tone that made everyone turn their attention to her. "It's because she's so devoted to Mother's gardens, you know. Anytime she can't be out digging in the dirt she becomes restless." Then she blushed. "Not that she likes being dirty, or rooting around in the mud," she clarified.

"Really, Petunia? I knew that you were fond of gardens, but I didn't know that you liked gardening itself!" Prince Grigori smiled at her, and Petunia gritted her teeth over the indulgent look on his face. He probably thought she liked picking flowers for table arrangements or some other ladylike pursuit.

"Yes," she said, slicing a sprout in half with unnecessary vigor. "I have been working with my father and our head gardener for several years in the hothouses, perfecting my father's hybrid roses. We're trying to create a yellow rose that blushes pink in the center."

To her satisfaction, this did appear to impress the prince.

"You are creating new roses?"

She liked that he did not seem surprised that *she* was the one creating the roses, but more that such a thing was possible. She nodded her head graciously at him.

"Yes, we are. It's quite exciting, really."

Orchid made a face. "It's really not, unless you're also obsessed with roses," she said.

Petunia glared at her.

"It's quite complicated," Rose put in. "And I do think my father is a little disappointed that the only one of us with a gift for gardening is Petunia. I think he hoped for three or four who would enjoy talking about grafting and cross-pollination."

"I have never heard either of those terms," Prince Grigori admitted.

"Then you should certainly have Petunia take you to the hothouses tomorrow afternoon and explain them," Pansy said with an excessive amount of enthusiasm. "And Galen and Heinrich should go with you; they've both worked in the gardens as well."

Petunia finally saw what Pansy was doing and tried to

kick her under the table but it was too wide. Pansy's voice was so bright it sounded strained. Petunia dropped her knife with a clatter.

"Clumsy!" she exclaimed, and snatched it up again. "I would be delighted to have a tour of the hothouses tomorrow, Grigori. But don't worry, I shan't think less of you if you aren't interested." She gave a tinkling laugh that was just as false as Pansy's bright tones, then quickly changed the topic. "Violet, would you like to play for us after dinner? The grand duchess's pianoforte is very fine."

"It is of Romansch make," the grand duchess said, as Violet and her husband, Frederick, exchanged eager looks. "My granddaughter Nastasya plays, but since she went back to Russaka, there has been no one to play for me."

"I would be thrilled to play," Violet said, and squeezed her husband's hand.

"I would love to play a duet with you," Frederick said, giving Violet a smoldering look.

"Oo-ooh," said Poppy, and winked at them.

"Poppy!" Daisy poked her twin in the side.

"And perhaps you could play for us while we have a little dancing?" the grand duchess asked. "There are not enough gentlemen to go around, but then, dear Petunia does not dance."

Petunia looked down at her plate and sighed.

"Petunia loves to dance," Lilac told the grand duchess. "For quite some time, she was the only one of us who did."

"But did your father not send a letter, Petunia, when you

172

were at court stating that you were not to dance?" The grand duchess's green eyes studied Petunia's still-red face.

"Petunia had been ill, we all had, but the effects hadn't lingered," Hyacinth said quickly. "Our father was rather overprotective of us, the way that fathers can be."

"I certainly know how overprotective fathers can be," the grand duchess said, her voice dry. "So if that is all it is, I would love to see Petunia dance with my Grigori later."

Just when she thought her blush couldn't get any hotter, Petunia felt her face absolutely burning. And it didn't help that she could not stop thinking of Oliver lying underneath her bed upstairs. Suddenly her made-over gown felt awkward, and the lace at the décolletage was scratching her.

"Are you all right?" Heinrich murmured.

"I'll be fine," Petunia said under her breath. She smiled brightly down the table at the grand duchess, who was also watching her. "Shall we have the dancing now, Your Grace?"

"Of course, dear Petunia," the grand duchess said with a chuckle. She rose and led the way into the drawing room.

Dancing with Prince Grigori was somewhat difficult. He was so tall that she had to either crane her neck to see his face or converse with his coat buttons. It was easier to dance with Galen or Heinrich, who were tall but not freakishly so. Heinrich, despite the old injury to his leg, was a steady, reliable partner, and Galen was quite skilled. Violet's Frederick was the shortest gentleman present, but he liked to add little flourishes when he danced.

Daisy took a turn at the pianoforte twice, to let Violet

dance with her husband, and Petunia even gave in to the grand duchess's urging and played a valse, the only dance music she knew.

"Now look at my Petunia," the grand duchess said. "She dances, plays music, gardens, and knits! Such an accomplished girl on top of all her beauty!"

Petunia didn't have to fake an embarrassed smile, fanning herself to cover her warm cheeks—would the blushing never stop this evening? Looking at Iris's face, Petunia could see that she was preparing some biting comment and frowned at her sister.

The grand duchess held out a slender hand, elegantly gloved in gray silk. "Dear Petunia, please help me to my room. I will retire for the night."

"Of course, Your Grace," Petunia said at once.

They all made their bows and curtsies, and then Petunia took the fine-boned hand and helped the grand dame to rise. They went out of the drawing room and past the stairs to the long hallway that led past the ballroom and the portrait gallery to the grand duchess's apartments. As she rang for the grand duchess's maid, Petunia tried to assume a casual air.

"Do you spend a great deal of time looking out at the gardens?" she asked as the grand duchess sank down on a sofa near the windows.

Petunia couldn't help but notice that, while the curtains were open, the windows were not. She was sure that the windows of her own bedchamber were wide open, letting in the icy air. And Kestilan.

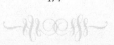

"Not during the winter," the grand duchess said with a chuckle. "At least, not during the Westfalian winter. So bleak! Russakan winters, you remember, are a fantasia of snow and ice. But this?" She shrugged one silk-covered shoulder at the window. "I don't know why my maid hasn't drawn the curtains tonight."

There was a faint scratch at the door, and her maid entered. The woman gave a dismayed shriek when she saw her mistress sitting before the uncovered windows and rushed to release the heavy velvet curtains from their embroidered ties.

"Still and all," the grand duchess said, ignoring her fussing maid, "these old bones do wish for a place where there is no snow or ice. Where there are only gentle winds to stir the branches of the trees and the sand along the shore of the lake."

"What lake is that?" Petunia asked, frowning. She had a sudden image of the black lake in the silver wood, but cast it aside. "Is that where you lived as a child?"

"Nowhere I've been," the grand duchess said, shaking her head. "Just a place I wish existed."

"Oh," Petunia said. Again she rejected a vision of the Kingdom Under Stone. The maid was now making motions about removing her mistress's gloves and jewels. "Well, good night, Your Grace."

"Good night, my dear Petunia," said the grand duchess. Her green eyes fixed sharply on the maid at last. "Good heavens, Ilenya, have you always been this incompetent?"

Petunia, forgotten, backed away. The grand duchess's

sharp tone and the flash in her green eyes made Petunia feel distinctly uncomfortable, but she couldn't think why. They reminded her of someone, but she couldn't recall who. Grigori's eyes were brown.

Petunia hurried up to her own bedchamber, where Pansy was already being undressed by Olga. Thinking that Oliver probably had not eaten all day, Petunia rang the bell and ordered the footman to bring a plate of something. The entire time, she was intensely aware of Oliver lying under her bed as Olga helped her and Pansy undress. Petunia forced herself to nibble one of the small sandwiches the footman brought, and Pansy took another, then they both protested loudly at the idea of having the plate taken away, though neither of them was touching the rest of the food. Petunia wondered how she would get the food to Oliver, or talk to him, if Olga insisted on sitting in the room, sewing all night, as she sometimes did.

Inspiration struck as Pansy knelt by the side of the bed to say her prayers. Petunia was not much for praying, personally, though she had had religious instruction by Bishop Schelker alongside her sisters. Still, she knelt beside Pansy and ignored her sister's startled look.

"I'm so tired, I think I will pray aloud tonight so that I don't drift off," Petunia announced.

"All right, but don't take too long about it," Pansy grumbled as she climbed into bed.

Petunia ignored Pansy and Olga, who was hovering nearby, and bowed her head over her folded hands. She took a moment to order her thoughts, and then plunged in.

176

"Dear God," she said loudly. "Please protect my sisters and their husbands and their husbands-to-be. Please bless my father, and Dr. Kelling, and Bishop Schelker. Please watch over all of us here at the estate, especially the grand duchess, because she is innocent and frail. Please watch over Prince Grigori, that he will not be tempted to do evil, and Olga, that she will also be good." Petunia shifted on her knees, feeling Olga's eyes boring into the back of her head. "Please guide Galen and Heinrich in their studies, since they do not know where to direct their attention at this time, and please help them find a way to guard us all from our nightmares. Amen."

"Forgive me, Your Highness, but Westfalian prayers seem very odd," Olga said, helping Petunia into bed.

"I would imagine that they do," was all Petunia answered. She could see by Pansy's face that her sister had understood the purpose of her prayer.

"If I may ask, Your Highness, what are the princes studying?" The maid's brow was creased with confusion. "I thought that they were past the age of school."

"They're studying magic," Pansy said, before Petunia could think of an evasion.

She looked at the maid quickly to see how Olga reacted. Olga snorted and rolled her eyes, as though Pansy were just being silly.

"Now could you please turn out the light?" Pansy snapped. "And don't you dare take those sandwiches, I might want one later!"

Pansy rolled over and went to sleep, but Petunia stayed

awake long after Olga left, and long after Oliver crawled out from under the bed, grabbed some sandwiches, and slipped out the door. She hoped that he was going to Galen and Rose's room, and she hoped, too, that he hadn't known she was awake when he had leaned over her and kissed her hair. She wanted to savor that touch forever.

Conspirator

Oliver had never had someone pray to him before. It had been slightly amusing until he realized that if Petunia was frightened enough of her maid to use such a ruse, Oliver really should be on his guard. When they first met, Petunia had pointed a pistol directly at his face without wavering for an instant, yet she was being terrorized by this Olga.

Did the King Under Stone have human servants outside of his kingdom who were helping him? If he did, this maid was certainly suspect. Oliver's experience with servants was limited, but it seemed to him that a good lady's maid wouldn't order her mistress around in quite the way that Olga did with Petunia and Pansy.

Once he was sure that the maid was gone and the princesses were asleep, Oliver rolled out from under the bed. He found the plate of sandwiches and shoved one in his mouth whole, wrapping two more in a napkin and stowing them in a pocket.

Chewing and swallowing quickly, he leaned over Petunia

and kissed her inky curls. He just couldn't help himself. His eyes had grown accustomed to the dark after a long day spent under the bed, so he could see her white face nestled in the blackness of her hair. He was sure she would wake if he touched her face, so he was careful only to press his lips to her soft hair, breathing in its scent of flowers and cinnamon, before he slipped out of the room.

He made his way down the hall, not sure where to find Galen or Heinrich. His every nerve was on edge—even though he was invisible—in case he stumbled upon Grigori. He listened at each of the doors, hearing nothing, until at the fourth door there was the sound of a woman crying and a man's voice speaking in soothing tones. He hated to interrupt such a scene but didn't know what else to do, so he softly knocked.

The voices went silent, then the man called out, asking who was there. It was Prince Heinrich, and some of Oliver's tension drained away.

"It's Oliver," he said, as loudly as he dared.

The door was opened immediately, and Heinrich peered out into the corridor. Seeing nothing, he stepped back, opening the door wider. Oliver slipped in, tapping the prince on the shoulder so that Heinrich would know where he was. The prince quickly shut the door and locked it.

Distinctly uncomfortable, Oliver undid the cloak and watched his body reappear. Princess Lily was sitting up in the bed in her nightgown, her eyes red from crying and her face pale and thin. Her hair, a rich dark brown, was loose and fell nearly to the bedclothes.

"I'm so sorry to disturb you," Oliver said, staring at his boots. "But I have information, and I needed to give it to you right away. I told Petun—Princess Petunia—but she hasn't been able to speak to any of you privately, so I thought I would come myself."

"You'd better fetch Rose and Galen," Lily said to her husband.

Heinrich left so silently he might as well have been invisible.

"If you don't mind, I'm going to put my dressing gown on," Lily said.

"No, I don't—oh!" Oliver quickly turned his back to the princess.

He heard her slip out of the bed and the rustle of her putting on a dressing gown. There was a flapping noise as she put on slippers as well.

"Thank you," she said.

Oliver turned around to find her in a lavender silk dressing gown. She expertly braided her long hair and tied a ribbon around the end, smiling at him as he watched in a sort of dazed fascination.

"Petunia's hair is too curly to braid," she said conversationally.

Oliver wasn't sure why, but that was what finally made him blush. Not barging in on her and her husband during a private moment. Not seeing her in her nightgown, but her mentioning Petunia's hair.

The hair he had just kissed.

He made a noncommittal noise and almost collapsed with

relief when the door opened a heartbeat later to admit Heinrich and the crown prince and princess. Galen was still dressed, though he was wearing a plain dark suit and not evening clothes. Seeing him, Oliver realized that Heinrich was dressed in much the same unobtrusive manner.

Rose was in a dark-red dressing gown with Far Eastern embroidery. She gave Oliver a warm smile without a hint of self-consciousness as she sat on the bed. Lily sat beside her, and they all looked expectantly at Oliver, who cleared his throat.

"I came to make sure that Princess Petunia and the rest of you were all right," he began, wondering how much of an idiot he was going to feel like before this was all through. "I went to the hothouse I told you about before, the one that I saw the shadows coming from, and I looked around to see if I could find anything."

"I take it that you did," Galen said, raising an eyebrow.

"Yes," Oliver said, encouraged. "At first I didn't think there was anything to find, but then I noticed that the floor was swept clean from the table in the middle to the door, but it didn't look like anyone had been in the hothouse since I was there two weeks ago. When I looked closer, I saw that someone had written on the floor with wax, but I couldn't decipher the writing."

The two princes exchanged looks.

"Do you . . . want me to show you?" Oliver offered, wondering if they were now about to thank him and then send him

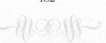

away. He wasn't going to leave Petunia, not while he still felt a pounding in his head that told him she was in danger.

"Yes," Galen said. "Just let me get something to light our way and we'll go." He took some of the tall white candles from a candelabrum on top of the desk and put them in a bag slung over his shoulder. "We'd better go out the window," he said.

"Do you want to wear the invisibility cloak?" Oliver held it out to him.

"Oh, no, but you had better," Galen said, clapping Oliver on the shoulder. "If Heinrich and I are seen, we're still invited guests. But you're supposed to be in Bruch."

"Have you been here all day, then?" Rose asked, getting up.

"Um, yes," Oliver said, praying that she wouldn't ask him where he'd been hiding.

"Are you hungry? Do you want us to find you something to eat?"

"Oh, no," Oliver said. "I have a couple of sandwiches . . . I brought with me." He patted his bulging pocket.

"That's very clever of you," Rose said. She had an amused expression on her face, though, that made Oliver wonder if she suspected where they had come from.

He bowed to the two princesses and put on the cloak, glad that they couldn't see his face anymore. Galen had turned out all but one small lamp and was pulling back the curtains so that they could go out the window.

"Here we go," Heinrich said with a groan.

When all three had reached the ground, they set off across

the lawns, Heinrich moving surprisingly quickly despite his limp. Oliver almost had to trot to keep up with them, the rustling he made crossing the winter-dead lawns telling the princes where he was. When they reached the little glass-paned house at the end, the one that Oliver was starting to think of as the Shadow House, he was panting, and Heinrich was rubbing his left thigh as though it pained him.

"Were you badly injured, in the war?" Oliver couldn't help but ask.

"An Analousian bullet lodged in the bone," Heinrich said. "But it's mostly stiff these days."

"We'll need to do this swiftly," Galen warned them both, handing out candles. "Anyone looking will see the lights through the glass walls, and they'll come to investigate at once. It will be a bit hard to explain what we're doing." He laughed.

As soon as they were all inside, Oliver tossed aside the cloak while Heinrich took matches out of his pocket and lit their candles. Oliver immediately squatted down and showed them the wax writing on the floor. It was easier to see by candlelight, to Oliver's relief. He'd been afraid that it would be too dark. Or worse, that he'd been imagining it all along.

"Here, hold this."

The crown prince handed his candle to Oliver. He got down until his nose was nearly touching the tiles, while Oliver and Heinrich held the candles high. Galen moved across the floor like a crab, studying the writing.

"Can you read it?" Oliver finally asked.

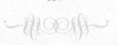

"In a way," Galen said. "It's not so much writing as a combination of words and symbols that form a powerful spell."

"What—what kind of spell?"

"Is it a summoning spell?" The shadows made Heinrich's face look hard and old.

"Worse," the crown prince said shortly. "It's a gateway."

"A gateway to what?" Oliver's voice shook when he said it, but he wasn't ashamed.

"A gateway to the Kingdom Under Stone," Galen said. "Or at least, a gateway *out* of it."

"We can't use it to get there?"

Heinrich sounded disappointed, and Oliver wondered if he was a little bit mad. Who would want to go to the Kingdom Under Stone?

"No, I think it can only bring the princes out, and not in their real forms," Galen said. Oliver thought he saw him sniff at the wax.

"Where—what—where *is* the Kingdom Under Stone?" Oliver wasn't sure how to ask the question, or what question he wanted to ask.

"The Kingdom Under Stone is the prison where Wolfram von Aue and his followers were exiled," the crown prince explained. "He was too powerful to be killed at the time, so he was locked into a place between worlds. I was fortunate that he had expended so much energy building his palace and stretching his bonds in order to father his sons. I was able to kill him with blessed silver inscribed with his real name, something that wouldn't have worked two hundred years earlier."

"I see," Oliver said, though he wasn't sure that he did. "So, his sons can only appear as shadows here in the ... real world?"

"Yes. Although they're not really shadows, they're ... well, they're not really shadows," Galen said with a small laugh.

"Could one have killed me?"

The crown prince looked up at Oliver, all traces of laughter gone. "Yes."

He took a clasp knife from his pocket and unfolded it. Grimacing at the sound it made, he began to scrape away the wax writing. "The princes were born here, but the king whisked them away moments later, otherwise they would have died when the sun rose. At night, though, if they can create a gate, they can reach our world in their shadowy forms."

"Why would you want to go to their kingdom, Your Highness?" Oliver looked at Heinrich, who also took out a knife and squatted down.

"To kill them," Heinrich said, his voice flat.

"Barring that," Galen said, pointing to a tile for his cousin to scratch at. "To seal them in their prison for good and all."

"Is that possible?"

"I did it once before," Galen said. "But my lock is breaking, or so I assume, judging by what's happening to my wife and her sisters. These shared nightmares," he went on, shaking his head, "they shouldn't be possible. And now a gateway, to allow the princes to leave ... it's only a matter of time until they can make a gateway to draw the girls in. We must reseal the prison."

"I don't want to reseal their prison," Heinrich said, beginning on another tile. "I want to kill them."

"Heinrich, you know that killing them may not be the best option," Galen said in a quiet voice.

"Fine then," Heinrich said. "I won't kill *all* of them. Just enough to make it easier to contain the rest."

"I want to help you," Oliver said.

"Why?" Galen looked up at him. "Because of Petunia?"

Oliver was relieved that the prince didn't seem to be skeptical about his conviction. He simply looked like he wanted to know, and so did Heinrich, when Oliver dared to look at the other prince. Oliver was very aware that Heinrich had known his father. Had known him better than Oliver had, in fact.

"Because of her," Oliver said at last. "Even though I have only met her twice, really . . . I just . . ."

"I risked my life to save Rose after only speaking with her twice," Galen said with a small smile.

Encouraged, Oliver went on. "But also because of my family. If it hadn't been for the King Under Stone and the trouble he caused with the worn-out dancing slippers, I would have been able to claim my title and take care of my people without resorting to banditry."

Both princes nodded as though this made perfect sense. And then the crown prince added fuel to Oliver's ire by saying, "And you have the King Under Stone to thank for the Analousian War as well. We don't know if he actually started it, but he kept it going for twelve years in order to further entrap Queen Maude."

Oliver stared at him, aghast. "Do you mean," and his voice was barely a whisper, "that the King Under Stone was responsible for my father's death?"

"And my father's," Galen said. "And my mother's, and my little sister's." He looked down at the tiles. "I think that's enough to prevent this gateway from working. Whoever did it will have to scrape all the tiles clean and start over."

Heinrich blew out his candle. After a moment Oliver blew out the ones in his hands as well. In the dark he felt something soft shoved into his arms.

"Take the cloak, lad," Galen said. "I hope you've got more sandwiches in your pockets. I'm sending you to Bruch."

"You are?" Oliver felt numb. They were sending him away from Petunia, away from the heart of the crisis? And what was he supposed to do, try to plead his case to King Gregor again?

"I need you to find Bishop Schelker," Galen said, to Oliver's surprise. "Tell him we need him. It's time."

"You have the spell ready?" Heinrich's brow creased. "I thought you and the others were still working on it."

Galen sighed. "We have *something*," he said. "There's no way to test it, of course. I can find a thousand excuses to read more books, spend another decade exploring more complex magic. But this," he gestured at the markings on the floor, "tells me that we've run out of time."

"And Schelker will know to bring the others?" Heinrich asked.

"Of course," his cousin replied. To answer Oliver's questioning look, he added, "The good bishop is a dab hand at

magic, but we're going to need all the help we can get. There are others with a stake in this who will be coming.

"And make sure the bishop arms you as well," Galen continued. "Bishop Schelker is also a dab hand at blessing silver daggers and bullets. Lily and Poppy are good with guns—all the girls are—but we can always use one more."

Gardener

Petunia dreamed of Oliver that night, a refreshing change from her usual nightmares.

They were walking in the forest, and everywhere they looked there were roses blooming. Blackened winter leaves were cold beneath their feet, but perfect yellow roses glowed from every bare bush. Petunia, laughing with glee, ran from one to the other, taking cuttings that Oliver gathered up in a flat basket. When she had taken a cutting from every bush that she saw, she stopped by one heavy-laden bush to catch her breath. Oliver picked several of the enormous flowers and tucked them into Petunia's hair.

"I wish that they were scarlet, to match your cloak," he said.

"But I like yellow roses best," she told him.

"Then I will fill your room with yellow roses," Oliver said, and leaned close as though to kiss her.

"Stop giggling," Pansy said, standing there in her nightgown with her hands on her hips.

Petunia turned in embarrassment to apologize to Oliver for her sister intruding on them, but Oliver was gone. The forest was gone. Petunia was suddenly awake, lying in her bed in the grand duchess's manor, and Pansy was standing over her, glaring.

"It's bad enough that we have the nightmares most nights," Pansy said crossly. "But now you've woken me from the best sleep I've had in weeks with your giggling!" She made a disgusted noise and stomped into their dressing room to use the water closet.

Petunia looked around groggily. Judging from the light coming in through a crack in the curtains, it was just after dawn. Then she had to gape: the curtains were not only closed, but the warmth of the room told her that the windows were still closed as well. What had come over Olga?

As though the thought had summoned her, Olga burst into the room and marched over to the window, yanking aside the curtains. Petunia covered her face with a small moan as the winter sun stabbed into her eyes. The maid ignored her and tied back the curtains, humming as she tidied the room.

"Isn't it rather early?" Pansy had come back from the dressing room and didn't seem all that thrilled with the open curtains either.

"But you're to have a very big day today, Your Highnesses," the maid said.

"We are?"

Petunia blinked at the maid. So far as she knew, they were

going to get a more thorough tour of the gardens . . . and that was more or less the extent of their plans.

A stab of anxiety went through her as Olga began to fiddle with the coverlet. Was Oliver underneath her bed? She hadn't heard him come back, but then, this was the best night's sleep she'd gotten in weeks as well—she prayed silently that Oliver hadn't heard her giggling in her sleep. And that she hadn't said his name aloud.

"What precisely is happening today?" Pansy asked.

Petunia got up and started sorting her knitting basket. It was on a chair across from the bed, and she contrived to drop a ball of yarn so that it rolled underneath.

"Clumsy!" She started patting around under the bed before Olga could offer to help.

"Prince Grigori has arranged quite the outing for you all," the maid said. "First you are to go riding in the forest with him, and then have lunch at his hunting lodge."

Petunia had writhed her way across the underside of the bed, but hadn't found any sign of Oliver. She crawled out from under the bed on the other side, making Pansy jump as she appeared, holding a ball of yellow yarn.

"Oh! What were you doing?"

"Getting my yarn," Petunia said meaningfully, tilting her head slightly at the bed.

"Oh. Oh!" Pansy appeared to catch her hint at last. "And did you find it?"

"Here." She held up the ball. "And the bed is very clean underneath," she said.

"I shall tell the chambermaid that you approve," Olga said, her voice flat. "Are you not excited to spend the day with Prince Grigori?"

"Of course we are," said Petunia brightly. She tossed the yarn into the basket. "Aren't we, Pansy?"

But Pansy's face was creased. "Is it safe? Aren't there bandits? And wild animals?"

"Prince Grigori is the greatest hunter in Ionia," the maid snapped. "If he says that you will be safe with him, then you will be safe with him!" And she swept out of the room.

"Well," Pansy said, her eyes wide. "I guess we'll be dressing ourselves, then."

"She's in love with Grigori," Petunia said slowly.

"I think she made that very plain," Pansy said, going to the wardrobe. "Are you sure Oliver isn't in here?"

"He's not under the bed," Petunia said. She went to the wardrobe and rustled the gowns about. "Oliver?" When no answer came, she pulled out her riding dress and threw it on the bed. "I don't know where he is," she said. "Or if he's coming back."

"I'm sorry," Pansy said, putting a hand on Petunia's arm. "But with things as they are, he's probably better off. I mean, we're dealing with the King Under Stone and his brothers, and the grand duchess might be—" Pansy stopped with a gasp, her eyes wide. "What *if* she's Rionin's mother?" Pansy's eyes got even wider, if that were possible. "Or worse—the mother of one of the princes we killed? She must loathe us!"

"The grand duchess is a rather strange old lady," Petunia

admitted, remembering their conversation from the night before. "But I can't imagine she would have anything to do with this. She doesn't have any contact with her . . . firstborn . . . I'm sure. How could she?"

This gave Pansy pause. "Well," she said at last. "I still think we need to be wary."

Petunia busied herself getting dressed, not wanting to start an argument. Olga soon returned and helped them finish dressing, doing their hair in simple styles that wouldn't interfere with their riding hats. Not that Petunia planned to wear hers. It was very stiff and the veil itched, and she never wore it unless one of her sisters fussed.

As soon as breakfast was over, they assembled in front of the manor. The presence of Prince Grigori and the grand duchess at breakfast had meant that Petunia had not been able to ask if anyone knew what had become of Oliver. She hoped that he had been able to speak with Galen, but Galen gave no sign at all.

All thoughts of Oliver were chased from her head when she saw the horse that Grigori wanted her to ride. Nearly the twin of his own enormous mount, it was a coal-black beast that towered above Petunia.

"Er," she said when the groom led it over to her. She looked at the other horses being brought forward for her sisters. They all seemed much gentler, and she watched with envy as Lilac reached for the reins of the smallest, oldest-looking horse.

"Oh, but you must try her," Prince Grigori enthused

about the black mare. "She is one of the finest in my stables. The full sister of my own favorite." He patted the nose of his horse, which looked like it was going to bite him.

"Er," Petunia said again.

"I would love to ride her," Poppy said with genuine admiration. "I'm afraid that I'm the horsewoman in the family."

"I can assure you, Petunia, she is as gentle as a lamb," Grigori said. The mare stamped her foot, and the groom took a step back. "And for you, dear Princess Poppy, I have an equally worthy mount." He gestured to a fiery-eyed bay.

"Ooh, lovely," Poppy said. She snugged on her leather riding gloves, an eager expression on her face.

"Poppy," Petunia whimpered.

Poppy looked from the bay to the black mare, then shrugged. "You'll be fine, Pet, just keep a firm grip on the reins." And she happily followed the groom to the mounting block.

Prince Grigori cupped his hands to help Petunia mount. She felt like she was preparing to be tossed over the moon as she put her knee into his hands. He lifted her into the saddle with a smile, and she scrabbled to adjust her cloak and get the reins in the right position. The horse shifted beneath her, and she broke out in a cold sweat. Her leather riding gloves felt thick and awkward, and she couldn't remember how to hold her hands, suddenly. Olga was probably watching her through a window, sick with jealousy, and at that moment Petunia wished she could trade places with the maid.

"Isn't she magnificent?"

Prince Grigori's face was alight with pleasure. Petunia wondered if he wanted her to fall to her death. Before she could say anything, however, Violet's husband, Frederick, started asking the prince questions about his horses' bloodlines. Petunia just sat there like a lump with the reins wrapped around her hands, worrying about whether she would even make it through the front gates without falling.

"Here, you," Poppy said, drawing up alongside her. Her horse was smaller, but that just meant that Poppy and Petunia were now the same height. She took the reins from Petunia, untangled them, and showed her how to hold them correctly. Fortunately, Prince Grigori was busy assigning horses to the others. Petunia refused to let him see how frightened she was. And not just of the horse.

"This seems like a terrible idea," Petunia said to Poppy in an undertone.

"Yes," Poppy said cheerfully. "That's why we're going to do it. He's clearly up to something, and the only way to find out what is to go along."

"And what if he . . . attacks . . . us?"

"Have you got your pistol?" Poppy looked scandalized at the very idea that Petunia might have left her bedroom unarmed.

"Of course I do," Petunia said, offended.

"Well then!" Poppy grinned. "We outnumber him and his little band of hunters, who can't be very impressive since Oliver and his men have kept right on thieving under their very noses."

Petunia looked around and realized that Poppy was right. Prince Grigori's hunters were a sullen-looking group of no more than six men. They were on very large horses, and armed, but as Poppy said, they had tried and failed for months to bring in a single one of Oliver's men.

And what were they going to do? Try to abduct the sisters on behalf of the King Under Stone? Did they even have a gate to the Kingdom Under Stone?

Petunia shook her head at her own fears and tried to concentrate on not falling off her horse instead. They left the estate and went into the forest, and Petunia discovered that if her horse kept moving it wasn't half so alarming. It helped that it was a beautiful day, with the sun shining brightly through the bare tree branches, and those birds that had not fled for warmer climes calling out to each other.

They ambled down a trail that led east, away from the Analousian border and deeper into the Westfalian Woods, which Petunia found reassuring. But as they rode, Petunia's relief at staying on Westfalian soil began to be replaced by a growing uneasiness. She knew that she had never been in this part of the forest before, yet it began to look increasingly familiar. She knew that there would be a small stream just ahead, and an elm that had been split apart by lightning, both halves of its divided trunk still reaching toward the sun.

Inside her gloves, Petunia's hands grew slick with sweat. The pins that held her hat in place stabbed into her head, and she reached up with one hand and pulled them out, jabbing them inelegantly into the crown before removing it entirely.

Violet was looking at her with concern, so Petunia didn't discard the hat but set it in her lap, taking up the reins with both hands again. The horse's ears flickered, as though sensing her uneasiness, and she prayed that it wouldn't take the opportunity to throw her off.

When they passed a rock fringed with moss in a way that made it look a balding man, Petunia knew how she knew this part of the forest. It was the forest she had seen in her dream the night before. There were no roses, of course, and she was with Prince Grigori and not Oliver, but this was without a doubt the place she had seen.

Violet drew her horse alongside Petunia's.

"Are you all right, Pet? You're very pale."

"I will be fine," Petunia said, taking pains to keep her voice even. "I am just worried that this horse is very tall and I . . . *there are yellow roses! There really are!*"

Her horse jogged sideways as she shouted this, and Petunia sawed at the reins to make it stop. It bumped into Violet's horse, which threw up its head in protest. Everyone halted as Petunia leaped from her own mount, even though it was still dancing around nervously. She narrowly avoided being stepped on, first by her horse and then by Rose's, as she bounded across the trail and off into the forest.

"Petunia! Where are you going?" Rose called after her. Petunia could hear their horses crunching through the dead leaves after her, but she didn't look back.

Just there, just ahead, where she had dreamed that Oliver

put roses in her hair, was an enormous rosebush. Despite the season, its leaves were a healthy dark green tinged with red, and it was covered with fat yellow blooms. They were precisely the glowing primrose yellow that Petunia and her father had been looking for.

"Petunia!" Galen's voice was sharp. "Don't touch those roses!"

But Prince Grigori just laughed. His enormous horse was between her and her sisters, and he leaned down and offered her a small dagger. "Take all you like, princess. It seems that they were meant for you."

"Thank you," Petunia said, taking the dagger without even looking at him.

She was studying the bush to find the best place to make a cutting. It was a pity that the bush was too big to transport whole. She wondered if they could come back later with better tools, to prune and uproot it. For now, though, a few slips would be sufficient.

She heard Galen's voice again as she separated out a thick stem crowned with blooms and began to slice through it.

"Petunia, stop," Galen said. "Roses don't bloom in winter; they can't be natural."

Petunia heard harnesses jingling as several of the others dismounted to come after her.

"Who cares?" she called out. "Father will be ecstat—"

Just as she heard Lily and Heinrich shouting almost in unison for her to wait, the ground opened up beneath her feet.

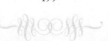

The thorns of the stem she was holding went right through her leather glove and into the palm of her hand, but she just gripped it tighter.

A heartbeat later, she landed with a thump on all fours on black soil that glittered faintly. She looked up through the silver branches that swayed over her head, but all was darkness above them, with no sign of the hole she had fallen through. She stood and shook the glittering dirt from her cloak and gown, leaning against one of the silver trees for a moment to get her bearings.

After a time, when no one else arrived, she made her way to the shore of the black lake. Across the lake, the jagged black spires of the Palace Under Stone cut the murky air, as familiar as her own home.

Kestilan was waiting on the shore with a single silver boat.

"Hello, beloved," he purred. "Welcome home."

Petunia didn't reply. What was there for her to say? Still holding the yellow roses in one hand and Grigori's dagger in the other, she stepped into the boat.

Tested

Oliver was nervous about knocking on the door of Bishop Schelker's modest home next to the palace. But he should have reckoned that the bishop, having been so long the advisor and confidante of the royal family, would have seen stranger sights than a wanted fugitive appearing out of thin air on his doorstep one morning.

"Come in," the bishop said as soon as he saw Oliver. He took Oliver's arm and pulled him into the cottage.

The bishop locked the door before he ushered Oliver into a small study. The windows faced the palace, and the bishop quickly closed the curtains. Then he breathed a large sigh and sat down behind his desk.

"Please have a seat," he said, indicating a comfortable chair across from his desk. "I would offer you something . . . but my housekeeper is in the kitchen just now, and I don't think she should see you."

"That's all right," Oliver croaked, sinking down into the chair.

He'd been walking for three days without stopping for more than a few minutes, and he was exhausted. Almost too exhausted to eat, though he wouldn't turn down a drink. His throat was so dry his thanks had come out as a croak. He'd thought about stealing a horse, but the only horses to be stolen in the forest had been the grand duchess's, and the risk of being captured was too great. What food he'd had had run out that morning, and once he'd reached the gates of Bruch, he'd rushed straight to the bishop's house without even stopping at a public well to drink.

The bishop noticed his dusty-sounding voice and poured him a glass of water from a decanter on the desk. "That I can help with," he said with a small smile. "It's what else you need that worries me."

Oliver downed the water before answering. "Well, Your Grace," he said when he could speak clearly. "I can assure you that I'm not here on my own behalf, to beg you to petition the king for my release."

Bishop Schelker looked at him with amusement. "The question of your release is rather moot, since you can come and go as you please with that particular item." His gaze sharpened on the dull purple cloak, which Oliver had laid over the arm of his chair. "Which belongs to Crown Prince Galen, if I'm not mistaken."

"Yes, Your Grace," Oliver said. "I wear it at his insistence, I promise."

The bishop relaxed. "I'm inclined to believe you. It's the sort of thing Galen would do. I suppose you were instructed to stay out of harm's way while Kelling and I soothed the king?"

"Yes, Your Grace."

"And yet you are here."

"Yes, Your Grace," Oliver said again. "Prince Galen sent me. He needs help."

The bishop sat forward. "What sort of help?"

Oliver rolled the glass between his hands, not sure why he was nervous. The bishop hadn't been surprised by his sudden appearance. He had readily believed Galen would loan Oliver the invisibility cloak. This seemed like one thing too many to ask a man of the Church to believe, however.

But it was for Petunia . . .

"Galen said that it's time, and that you were to come with me. He also needs all the silver bullets you have. Also daggers. And there is a list of herbs. . . ." Oliver trailed off.

The bishop was looking at him with his face completely blank. Not confused, not alarmed, just blank. Oliver wondered if the bishop had any idea what he was saying. Oliver didn't know where to find the herbs, let alone bullets made from silver, so he'd been hoping that the bishop would understand everything that the crown prince had asked for. But the way the bishop was looking at Oliver made him wonder if he was about to ring for help in restraining a madman.

"Anything else?" Bishop Schelker's voice was as carefully blank as his face.

"He said that you were to . . . summon . . . the others."

"The others?"

"The others," Oliver said firmly.

"Why are you doing this?" The bishop folded his hands on the desk blotter and looked at Oliver. "The palace is right there. His Majesty has just returned from the fortress, which calmed him only slightly. If I choose to raise the alarm, you will be executed tomorrow morning. Why did you come all this way to carry this very cryptic message? One which, might I add, Galen could have sent in a letter."

"I—I— Well, you see—" Oliver stammered for a moment. He looked at the bishop's earnest face. He remembered that the bishop had been the one to take his side that day in the council room. Oliver's heart tried to pound its way out of his ribcage, but he ignored it. "I'm in love with Petunia," he announced. "And I want to help her."

Bishop Schelker got to his feet. Oliver scrambled to follow, and his tired legs nearly buckled and dumped him on the floor. He steadied himself on the edge of the bishop's desk, but Schelker didn't seem to notice.

The bishop took a key from his pocket and opened a cabinet behind his desk. Oliver wondered if he was going to pull out a weapon or perhaps restraints. Instead the older man took out several small knitted bags on long cords, some dried herbs, and a stack of pasteboard boxes and laid them carefully on the desk.

Schelker leaned his hands on either side of the strange pile he had made and looked sternly at Oliver for a long time.

Oliver sank back down in his seat, tired and uncomfortable and not sure which was worse.

"I have known Petunia a long time," the bishop said. "All her life, in fact. I have known all the princesses since birth. They are as close to me as my own daughters would have been, had I married.

"I was a young priest when Queen Maude came from Breton with her bevy of attendants, of which your mother was one." He merely nodded at Oliver's surprise. "Lady Emily Ellsworth, a lovely girl. They were beautiful, and rather silly, and everyone loved them, myself included. We Westfalians can be a grim people, but they brought life and joy to the court. I was there when your father and mother defied their parents and eloped.

"I would have helped your mother after your father's death, if she had only come to me. We were all devastated by the loss of Maude, and by the effects of the war. But still, if she had come to me I would have tried."

"I'm . . . sorry," Oliver said.

He didn't really know what he was. Confused, mostly. But anger and anxiety warred inside him as well. What was the bishop getting at?

"It isn't your fault," said Bishop Schelker, as though surprised that Oliver would feel the need to apologize. "We each make our own choices. That's what I'm trying to say. Your parents chose their path, and Gregor has chosen his. And you, born an earl, trapped by the choices of others, chose not to flee, not to give up, but to take care of your people the only way you could. But now you are making new choices, to confess of your crimes, though apparently not to take the punishment for them—"

Oliver started to protest, but the bishop held up a hand to stop him.

"I understand why," Schelker said. "Of course I do! What man can say he wants to be executed? And you wish to protect a beautiful princess, with whom you have fallen in love. But do you understand how dire the situation is? Her life and the lives of her sisters are hanging in the balance. You yourself risk death if you choose this path."

"I don't care," Oliver said. He stood up and faced the bishop. "I don't care! I love Petunia, and this is what I'm choosing, right here and now."

"I like this boy, Michael," said a voice from behind Oliver. "He knows when to hold his tongue and when to speak. A valuable quality in the young."

Oliver lurched to his feet and spun around. The bishop's housekeeper was standing in the doorway of the study. She was dressed in a ragged blue gown with a blue shawl around her thin shoulders and looked like she was nearly a hundred years old. She smiled toothlessly at Oliver, but then her sharp eyes saw the purple cape on the chair.

"My cloak!" She stepped around Oliver with much greater speed than he would have given her credit for and snatched up the cloak, inspecting it with narrow eyes. "Still in good condition, I see, despite having been who-knows-where."

Oliver's fingers itched to snatch the cloak back from the old woman, but he didn't want to antagonize her. If she sent word to the palace, Oliver would be dead by noon.

"Thank you for coming, good frau," said the bishop with a slight bow.

Oliver wondered if he were always so formal with his housekeeper. She was still clutching the cloak, but now she was raking Oliver with her dark-eyed gaze.

"I didn't know it was yours, good frau," Oliver said, feeling dazed. "If the crown prince had told me that Bishop Schelker's housekeeper was such a resourceful—"

"His housekeeper? His *housekeeper*?" The old woman made a noise of disgust and flapped her hand at Bishop Schelker. "Hardly! Perhaps this boy isn't as clever as he seems."

"I believe he is quite clever enough," the bishop said mildly. He turned to Oliver. "But no, the good frau is most assuredly not my housekeeper."

"Oh!" Oliver blushed. "I'm so sorry, good frau."

She grabbed his jaw and studied his face closely. "Very handsome. But then, the princesses do have such fine taste in young men," she said with a cackle of laughter. "I nearly kept Galen for myself, you know." She winked saucily at Oliver, who felt his jaw sag in reply.

"I am more concerned about the moral character of their suitors," Bishop Schelker said in a rather pained voice.

"You would be," the old woman said rather rudely.

"Where is Herr Vogel, good frau?" Bishop Schelker changed the subject. "Did he not come with you?"

"He's visiting his gardens," she said, waving a gnarled hand at the window. She shoved the purple cloak up beneath her shawl, making her look like a hunchback. "Like my shawl, do you?" She turned around so that Oliver could admire it. It was blue, with ruffled edges. "One of the girls made it for me. I don't know which one. All those foolish flower names are impossible to keep straight!" Another cackle of laughter.

"Walter Vogel, the gardener?" Oliver remembered the name his mother had given him, the name of the gardener she thought could help.

"Is there any other?" The old woman crowed.

"We had better arm ourselves and be going," Bishop Schelker said. "Young Oliver will need the cloak until we are out of Bruch, good frau."

"I will?" Oliver's voice rose embarrassingly on the second word. His blood pounded at the bishop's words: *until we are out of Bruch.*

"Yes, yes," the old woman said. "He can have it when he needs it."

"So, you mean that I will be going with you? To help? You trust me?" Oliver looked from the bishop to the old woman and back again. Galen had said Oliver would join them, but until that moment he had been afraid that Schelker or one of the others would decide to dismiss him.

"Here," the bishop said by way of an answer. He handed Oliver one of the small bags. Whatever it held crackled and released a scent of cooking herbs. "Wear it around your neck, under your shirt. And take a box of bullets; we'll get you a pistol in a moment."

Oliver slipped the cord of the little bag around his neck and took the pasteboard box of bullets before he could tuck the bag out of sight. Judging from the weight and the noise the box made, it did indeed contain bullets, which he assumed were silver as the crown prince had requested.

"It seems you passed muster, lad," said a gentle voice as another person came into the room, making the small study rather crowded.

"You're late, Walter," the crone snapped.

The newcomer was an old man with a peg leg and the weathered face of someone who spent his days in the sun. "We need all the help that we can get," he said.

"When we're in the palace, we will have great need," agreed the crone.

Captive

When Kestilan brought Petunia to the Palace Under Stone, she was taken to the very bedroom that she had dreamed about the night when she had tried to shoot Rionin in her sleep. She laid the bunch of yellow roses on the black-lacquered dressing table with shaking fingers. Kestilan left, to her relief, but then the ladies of the court came flooding into her room.

There were few servants in the Kingdom Under Stone, mostly silent musicians and footmen at the Midnight Balls, and the sisters had long suspected they were magical constructions: shadows brought to life. It was the courtiers, the immortal followers of the first King Under Stone who shared his exile, who had waited upon the sisters. The court ladies had taken away the princesses' clothes that terrible night they had spent in the castle before Galen had helped them escape. And it was the court ladies who came now, screeching with triumphant laughter, and stripped Petunia of her clothing.

They dressed her in a midnight-blue gown laced with dull silver and put silver slippers on her feet. Then they scraped her curly hair up into a coiffure so rigid that she felt like she could lower her head and run one of them through like an angry bull. They gave her a necklace and earrings of sapphires that looked faded with age, set in tarnished silver, and then they gathered up her old clothes.

Petunia had no particular fondness for her riding habit, but when one white-faced gloating woman tried to fold up her scarlet cloak, Petunia snatched the heavy velvet out of her hands. The woman actually hissed at her, like a cat, but Petunia would not let go.

"I will kill you if you touch it again," she snarled at the woman.

Her heart was racing, not just because she wanted to keep her cloak, but also because she didn't want them to feel the heavy lump in the inside pocket. The pistol-shaped lump. They'd taken her silver dagger with clear distaste, but they had left her specially knitted garters, which seemed to irritate their fingers as they changed her stockings. So the garters had worked a bit, at least, even if they hadn't prevented her from being brought here.

"There are some who would give a great deal to join us here," the woman said with a sneer. She seemed to be the leader of the ladies, a tall creature with unnaturally red hair and eyes like chips of ice.

"Name one," Petunia snapped.

"That maid," the woman said. "Olga."

Petunia's head jerked at the news. She wasn't all that surprised, just startled at having her suspicions confirmed.

"It will be so nice to have a maid again," sighed one of the women, a shrill little creature who reminded Petunia of a rat.

"Olga is really that eager to leave the grand duchess and be a maid here?" Petunia could hardly credit such a thing. What sort of appeal did a world without sunlight have for Olga? Especially since she would be the only maid, with more than two dozen cruel mistresses to order her around.

"Well," the tall leader of the ladies said in an artful voice, toying with the tattered lace of her sleeve. "She may have gotten the wrong impression about the offer. She may have thought she was to be a lady . . . even a princess."

Screams of laughter pummeled Petunia's ears, and she took an involuntary step back, bumping into one of the ladies behind. The woman growled and pushed her back, and Petunia stepped on the hem of her own gown and almost tripped. The leader watched Petunia right herself with hooded eyes.

"You're very short, aren't you?" She smirked at Petunia.

"And you've got a nose like a stoat," Petunia replied. "But I can always have my gowns altered."

"Dinner is in an hour," one of the other women told her while their leader swelled with anger. "You will eat with the princes." She gave Petunia a spiteful look, as though angry that Petunia should be so honored.

"And tonight there will be a ball, of course," their tall leader added, now that she had recovered herself.

"Am I expected to dance with all the princes?" Petunia couldn't resist asking.

"You will dance with your betrothed," the woman snapped.

"But he isn't here," Petunia said, blinking at her innocently.

She knew that the ruse would mean little to Kestilan, since Rionin was not even deterred by Lily's marriage to Heinrich. But she wanted to give them something to chew on. Kestilan *wasn't* the only man interested in her, after all. There was Oliver, and Prince Grigori . . .

Prince Grigori, who had clearly led them into the forest for the sole purpose of sending Petunia to the Kingdom Under Stone. She had been right: he was in league with Rionin. But what had he been promised to make him do such a thing? Petunia had been certain that he truly liked her; why would he give her up to Kestilan? And why not capture Lily instead?

"This betrothed of yours, what is his name?" The freakishly tall lady asked.

Petunia opened her mouth to say Oliver's name, and a face flashed before her eyes. Prince Alfred, their horsey-looking second cousin, who had come to solve the mystery of their worn-out slippers when she was just a little girl. Come to solve the mystery and died for his efforts, so that the first King Under Stone could show the sisters the power of his displeasure. Alfred's face, blurred by time, was followed by other blurry images: a Belgique prince who had tried to spy on Rose while she was ill, a foppish Spanian with more luggage than all twelve sisters put together. All dead now, because of the King

Under Stone. And, to be honest, because of Petunia and her sisters.

"I'm not going to tell you," Petunia said, not caring if she sounded childish. "The king will probably try to kill him."

"Probably?" The women all shrieked with laughter as their tall leader leaned over Petunia. "There is no 'probably' about it. You and all your sisters need to be taught a lesson about where you belong, and *whom you belong to.*" The woman's long nose was almost touching Petunia's now.

"I don't belong to anyone," Petunia said, gripping her cloak in both hands and resisting the urge to pull out her pistol and shoot the woman. "But if I do marry Kestilan, I shall order you flogged in the middle of the ballroom as a wedding gift."

"Marrying one of the princes does not give you the right . . ."

"Are you completely sure of that?" Petunia raised one eyebrow at the woman. "I can hardly see the king objecting. Rionin strikes me as one who would enjoy that sort of thing."

The woman's face paled under her heavy powder, and Petunia knew she had struck a nerve. Petunia smiled at the woman, who was the one to take a step back this time.

"Dinner in an hour?" Petunia made a pretense of yawning. "You can go now."

She shoved her way out of the ring of ladies and went to a chair, where she lovingly laid her cloak on the seat. Then she turned and watched them file out, her arms folded and one foot tapping. Their expressions were by turns horrified or enraged, but Petunia didn't care. She was done with being bullied by tall people.

Dinner that night was awkward and silent. She was the only lady, and though Rionin didn't join them—she got the impression that he didn't need to eat anymore—the mood was oppressive. Even Kestilan had given up his usual insinuating banter and ate in silence. When she was done eating the flavorless, unidentifiable food, Petunia got up and left the table without a word. She found her way back to her room and barred the door with a chair, since it didn't lock.

Petunia toyed with the idea of staying there all night, refusing to come out for the ball, but knew that it wouldn't work. They would simply break down the door and drag her out by the hair.

She occupied her time by taking the bullets out of her pistol and using a long hairpin to scratch the names of the princes on them. The bullets weren't silver, which were far too costly to carry all the time, but they would still kill the princes if she hit her mark. She didn't need to use their names, either, but she didn't care. It gave her something to do. Something other than just starting the palace on fire and walking away.

That thought gave Petunia pause. Would the twisted stones and slick wood of the Palace Under Stone burn? She had matches—she always had matches, considering them quite as essential as protective garters or a pistol—but did she dare set something alight?

No. Not just yet.

She went back to etching her bullets, occupying her hands again while she wondered, could she kill someone? Kestilan?

The others? That horrible court lady? She just didn't know. Poppy could shoot without hesitation, Petunia was sure, and Lily had already killed at least one of the princes. But Poppy and Lily were endlessly brave and the best shots in the family besides.

"The time is coming for you to choose, my girl," she scolded herself. "Are you always going to be little Petunia, who nearly burned down Papa's hedge maze and likes having dirty hands, or are you going to stand up and be one of the brave ones?"

"She's talking to herself and she's only been here a few hours," Poppy said from the doorway. "I'd worry, but I can hardly blame— *Oof!*"

Petunia flew across the room and embraced her older sister tightly. Poppy squeezed her right back, belying her joking words. Then Petunia felt other arms around her. Looking up from Poppy's shoulder, she saw all her sisters gathered around, their faces variously white from strain or red from crying.

"What's happened?" She drew back, looking at them all in horror. "Why are you all here? How did Grigori trick you all?"

Rose smiled, a slight expression that quickly passed. "He didn't trick us; he told us the truth. And we chose to come here."

Petunia felt like the floor was tilting and thought she might faint for a moment. Rose quickly helped her over to a chair, and the rest of her sisters crowded into the room. Hyacinth shut the door and stood ready to bar it with her slight frame if anyone should try to enter.

"You *chose* to come here?" Petunia choked on the words. "Why?"

"To find you," Rose said simply. "But don't feel guilty, dear, that's not the only reason."

"What are the other reasons?"

Petunia looked at her sisters with a growing feeling of despair. She didn't know how long they had been here, but they were already gowned in the slippery, bleak gowns of the Kingdom Under Stone. Their hair, too, was scraped into high twists and topknots, and they wore cracked and dulled jewels. Petunia knew that their weapons were probably gone, and thought she had better give her pistol to Lily or Poppy before someone came for them.

"After you disappeared," Rose said, "Prince Grigori told us that you were safely where you belonged in the Kingdom Under Stone."

"At which point, I nearly killed him," Poppy muttered, and Daisy shushed her.

"We disarmed his men, tied them up, and searched the entire area," Rose continued, "but it was as though you had been swallowed up by the earth; there was no sign of any gate. Grigori seemed very pleased with himself. We were all a bit in shock as well, so at his urging we went on to his hunting lodge, as it was only a few minutes away. He calmly informed us over refreshments that he had been working for Rionin for several years."

"I will never get over him sipping his tea while Heinrich

held a gun to his head," Hyacinth said in a low voice. "He's mad, or he has no soul."

"Grigori— he— what?" Petunia could suddenly not take it all in.

"Grigori has been promised rewards beyond his wildest dreams if he helps bring us back here," Rose said.

"Then why did you give in?" Petunia felt like crying. "Why did you come here?"

"To save our husbands," Hyacinth said.

Petunia's heart shuddered. "No," she said, shaking her head. "No, no, no, he didn't!"

"They're well enough, for now," Lily quickly assured her. "But we could either follow you, or the King Under Stone will kill our husbands and everyone else we love. Including Father."

"He's lying," Petunia said, trying to swallow. "He's lying! He doesn't have the power! Why wouldn't Rionin have killed Father years ago, then? And Galen and Heinrich?"

"He's not lying," Rose said, putting a slender hand on Petunia's shoulder. "At least, *Grigori* isn't. He truly believes that Rionin can do this. But it does make sense: why would Rionin waste his power killing our father or our husbands, if he didn't have a way of bringing us here yet? He's only just redis-covered how to make a gate."

The rug in their sitting room had transformed into a stairway that led to the Kingdom Under Stone. It had been created for their mother by the first king, and she had taught them how to use it before her death. Galen had destroyed it after rescuing them ten years before.

"The first king had never taught his sons how to make such magic," Rose explained. "But Rionin figured out how to do it at last. There was a temporary gate placed under the dead leaves around that rosebush you found. And a permanent one in Grigori's hunting lodge. They thought that if you, the youngest, were taken first, it would inspire us all to follow and protect you."

"And it did," Pansy said. "We didn't just come because Grigori threatened Papa and the others."

"Thank you," Petunia croaked. "But what now? What can we do? How can we fight this?"

"We will find a way," Rose said at her most no-nonsense. "We did it before, and that was with only Galen to help us, and none of us able to tell a soul what was happening. We'll do it again, older and wiser and with more help coming."

"Unless Grigori killed your husbands after we left," Jonquil said bleakly.

Hunter

Oliver had been robbing coaches since he was thirteen years old. He knew every inch of the forest along the highway. And yet that journey through the Westfalian Woods was the strangest two days of his life. Oliver found himself riding on a fine horse, dressed in his faded leathers, wolf mask bobbing on his shoulder, in the company of an extremely old woman, a one-legged man, and a heavily armed bishop who rode what looked like a cavalry horse.

Despite the seeming fragility of the old woman—who apparently didn't have a name and was merely referred to as "good frau" by everyone—she proved to be a skilled rider. Walter Vogel, too, was at ease on a horse even though Oliver would have thought that his peg leg would be a hindrance. And it seemed that Bishop Schelker's father had been a general and had insisted that all of his sons learn to ride and shoot, no matter that one of them had been called to the Church at a young age.

They set a swift pace, and as they rode, Walter Vogel, who had once been a gardener at the palace but was also a sorcerer or some such improbable thing, explained to Oliver that if the princes Under Stone could come out of their prison through the hothouse, it might be possible to get into the Kingdom Under Stone through that same hothouse.

"Why would we want to do that?" Oliver looked over at the old man in consternation. "Shouldn't we just scrub away that spell and keep them in there for good?"

"Whoever created a gate in the hothouse will just make another," Walter said. "The best thing to do is to reseal the prison."

"Or kill them all," Oliver said.

They had slowed to a walk to rest their horses before Walter answered Oliver. He brought his horse in close to Oliver's, his face grave.

"Wolfram von Aue summoned terrible powers from spirits of the dead and other unholy sources," Walter said in a lecturing tone. "He held all these powers within him, gathering more strength by feeding off the energy of his followers. That power still exists. It needs to be contained. If it gets loose, it could destroy all of Westfalin."

"Westfalin?" The good frau had brought her horse close along Oliver's other side. "Don't coddle the boy! If the powers that Wolfram gathered get loose, *Ionia* would be a smoking pit in the ground!"

"Galen was lucky," Walter went on. "Very lucky. He killed Wolfram when his oldest son, the perfect vessel for those

powers, happened to be standing right at hand. If Wolfram's sons had not been there, the powers might have scattered and broken out of the cage we created. Or they could just as easily have gone into Galen, twisting and using him even as Wolfram had twisted and used them."

"I wonder," Bishop Schelker said from Walter's other side, "if Galen would have killed the king so readily, had he known the danger he was in."

"And young Rose," said the crone. "If we had had a Queen Under Stone, would that have been any better?" She clucked her tongue in disapproval. Her horse took it as a sign to move back to a canter, so they did.

As they moved steadily down the road into the depths of the forest, Oliver pondered everything that he had now learned. They could not kill the dark king or his brothers, at least not all of them. One of them would need to remain alive to hold the power in check.

"What are we going to do?" Oliver asked all three of his companions as they slowed again. "If we can't kill them, and they've broken the lock on the prison, what do we do?"

"We remake the walls of the prison, stronger than before," Walter Vogel answered.

"But how?" Oliver looked at his horse's mane in despair. "According to a book Princess Poppy gave me, most of the wizards who made the prison died working the magic! And those who survived have been dead for centuries now anyway."

"The young are so sure of themselves, aren't they?" The

good frau sucked her remaining teeth and rolled her faded eyes. "Dead for centuries, bah!"

"Indeed, good frau," Oliver said, his voice strained as he tried to conceal his frustration. "Wolfram von Aue was imprisoned well over fifteen hundred years ago."

"Has it really been so long?" Walter studied his own horse's mane for a moment. "I suppose it has."

"I don't worry about such things as age or death." The old woman sniffed. "I have too much to do yet."

"Er," Oliver said.

"He talks even less than the one Lily married," the crone remarked to Walter. "Though when the mood strikes him, he asks just as many questions as Galen."

"I'm sorry," Oliver said weakly.

The old woman nodded. "You are forgiven," she pronounced in queenly tones. Her sharp eyes bored into his. "And that is because once I was a queen." And with that she spurred her horse to a gallop.

Oliver looked over at Walter, concerned that the woman's mind was as feeble as her body appeared. But Walter was rubbing at the leg that terminated in a polished wooden peg and gazing after the crone with a wistful expression.

"Long ago we were all something else," was all Walter said, then he too sent his horse forward, leaving Oliver and the bishop to catch up.

They rode in silence the rest of the way to the estate, but just when they could see the stone fence peeking through the trees, bandits surrounded them. Oliver and his companions brought their horses to a sharp halt on the hard road as men in wolf masks stepped out of the trees on all sides. Oliver looked around, nonplussed. They had to have recognized him: he recognized them even with their masks in place. He was about to call out to Karl, who stood directly in their path, when Karl unmasked and spoke.

"All right there, Oliver?"

"I'm well," Oliver replied. "Yourself?"

Karl nodded.

"What's the reason for this?" Bishop Schelker looked around. "Aren't you Lord Oliver's men?"

"Indeed we are," said Johan, taking off his own mask. "And that's why we're here. Lady Emily told us that you intend to rescue the princesses. If that's so, then that is the path you must take." He pointed to a narrow side road, little more than a deer path, that skirted around the back of the estate wall.

"What's down there?" Walter peered through the trees.

"That Russakan prince's hunting lodge," Karl said with a grunt. "He took them all there, four days ago. Though not all of them made it." He looked pained.

"What do you mean?" Oliver's mouth went dry.

"The littlest princess, your Petunia, Oliver," Karl said. "She disappeared somewhere along the trail."

"How should you know such a thing, Karl Schmidt?" The good frau narrowed her pale eyes at him.

224

"How did *you* know his name?" Johan glared at the old woman.

"I know a lot of things, Johan Mueller, and most of them would turn your gray hairs snow white," the crone retorted.

"It's all right," Karl said, swallowing loudly. "We've kept a watch on the princesses, good frau. Lady Emily ordered us to do it."

The old woman looked at Walter. "Emily? The skinny one with curly hair?"

"Yes," Walter said. "She married the Earl of Saxeborg-Rohlstein."

"And then gave birth to him?" She jerked a thumb at Oliver.

"What do you mean Petunia disappeared?" Oliver demanded, ignoring the good frau. "Tell me exactly what you saw, Karl!"

"They were taking a picnic to the hunting lodge, so far as we can tell, with six of Grigori's men as escort. We followed, staying in the trees. They were within a few minutes' ride of the lodge when Petun—Princess Petunia—stopped and got down from her horse. She went into the trees and was cutting some flowers. They were roses, yellow roses in full bloom," said Karl, his voice taking on a hint of wonder. "The others yelled at her to stop, and she just . . . disappeared. They searched for her but there was nothing. Then they continued on to the hunting lodge, but we haven't seen or heard from any of them since."

"Petunia wouldn't have been able to resist a rose that bloomed in the wintertime," Walter said quietly.

"We went to have a look, once the others had gone," Johan put in. "We found the bush, but it was winter-dead just like everything else. And I will swear to there being yellow roses and green leaves all over it just a moment before."

"We have to go find her," Oliver managed. He started to turn his horse.

"No need," Walter said, his voice kind. "We know precisely where she is. It's getting her out that's going to be the difficulty."

"Where are the others?" Bishop Schelker asked. "Galen? Heinrich? The rest of the princesses?"

"As I said, they're at the hunting lodge," Karl said, adding a belated, "Your Grace. Except for the Russakan prince's men. We were about to step in to help, but quick as a blink, those princesses had drawn pistols on the men, had them off their horses and tied to a tree!" He chuckled. "Now there was a sight!"

"A sight indeed," Johan said uneasily. "The men disappeared that night, and not a footprint to be seen."

"Are you sure?" Oliver couldn't keep the strain from his voice.

"Sure as sure," Johan said. "We've had every man available keeping a watch on the forest, and no one's seen them or the old lady."

"You mean the grand duchess?" Bishop Schelker raised his eyebrows. "Did she go with them to the hunting lodge?"

"No, Your Grace," Johan said. "She stayed behind at the estate, and we've had a pair of men watching there as well. But

they haven't so much as glimpsed her passing a window since yesterday. The house has that look about it, you know? As though no one was at home."

Bishop Schelker looked at Oliver and then Walter. "I say that we make for the hunting lodge with all possible haste."

"I'm already there," Oliver said.

He dug his heels into his horse's flanks and sped down the path. He heard the others call out behind him, but he ignored them. He was sure that Karl and Johan and the others would have searched the rosebush and that entire area carefully enough; there was nothing to learn there. But he wanted to get to the hunting lodge, to find Prince Grigori and punch him in the nose for losing Petunia, and then to make certain that her sisters were all right.

And then he would find Petunia, and he would bring her home.

Dancer

My one consolation is that the princes are all very good dancers," Orchid remarked to Petunia as they entered the ball.

"There is that," Petunia agreed.

"I think it's awful, and you're both awful," Pansy said shrilly.

Petunia tried to put her arm through Pansy's, but Pansy shrugged her away and went to Lily's side. She had always been Lily's pet when she'd been small, and now that they were back in the Palace Under Stone, Petunia suspected that Pansy was returning a bit to that time in her mind. Pansy had never quite recovered from the Midnight Balls to begin with: she had always been plagued by night terrors, even before the dreams had begun. And Pansy had never liked dancing, so Petunia could hardly fault her for being upset now.

"There you are, my dove," Kestilan said caressingly as he came to draw Petunia away from her sisters and into the figures of the dance that was just beginning.

Petunia gritted her teeth and took his hand and tried to ignore him as they danced. He refused to be ignored, however, lavishing her with praise and running through an apparently endless list of endearments until Petunia wanted to scream. All around her, the members of the court swirled in the steps of the dance, her sisters mingling among them, their princes by turn sullen or equally flirtatious. Petunia was not sure which was worse, and when Kestilan called her his "sugar lump," she knew that she had had enough.

She yanked her hands out of Kestilan's grip and stood still and straight in the middle of the worn marble floor. When the dancers around them had been forced to stop as well, lest they trample Petunia, and she saw even Rionin's gaze on her from the dais, she raised her voice so that they could all hear her.

"I am not your sugar lump," she said. "I am not your dove, your flower, your amour, your jewel, your sweetmeat, your pigeon, or your delight. I am here as a prisoner, as are my sisters. I will wear this awful gown and eat your terrible food and sleep in that cold bed, and I will dance when I am bid to dance. But I will not endure this grotesque attempt at seduction. Is that understood?"

"Is there a problem?" Rionin drawled from his throne. Then he summoned both Kestilan and Petunia to the dais with a look and a languid wave of one hand.

Petunia went willingly, but Kestilan scuffed along behind her like a young boy caught in some mischief. Rose abandoned her partner and followed, and so did Lily. Lily was dancing with some gaunt member of the court who looked relieved when she stepped toward the dais, Petunia noticed.

"My queen," Rionin said with a smile at Lily. "Won't you sit beside me?"

Another gesture, and a small, crook-legged chair was brought and set beside the tall, angular throne. Lily went to it and sat without comment, but Petunia could see that her sister's thin hands were clenched in her violet skirts. There were dark circles under her eyes, and she had lost weight in the past weeks. Petunia could hardly fault her for taking the seat, close as it was to the throne.

"Now," Rionin said with a kindly air that set Petunia's teeth on edge, "what seems to be the trouble?"

"The trouble," Petunia said over Kestilan's protest that there was none, "is that we are here against our will. You know it, we know it, *everyone* here knows it. For four days I have endured his horrible playacting, calling me little pet names and pretending at courtship, and it is vile beyond even your usual vileness. I will dance all night if that is what is required of me, but I refuse to do so while Kestilan hisses in my ear about my being his kitten."

The King Under Stone was looking at Petunia as though she had suddenly sprouted a horn from the middle of her forehead. "Who knew that little Petunia would grow up to be such a bold creature?"

"Anyone who ever spoke with her from the time she said her first words," Rose said crisply. "Now, if you will make your brother promise to stop his awkward flirtations, we will continue to dance."

"Very well," the King Under Stone said, looking amused. He raised his voice so that it carried to all the corners of the ballroom. "The princesses have asked that all endearments and flirtations be halted, and we will abide by their wishes," he said.

There were hoots and catcalls from the court, and several of them called out alternate names that the princesses might enjoy. Petunia was shocked, not just because of the crassness of some of the names, but also because the first King Under Stone would never have allowed such behavior.

She was about to say something, when Rose squeezed her elbow in warning. Petunia glanced up at her oldest sister, who didn't look at her but continued to gaze at Rionin with vast disapproval.

Had they not been standing on the dais, Petunia would not even have seen it. But under the weight of Rose's stare, the King Under Stone's pallid cheek showed the faintest hint of a blush. The sight of it gave Petunia a small glow of hope. She reminded herself once more that he was human, at least half-human, and susceptible to human weaknesses and mistakes after all. He'd been trying to taunt the princesses with his announcement, but instead it had only underlined how tenuous his control was.

Rose let go of Petunia's elbow, and Petunia turned on her heel and stepped off the dais without waiting for permission.

She snapped her fingers at Kestilan, who followed her with an expression of deep astonishment. As they rejoined the dance, Petunia wondered if she'd gone mad. Even as a child, when she knew that she had had no real idea of the danger they were in, she never would have dared to argue with or turn her back on the king.

But she was not a child. And Rionin was not the king who had terrified her then.

After the ball, Petunia went back to her room alone. They usually met in Rose's room once they were sure the princes were abed. She had just closed the door and was thinking of blocking it with a chair, when it swung open and someone walked in. She tensed, but it was only Poppy.

"Want me to help you undress so that you don't have to have one of those horrid court ladies snatching at you?"

"Oh, yes, please!"

Petunia turned so that her sister could undo the dozens of tiny hooks that held together the bodice of her gown. But instead of feeling Poppy's deft fingers at her back, Petunia stood alone in the middle of the room until she finally heard her sister's hushed voice.

"What in the name of all that is holy is that?"

Petunia turned and saw Poppy pointing at something lying on her dressing table. Poppy's face was twisted with revulsion, and Petunia could hardly blame her. The blackened mass defied recognition, and she wondered if one of the court ladies had put it there as a sort of petty revenge. She sidled closer and poked it with the end of her lace fan.

"Oh," Petunia said after a moment. "It's the roses."

"Roses? It looks like a decomposing weasel," Poppy said. She put a hand to her nose. "It smells like a decomposing weasel too."

The poke from Petunia's fan had indeed released an odor of extreme decay into the room, and Petunia gagged and covered her nose and mouth with her handkerchief. She dropped the fan next to the roses, resolving to never touch it again, as some of the rose petals had broken off and were now stuck to the folded lace.

"Are those the roses you picked in the forest?" Poppy's voice was choked, and the smell was getting stronger.

"Yes, but I don't think they're really roses," Petunia said.

"Clearly. Scoop them into the chamber pot?"

"They'll just fall apart," Petunia wheezed. "Get the water pitcher."

"Washing won't help," Poppy said, but she went over to the pitcher all the same.

"I'm not going to wash them; I'm going to burn them," said Petunia.

Still holding the handkerchief over the lower half of her face, she went over to the bundle of her cloak. Galen had once told her that a good soldier never went anywhere without waterproof matches, and she had started carrying a box immediately. Later she realized that this was to stop her six-year-old self from demanding a pistol, but she continued to carry them all the same. She was rather proud of the fact that she could light a fire anywhere, and with any type of kindling.

"Step back, but keep the water ready," she instructed Poppy.

Seeing the matches in Petunia's hand when she turned around, Poppy nodded. She hefted the full pitcher of water in front of her, but stepped clear of the dressing table. Petunia realized she would need two hands, but instead of tucking her handkerchief away, she dropped it on top of the rotten flowers and the fan. Then she tapped out a match and struck it on the rough side of the box. It flared to life and she set it atop her little pile.

The whole mess flared instantly. Petunia leaped backward, stuffing the box of matches into her bodice and reaching for the pitcher of water. She hadn't expected it to burn so quickly or so high, and she could tell that Poppy was just as stunned.

But before she could grab the pitcher to pour it over it, the door flew open and the princes filled the room. One of them tossed something soft and gray, like a massive cobweb, over the flames. The fire died and noxious smoke filled the room, far more than was warranted by the blaze Petunia had created.

The King Under Stone swept in, his face so twisted with rage that Petunia was as frightened as she ever had been of his father. He looked at her, and then at Poppy, still standing frozen with the pitcher of water in her hands. Rionin snatched the pitcher from Poppy and threw it against the wall. The porcelain shattered, sending water and tiny shards of blue porcelain flying across the room.

Then the king rounded on Petunia, and his face no longer bore any semblance of humanity. Petunia tried to step back,

but the high bed was right behind her, and she had nowhere to go. Poppy tried to move closer to her and Blathen caught Poppy's arm, his own face a rictus of fear.

"We do not light fires in this place," the king hissed. "Not ever."

"But I just wanted to—"

"I don't care what you want," snarled the king. "No one here cares what you want. Now give me the matches."

Petunia went cold all over. She didn't want to give up one more thing—not her matches, not her pistol, not her cloak. But if he searched the room for the matches, he would find the pistol.

"She only had the one," Poppy blurted out.

"Yes. I had a match," Petunia said, scrambling to think of a story. "When I came here I had a whole box in my pocket, but the ladies took it when they took my clothes. One fell on the floor and I—I saved it. When I saw the flowers had gone rotten, I used the match on them."

She thought that this was the stupidest thing she had ever said. It was plain that she was lying and she almost closed her eyes, certain that Rionin was about to murder her with his bare hands. Knowing that would make her look even guiltier, however, she managed to keep them open.

It occurred to her that there were no fireplaces in the palace and the lamps all burned with a pale glow that gave off neither heat nor smoke. She had never seen anyone light one of the lamps, and wondered if they used matches or if it was some kind of magic.

"Very well," the king said at last. "But if you ever light a fire in my kingdom again, I will make you suffer for it."

Petunia swallowed, and nodded. The king stalked out of the room, his brothers following without a word. When the door had slammed behind them, Petunia gave a faint scream and collapsed on the bed.

"That was very interesting," Poppy said slowly, sinking down next to Petunia. She hummed under her breath for a moment.

"Interesting?" Petunia's voice came out as a shriek, and she laid her arm over her eyes.

Poppy asked a little while later, "How many matches have you got?"

Hero

The hunting lodge was locked tight, and all the curtains were drawn. It looked as though no one had been there for a month at least. There were even dried leaves blown across the front steps, the sight of which was apparently hilarious to the crone.

"A very nice touch," she cackled. "But never fear, young hero, someone is inside."

"Are you sure?" Bishop Schelker's face was tense.

They were all tense. As soon as Oliver had spurred his horse along the track, the others had followed, arriving only a heartbeat after. Karl and Johan and the rest of Oliver's men were not far behind, either, even though they were on foot.

The crone didn't even bother to answer Schelker. She climbed down off her horse and tied it to the long rail in front of the lodge, then pointed to Oliver.

"Boy! Hero! You have nice, broad shoulders: see if you

can't get yourself through that door." She made an encouraging gesture.

Oliver got down from his own horse and tied it to the rail. He looked helplessly at the door, a massive thing of aged oak and iron. He could try ramming his way in, but he knew full well that his bones would break before the wood so much as splintered.

"Stop toying with the poor lad," said Walter Vogel as he dismounted.

He threw his reins to Oliver, who tied up the old man's horse as Walter hobbled up the steps to the door. He did something for a moment with the lock, and the door swung open.

"Magic," Oliver breathed as Bishop Schelker tied his horse beside Walter's.

"Picked the lock, more like," the bishop snorted. "Herr Vogel has many talents. Not all of them that mysterious. Or very honest."

"Oh," Oliver said, feeling foolish.

"Come along." The good frau stalked up the stairs to the door.

Oliver and the bishop hurried after her. Oliver drew his pistol and was pleased that the bishop did the same. He wasn't being overly cautious then. Their bullets were silver, which the bishop had blessed, but that would hardly keep them from being effective on an ordinary man.

Like Grigori.

"Hello the house," Walter called out cheerfully. "Anyone at home?"

Silence.

Complete and utter silence. Not a single footstep could be heard that was not their own. No bustle of servants, no sound of a small caged bird twittering from the parlor, no hiss of a teakettle from the kitchen. The hair on Oliver's neck stood on end, and he knew that they were all gone: Grigori, his men, everyone. But where had they gone without Oliver's men seeing?

"I think we'd—" Bishop Schelker began, but Oliver silenced him, holding up one hand.

Oliver was sure that he had heard something, but he wasn't sure what or where the sound was coming from. They all froze in the middle of the front hall, heads cocked and eyes unfocused. Then Oliver heard it again: a scraping noise that came from a room on the left.

Oliver readied his pistol and crept toward the room with Bishop Schelker just behind. Oliver crouched down and peered through the keyhole but couldn't see anything. He tried the door latch. It opened easily, and Oliver jumped into the room with his pistol cocked.

Three men were lying bound and gagged in the middle of the floor. Oliver recognized Galen and Heinrich and assumed that the third man was another of the royal husbands.

Oliver holstered his pistol and pulled out a hunting knife. He ran to Prince Galen and sawed through the ropes that bound his hands while Bishop Schelker rushed to Prince Heinrich.

"This is a fine state of affairs," said the crone as she came into the room. "Got the drop on you, did he?"

"Yes," the crown prince said with disgust, removing his gag. "He did."

"In all fairness, he did have a small army," Prince Heinrich said.

"He . . . what?" Oliver looked around.

The hunting lodge showed no sign of a scuffle. Oliver's heart clenched as he noticed a small marble statue of a stag in the corner of the room. He was almost certain that had belonged to his father.

"We followed Grigori here because we had his people tied up in the woods," Galen said, as he massaged his hands and wrists. "We outnumbered him fourteen to one! Heinrich had a gun to his head! Then, when darkness fell, the room was filled with people—"

"Those weren't people," the prince Oliver didn't know interrupted, his voice dark with revulsion.

"Under Stone's court," clarified Heinrich. "They surrounded us, tied us up, and then they were gone in a matter of minutes."

"Where are the princesses?" Walter's voice was as sharp as Oliver had ever heard it.

"They're gone," said the other prince as the bishop freed him. "They went to Under Stone to be with Petunia, before we were ambushed."

"Ye gods," Oliver said, feeling sick.

"Begin at the beginning," Bishop Schelker urged.

Galen leaned back against the sofa, still sitting on the rug. His skin looked grayish, and his voice was raw, but he waved

away Schelker's waterskin. "We were coming here for lunch," the crown prince began. "Halfway here, Petunia saw a rose-bush in full bloom and tried to pick some of the flowers. We tried to stop her, but Grigori interfered. Before we could get to her, the ground opened up and she fell."

"We know," Walter Vogel said. "Oliver's men were watching."

"We came here, and when the courtiers arrived," Heinrich said, continuing the story while Galen finally took a drink from the waterskin, "we were overpowered at once, all of us. Galen, Frederick, and I were tied up, and we could hear Grigori talking to the girls in another room for some time. They must have agreed to go after Petunia, because after a while, we heard only Grigori and his men. Then they disappeared too."

"I'm amazed that Poppy didn't just shoot Grigori," Bishop Schelker said.

"She almost did. And so did I," Galen told them. "But he is the only one who knows where the new gateway into the King-dom Under Stone is."

Prince Frederick sighed. "But now they've gone, and we still don't know where the gate is."

"We are not entirely without hope," Walter assured him. "The gate is somewhere in this lodge. Oliver's men haven't seen any sign of anyone leaving."

"Oliver's men again?" Heinrich murmured.

Oliver was strangely embarrassed. "They were worried about Petunia," he muttered.

"And a good thing too," Frederick said.

241

"We'd better find that gate," the crone said. She turned and started out of the room.

"Hold a moment," said Heinrich. He got to his feet, nearly falling against the sofa as he did so. He stretched and rubbed his bad leg for a moment, a frown creasing his face. "What do we do when we get there?"

"Whatever needs to be done," Walter Vogel said.

"Not good enough," said Heinrich. "What will need to be done to stop this from happening over and over again?"

"Seal them all up once again, and this time we'll make sure it holds," the old man said, rubbing his seamed face.

"Can you be sure?"

"I haven't spent the last fifteen hundred years learning to knit my own socks, boy!" The crone looked like she might box Heinrich's ears, if she could have reached them.

Heinrich didn't look pleased; he looked even grimmer, if that were possible. "You've found the way? Galen's studies—"

"Galen's studies are a wonder," said Walter Vogel gently, "but as the good frau has said, we have had centuries of time to perfect our original spell."

"Last time it took a dozen practitioners, and most of them died," Galen pointed out. He put a hand on Walter's shoulder and squeezed it. "If we dared to take more time—"

"What did I just say to the other one?" The old woman jerked a gnarled thumb at Heinrich. "We wouldn't have come if we didn't think we could succeed."

"The power will mostly pass through the good frau and

myself," said Walter. "The rest of you will be quite safe." He leveled his gaze at Oliver. "But we will need all of you."

"Of course," Oliver said, getting to his feet. He tried not to show how stiff the ride had made him. "Of course I'll do whatever necessary."

"And if you're wrong, Walter? About the focus? About the effectiveness of the spell?" Heinrich's frown had never left his face.

"Have we ever been wrong before?" The good frau smacked him on the upper arm, which was as high as she could reach. She looked at Galen. "Well? Tell him!"

"No, good frau," Galen said, with a faint smile that didn't reach his eyes. "You never have been wrong."

"I have everything here that Walter and the good frau have asked for, and the items that you sent for as well, Galen," Bishop Schelker said, indicating a satchel slung across his chest. "Let's find the gate and go. The princesses have spent long enough below."

They tramped from room to room, looking for a way to reach the Kingdom Under Stone. In every room, Walter Vogel and the good frau would stand with their heads cocked as though listening to something. Then they would shake their heads and move on.

"The whole house reeks of magic," the crone complained after a few minutes. "Did Under Stone's men tramp through every pantry and water closet?"

After they had searched every room in the house, they

went back through the front hall. Walter decided that Prince Grigori had destroyed his gate after he and his people went through, and there was no point in lingering.

They would have to make their own way Under Stone.

Frederick moaned. "How long will that take?"

No one answered him.

"As there is no food here, we could go to my hall," Oliver offered. "It's not very fine, but you could work there unmolested as long as you needed."

Oliver couldn't bear to look at Galen's or Walter's faces as he said this. He could see that they were thinking that making their own gate would take not a matter of hours or days, but months or years. It didn't bear thinking on.

He reached out and nearly brushed the canvas of an enormous painting that hung on the nearest wall. It was a hunting scene and looked very familiar. He was almost certain that it had belonged to his family. In fact, one of the figures wore a dark tunic that clearly had been painted over, and he thought it had borne his family's coat of arms before. He squinted at it. The paint in several places looked wet, now that he gave it closer scrutiny.

"Shall I return to Bruch, while the rest of you go to this hall of Oliver's?" Frederick asked.

He started to add something more, but Karl and the rest of Oliver's men burst through the front door. Karl had an ax in one hand and a pistol in the other, and all their masks were in place.

"What's afoot?" Karl demanded.

"Ah, an escort back to the young earl's hall," said Walter Vogel with a laugh.

"Karl," Oliver said, holding up his hands. "Hold your fire!"

When he lowered his arms, his elbow passed right through the painting as if it hadn't been there. Oliver slowly removed his arm, then he plunged his hand in. It was as though there was no paint, no canvas, and no wall behind. It just kept going.

"I believe I've found the gate," Oliver said.

He moved his arm back and forth. The gate was as high and as wide as the painting, and Oliver held his breath as he thrust his head in to look around.

"Oliver! What are you doing?"

He heard Karl shout, but it wasn't necessary. He could see quite well, and there was nothing to alarm him. Just a stairway of gold that descended toward a silver gate. Beyond the gate he could see a wood, also of silver, and beyond that the spires of a black palace. He drew back.

"That's the gate all right," he told them, feeling almost giddy.

"How in heaven's name?" Prince Heinrich's mouth was agape. "They walked through a *painting?*"

"And not a very good one, either." The crone sniffed. "Those horses have stumpy legs, and what are they hunting? I can't tell if that's a fox or a polecat."

Oliver bowed to the old woman. "When this is all over, I shall replace this painting with a portrait of you, good frau."

"Well!" That seemed to please her. "Help me over the frame, then."

Arsonist

Petunia was crouched in a corner of Rose's bedchamber, trying to light the leg of a small table on fire. Her sisters all
stood watch, except for Poppy and Violet, who had gone off
on some mission of their own. This made Lily even more nervous than did the prospect of setting Rose's room on fire, for
as she said, "Anytime Poppy gets that look in her eye, it
makes me nervous."

"Just light it already," Jonquil shrilled. "And try not to use
up all the matches!"

"Thank you, Jonquil," Petunia snapped. "I hadn't thought
of that."

"Be nice," Daisy whispered. She was standing next to the
chair with a pitcher of water, ready to douse the experiment.

But there was no fire. Petunia had even shredded a handkerchief as kindling and wrapped the bits around the leg of
the chair. They had no books in their room, though Rose
swore she had seen some of the princes reading when they

had been trapped in the palace as children. Even if the slick wood of the chair was reluctant to burn, the linen—or whatever it was the handkerchiefs were made of in Under Stone's realm—should have caught fire by now; she'd placed three matches directly on the threads.

"I don't think it will work," Petunia admitted. "And Jonquil's right: I shouldn't use up all my matches just playing around. I've never seen them so frightened; there must be some way to use that against them." She closed the little box of matches and put it in her bodice.

"What was it exactly that you started on fire last night?" Rose's forehead was creased with concentration.

"The horrid flowers that I had picked in the wood," Petunia recited. "And my fan from the ball, and my handkerchief."

"Did it all burn?"

"Yes!" Then Petunia stopped. "No," she said more thoughtfully. "I don't really think the fan burned. But that handkerchief—wait! That handkerchief was one of mine! It burned and so did the flowers. There was a nasty mess on my dressing table afterward; I could see it through the webby thing that Rionin put over it all. I don't know if the sticks of the fan burned; I could see its shape through the web. But a footman cleared it all away before I got a good look at it."

"If they are so afraid of fire," Orchid said, "it might be that things here aren't meant to burn. They might have some chemical on them, or be made of things that aren't naturally flammable." She pushed her spectacles up higher and nodded.

"What isn't flammable?" Petunia frowned at her.

She'd never heard of such a thing. Her father had lectured her at length when she was a child about how everything had the potential to burn, and burn out of control, from green wood on down a list of household items he thought she might try her matches on.

"Wool doesn't burn," said Orchid. "In fact, it smothers fires."

"I don't think this is wool," Petunia said, fingering the slippery shreds of what had been a black handkerchief edged with rather tatty lace.

"Silk burns," said Orchid. "But not very well." She squinted at the mess around the table leg. "Did that even singe?"

"Not a bit," said Petunia with despair.

"It makes sense that they wouldn't have clothes and things that could burn, if they're afraid of fire," said Hyacinth. "Which is a shame, since we shan't be able to burn this place to the ground after all."

The others all stared at her in surprise, and she flushed.

"Well, there must be something around here that burns," said Lilac, disgruntled.

"I'm not sure that this chair is even really wood," said Petunia, chipping at the lacquered leg with a fingernail.

"If something did burn, how could they replace it?" Rose pointed out. "I don't know how the first king created all this, but I doubt Rionin has the power to do the same. There's no quarry to get new stone, no forests other than the silver wood."

Petunia's head snapped up and she blinked at her oldest sister. "The silver wood! Do you think that would burn?"

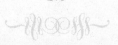

"It's *silver*," Iris said. "Metal doesn't burn." She was rearranging her hair in the dressing-table mirror. "But I do wish we could go across the lake to the forest. I want some knitting needles."

"What are you going to knit?" Lilac wanted to know. "A nice scarf for Derivos?" Her voice was thick with scorn.

"No," Iris retorted, "I want something that doesn't look like a weapon so that they won't take it away from me, but I could still stab someone with it."

"I just want clothes that don't scratch at me," Jonquil fretted. Her pale skin was red where the lace of the bodice chafed, and she was so thin that the gown hung off her shoulders, though Lily had tried pinning it up as best she could.

"I wonder," Petunia said, tucking the box of matches into her own bodice and getting to her feet, "if they would let us go over to the wood if we said that we wanted knitting needles."

"It can't hurt to ask," Rose said, her eyes gleaming.

"Someone's coming," Lily whispered, and hurried to sit on the end of the bed by Pansy.

The door was thrown open, and at first Petunia wasn't sure what she was seeing. It looked like a mountain of clothing had come to life and was about to attack them. Then she noticed a high pile of black curls atop the pile—Poppy. And some of the clothing was familiar too. . . .

"My riding gown!" Pansy leaped up to seize a pale-yellow gown from the middle of the pile.

"Careful!"

Poppy tipped forward and all the gowns spilled on the

floor. She came all the way into the room, kicking the pile ahead of her, with Violet on her heels holding a lumpy bundle wrapped in a petticoat.

"The good news," Poppy said, closing the door behind Violet, "is that Blathen is the worst poker player in the history of the game. I mean, really, Violet and I simply slaughtered him and Telinros." She smiled at the memory. "The better news is that I won back all our clothes, including our boots, as you can see." She made an expansive gesture at the pile on the floor, and the bundle that Violet was putting down with greater care.

"If you're good with numbers, poker isn't all that difficult," Violet said. She shook her head over the princes' lack of skill but couldn't hide a pleased smile.

The sisters quickly shed their Under Stone gowns and put on their own things. Even Jonquil, the most fashion-minded among them, didn't complain about wearing a riding habit and boots indoors. Instead, she smiled for the first time since they had arrived, and Poppy hugged her in an uncharacteristic show of affection.

Petunia even tied on her scarlet cloak. She had brought it with her to Rose's room, not wanting to let it out of her sight. She had been using it as a blanket at night, instead of the thin, slick covers on her bed, which gave off little warmth and smelled like pond water.

Once she was dressed, Pansy looked around nervously at her sisters. "Shall we all go together?"

"Go where?" Poppy looked up from putting Petunia's

pistol in a pocket that tied around her waist under her gown. "Are we going to try to rush out the front door?" She looked rather excited by this idea. "I still say they won't expect it, always a benefit in any battle."

"We're going to ask if we can go to the wood," Rose said. "And gather twigs to use as knitting needles."

"And then we're going to stab Rionin with them," said Jonquil firmly.

"I love this idea," announced Poppy. "Let's all pick a prince, inscribe his name on our needles, and then attack tonight during the ball. If we all strike at the same time, no one will stop us until it's too late. Then we run for it. If there are ways in, there are ways out."

Petunia felt a chill at Poppy's cheerful words. It seemed far too easy. If there was a way in and out, shouldn't Galen and the others have found it by now? It had been almost five days! At least carrying some kind of weapon would make her feel safer.

So they all trooped out of Rose's room and down the corridor, until they found where the princes were gathered. Their request to cross the lake was met variously with unease or hilarity, however, until at last Hyacinth's partner Stavian silenced his brothers with a loud hiss.

"You cannot leave the palace," he told the princesses.

"If we are to stay here forever, we will need some things," Rose said evenly.

"You have been given clothing, and your old things were just returned to you," Telinros said. Petunia noticed that his

fists were clenched: he probably had not enjoyed losing to Poppy and Violet.

"I refuse to wear someone else's stockings," Lily said with a snap in her voice that Petunia had never heard before. "If I am to be your queen, I will not wear tatty old stockings and garters made to fit some common courtier with elephantine legs!"

Everyone gaped at her. Derivos actually let out a little bray of laughter.

"I don't know where your clothing comes from," Lily went on, "or how to get more, but if you provide us with yarn and needles we will make our own. And the best, sharpest needles to be had are taken from the branches of the silver trees across the lake!"

Petunia cringed and just behind her Daisy sucked in her breath loudly. Even Lily's face had gone rigid, and Petunia knew that her sister had gone too far. The princes would surely guess why they really wanted twigs from the silver wood, now that Lily had reminded them all of what had happened the last time someone had used the silver wood for knitting needles.

"Do you think we are fools?" asked Stavian.

"Princess Rose has made it clear before that she does not find us all that intelligent," remarked the King Under Stone as he strolled into the room. "Isn't that right, dear Rose?"

A chill went up Petunia's back. "Dear Rose" had been the first king's way of addressing Rose. In the grayish light of the sitting room, Rionin looked even more like his father

than he had in the ballroom. She nudged Poppy, whose hand was already hovering near her right leg. Petunia wondered if Poppy had cut a slit in her riding gown so that she could reach a pistol more easily. Poppy moved to the front so that she had a clear view of Rionin.

"What is it that our dear brides wish?" Rionin smiled at them with pointed teeth.

In the days since they had arrived in the Kingdom Under Stone, he had glutted himself on the power from their dancing. His hair shone silver, and his eyes blazed green. He reminded her of someone . . . not his father, but someone else she couldn't quite put her finger on.

"They want to go to the silver wood to make knitting needles," said Derivos.

"We need stockings that fit," said Pansy, her voice little more than a squeak. She was holding Lily's hand.

"Naturally you do," said the King Under Stone. "And it would be wise to find something to occupy you during the days. Can't have you wandering about the palace, plotting mischief, now can we?" His cold eyes fixed on Poppy, and he snapped his long fingers.

In an instant Blathen had leaped at Poppy and wrestled her to the ground. Rose flung herself at him, hammering his back with her fists. Daisy kicked him in the side with her riding boot and shouted for him to let her twin go. Poppy was screaming obscenities and pulling at Blathen's ears so hard that Petunia, who was frozen in place, thought they might come right off.

"Got it," Blathen panted, slithering away from his assailants.

He held up the heavy pistol, triumphant despite his scratched and bruised face. Rose helped Poppy to her feet, and to Petunia's increased horror, Poppy was sobbing.

"Never touch me again," she choked out.

Blathen just leered at her.

The others circled around her, Daisy taking Poppy in her arms and rocking her. But Petunia couldn't keep her eyes off of Rionin, and Rionin was staring right back at her.

"Pet . . . isn't that what they call you?"

"*They* do, but not you," Petunia said, but her bravado was ruined by her shaking voice.

"Dear little Pet," said the King Under Stone, smiling even wider. "I think you would be the perfect choice to go and fetch some twigs from the wood. And your betrothed can accompany you."

"I want Telinros or Derivos to come as well," Kestilan said, looking uneasy.

"Take them both, if you are feeling cowardly. Although I fail to see how one little girl can do much harm," the king retorted. Then he swept out of the room, and the sisters weren't the only ones who sighed with relief when he left.

$\mathcal{W}$oodsman

$\mathcal{S}$o this is Maude's forest," Bishop Schelker said wonderingly.

"An inadvertent gift to her daughters," Galen said.

They moved through the silent woods, the tree branches swaying over their heads in a breeze that could not be felt. Oliver had never seen anything like it. The trunks of the trees were softly gleaming, and the leaves were shaped like hearts, each one the length of his thumb. It looked like the work of a silversmith, but he could see where their roots were digging deep into the black soil.

Walter led them into the woods a little way so that they were hidden from the path that wound through it. He took a saw-edged knife from his belt and reached up, cupping a hand gently over a low-hanging branch. With a deep breath, he began to cut.

Oliver watched with a faintly sick feeling as Walter's knife rasped through the silver tree. Then he chose a thicker tree branch. He'd taken Karl's ax before sending his men, with Prince Frederick, to the grand duchess's estate. Oliver hesitated, aiming the ax at it several times, before a nod from Galen gave him the encouragement he needed. He swung and took the branch off with one blow.

The crone gave an appreciative whistle.

"I've been taking out my frustrations on firewood since I was twelve," Oliver told her. He braced his foot on the fallen branch and cut it in half with another blow.

"I don't know how inadvertent this was," Bishop Schelker said, fingering some of the silver leaves.

"What do you mean?"

Oliver picked up the smaller part of the branch he had just severed and studied the end. The wood, if wood it was, was silver clear through and didn't have rings, so there was no way of telling how old it was. A few strange, soft fibers poked out of the cut, and the branch felt like neither metal nor wood, but a mixture of both.

"I didn't know what she was doing at night, of course," the bishop said, "nor why she was becoming more sorrowful even as her beautiful daughters were bringing such joy to Gregor.

"She told me that she was troubled by dreams. I knew she was holding back, but only now do I realize how much." Schelker kicked at the sparkling black soil at their feet.

"In one of her dreams," the bishop continued, "she said that she planted the silver cross I had given her. The cross sprouted into a shining forest that brought hope and protection to her

children. She was expecting at the time . . . Lilac, as I recall . . . and I assumed that it was the fancy of a woman in her delicate condition." He grimaced and snapped off a twig to add to the crown prince's growing pile. "I assured her that her children were in no danger. I remember how sadly she looked at me, as if I had disappointed her. A few days later she stopped wearing the brooch. I thought she had put it away because I had upset her."

"Lily always said that her mother had dropped the brooch returning from the Midnight Ball," Heinrich said. "But perhaps she decided that her dream was more than just a dream and planted it on purpose."

"I rather suspect that she did," Bishop Schelker said.

"Of course she did," Walter grunted. He was stripping leaves from the branches and putting them in his bag. "Maude believed in dreams, and magic, or we wouldn't be here."

"Should we be watching for . . . guards or anything?"

Oliver had been about to take a swing at another branch, but wondered if the noise they were making would attract unwanted attention. Everything was so still and silent without birds or insects or even a real wind that the sound of Walter picking leaves was making him twitch.

"There are no guards," the crown prince said. "There's the king, the princes, and the court, but they never venture across the lake."

"Hurry and get a few more branches if you would, Oliver," Walter Vogel said. "Then we'll find a place to make our preparations."

"How large is this wood?" Oliver asked.

He took a few steps farther into the thick of the trees. They had been taking leaves and cutting branches right beside a narrow path, and he worried that Grigori or someone else who used the same gate would notice. A few steps in he selected another branch and lopped it off near the trunk of the shining tree.

"I don't know that anyone's ever explored it," Walter said. "Galen and the girls were too busy running to really take it all in the last time." He gave a dry chuckle.

"Running and shooting," the crown prince said.

"Aren't we glad that I taught Lily to shoot?" Heinrich was gathering up handfuls of black dirt to fill small leather bags.

"Not a day goes by that I don't give thanks for that," his cousin said fervently.

"And then you taught the other princesses to shoot afterward?" Oliver dragged the branch he had cut back to the path.

"Yes, after what happened the king was quite adamant that they all learn," Galen said. "That's why I'm surprised that you, er, abducted Petunia. Wasn't she armed?"

"Yes, she was," Oliver said, smiling to himself. "The first time I saw her, she had a pistol aimed directly at my face. But I jumped down out of a tree later and caught her off guard," he explained.

The others laughed at that, which reassured Oliver. If they could laugh, if Walter Vogel could hum as he gathered up the twigs, then Oliver felt that this might all turn out all right.

When they had gathered the wood, leaves, and soil that

they needed, they continued down the path until they came to a lake of black water. Rising from an island at the center was a palace, ragged and menacing against the dull-gray nothingness that formed the sky. Oliver felt prickles of ice go down his spine.

"Stay in the trees," Walter Vogel cautioned. "They can see us from the palace. We'll need to move just around here a ways, to find a place to work."

Reluctantly, Oliver pulled back into the trees with his armload of silver wood. He tripped several times trying to crane his neck and keep the palace in sight. It didn't seem to have any windows, only a single large door, but still he wished for a glimpse of Petunia. Was she all right? Had they hurt her?

"They are well," Heinrich said quietly, walking along beside Oliver. "It's thin consolation, but the princes do want their brides unharmed."

Oliver cringed. Their brides. And Petunia had been six when they'd first stolen her away to make her a bride. Now she was barely sixteen, and he still could not fathom it. She might show a bold face to the world, but she was still so very vulnerable.

A flash of red caught the corner of Oliver's eye. He turned his head toward the palace once again, thinking that he had only conjured the color out of his memories.

But no.

Someone in a red cloak was emerging from the palace doors, a tall figure in black on either side. Oliver knew it was Petunia in the red cloak. It had to be. The smallness of the

figure, the sweep of the cloak . . . he would know her no matter the distance.

"That's Pet," breathed Heinrich, standing close by Oliver. "But where are they taking her?" Every line in the prince's body was taut.

There was a row of small boats beached on the shore. One of the tall black figures helped Petunia into the bow of a boat, and then sat in the middle seat with a hand on each oar. The other tall figure pushed the boat out and leaped into the stern. The rower pulled them toward the wooded shore with firm strokes, and Oliver and the others drew back into the trees.

"We have to move farther away," said Galen in a barely audible whisper. "We can't risk them seeing us now."

"But we could rescue her," Oliver insisted in a harsh whisper of his own.

"She doesn't need rescuing right this very moment," Galen said, taking Oliver's upper arm in a tight grip. "And if we killed those two and took Petunia with us, the king would soon miss his brothers, and he would come looking for them. We would never be able to get the other girls out then."

The other girls. Beautiful, queenly Rose. Poppy with her mischievous smile. She and Princess Daisy were to be married in the spring. Oliver had seen Princes Ricard and Christian in Bruch. He had seen the way they smiled at their princesses. Did they know what had happened, or were they still going about their ordinary duties, oblivious to the danger their brides were in? Oliver swallowed, his throat dry.

Suddenly, getting all twelve princesses safely out of the black palace seemed insurmountable.

He watched Petunia climb out of the boat without any assistance, his eyes searching her for any sign of pain or fear. She moved easily, but her hood hid her face. The swirls of silver embroidery around the edges of the hood matched the silver of the trees, and the scarlet velvet stood out against the black soil. When she started toward the trees with her escort, Oliver allowed himself to be drawn back into the thick of the woods.

They found a small clear space some ways away, and Walter Vogel set them each to a task. Oliver's was to cut the silver twigs to a certain length, and then to notch them in a pattern that looked like a line of fence posts.

"Well! What did you think they were?" The crone whacked him over the head with one gnarled hand. "New fence posts to hold them all in, the awful old things."

Oliver used great restraint to avoid sidling away from the crone. He didn't care if she was a revered sorceress; his head smarted where she had hit him. But he supposed being several centuries old would make your moods unpredictable.

The two princes busied themselves with the small bags of soil and the leaves, and Bishop Schelker cut marks into the ends of the larger branches that Oliver had chopped. Their preparations weren't taking very long, and Oliver was hopeful that they would be able to finish refreshing Under Stone's prison before nightfall. Then he supposed they would just have to worry about actually fetching the princesses, and they could finally leave.

And it seemed that Walter and Galen had a plan to get the princesses out of the palace as well.

"We'll need to sneak inside the palace, and there's only one invisibility cloak," Galen said when they had finished preparing the wood and soil. "Although I do have this." He reached into the satchel that Bishop Schelker had brought and removed a lightweight shawl of gray wool. "Which should work just as well."

"It's not as stylish as my cloak," sniffed the good frau.

"I wouldn't think to upstage your fine cloak," said Galen with a little bow.

"I stole that off a Romisch cavalry officer when I was a young lass," she told Galen with a twinkle in her eye. "Of course, it had no magic then. I just liked the color."

"It was always a very good color on you," Walter Vogel said.

Oliver thought about asking them how long they had known each other, but decided he didn't want any of the details that the good frau might actually offer about their relationship.

"Two of us will be invisible," Galen continued. "But unfortunately only two of us. Another reason why I sent Frederick to the estate with Oliver's men: he would have tried to come with us, and there isn't a third cloak.

"We'll try to get in at the end of the ball and bring the girls out when everyone is dispersing for the night," Galen went on. "Someone will need to wait by the gate to make certain they all get through, and then we'll close the prison."

"I want to go into the palace," Oliver said.

At the same time, Heinrich reached for the gray shawl.

But Galen was shaking his head. He pulled the gray shawl away from his cousin. "I'm sorry, Heinrich. I'm giving the cloak to Oliver, and taking this myself."

"But Lily," began Heinrich.

"Heinrich, how fast can you run?" Galen looked as if asking the question pained him, but his eyes never wavered from his cousin's face.

"Damn Analousians," Heinrich said, and let go of the shawl. He pounded the thigh of his bad leg with a fist and winced.

"Heinrich, after you help to place the new fence posts, you'll wait at the gate," Galen said. "And get all the girls out. And yourself."

"I thought you needed my help with the spell," Heinrich protested.

"We could use you," Walter Vogel admitted. "But we can also do it without you."

"And I would rather that you made sure that Rose didn't try to come back," Galen said. "It will be easier for me knowing that you and the girls are all safe. And alive."

Oliver looked down at his hands. He knew there was a chance he wouldn't survive this. Especially if he helped to seal the Kingdom Under Stone. That had been another reason why Prince Frederick had been sent away, for some of their husbands would need to survive this. But if Petunia and her sisters could be free, it would be worth it, Oliver decided.

To his surprise, the good frau put one hand over his in a comforting gesture. He looked at her, but just as she opened

her nearly toothless mouth to speak, there was the sound of shouts and then the crack of a pistol firing.

"That wasn't the palace," Heinrich said, struggling to his feet.

"It came from over there," Bishop Schelker said, pointing through the trees where they had last seen Petunia.

Out of habit, Oliver pulled his wolf mask over his face and fastened it. He grabbed his pistol, shifting it to his left hand. He hefted Karl's ax with his right. "I hope this doesn't ruin your plans too much," he said to the crown prince, and then he raced off through the woods.

Prize

Petunia was having quite an enjoyable time pretending that Kestilan and Telinros didn't exist. Telinros was returning the favor, but it frustrated Kestilan and he kept trying to make conversation, or at the very least make her look at him.

She went a little way along the path that wound from the black shore through the silver wood. It was the same path that she and her sisters had always used, a path she hadn't walked in ten years.

"Petunia, come back here!" Kestilan called.

That decided her. She went along the path to its end, with the princes trailing behind. Kestilan continued to plead with her to turn back, but Telinros just looked angry when she peeked at him. She straightened her cloak and kept going.

At the end of the path she found the silver gate, set with pearls, that even after all these years was as familiar to her as her own bedposts. Wrapped around the gate was the chain of boiled wool links that Galen had used to seal it shut, the knot pinned by a silver knitting needle.

She reached out and fingered the scratchy, boiled wool of the chain. She remembered watching Galen knit it at dinner, the night before the old king had forced them to stay Under Stone. At the time she'd thought he was only amusing her and her sisters, the way he had earlier by giving Pansy a red yarn puffball when she was crying. It wasn't until later that she understood what he was doing, his calloused fingers working away with the yarn that was so much more than just wool.

Petunia's mouth went dry. She whirled, grateful that her sweeping cloak hid the chain from the two princes. Their faces were white and strained, as though it hurt them to be so close to the gate, and she felt a small surge of triumph even as she brushed past them, hurrying back along the path and hoping that they would follow. She snapped her fingers to speed them along.

The chain was knotted and pinned on the *inside* of the gate now.

Halfway down the path she noticed something else that she did not want the princes to see. Someone had chopped a branch off one of the trees. The scar on the trunk was plain to her eyes, glittering slightly. The shimmering black soil was swirled and scuffed as though several people had been there. She immediately went to the other side of the path and began testing the branches, moving with light steps.

"Don't go into the trees," Kestilan said.

"Stop her," Telinros ordered his brother.

Petunia looked back and saw them both standing at the edge of the path, their faces twisted with pain. Kestilan took one step off the path, between two arching silver trees, and hissed. He glared at Petunia.

"Come here."

"No," she said. "I'll come when I've finished gathering twigs."

"Gather them from the path," he snarled.

"No."

She kept walking deeper into the woods. She heard slow steps behind her: Kestilan braving the blessed silver. She hoped the pain was excruciating.

"Petunia, come back here!"

"No!"

"Haven't you learned not to wander into the woods?"

That brought her up short.

It was true that she was in the Kingdom Under Stone because she had been picking flowers that any sane person would have known signaled a trap. But how could she get into any more trouble? And now she was walking in her mother's silver wood, perhaps the safest place in this realm.

She went forward and came through the trees into a clearing. In the middle of the clearing was a beautiful little house, like an Analousian chalet with a sloping roof and ornately carved wooden balconies. It was all in black, and there was none of the traditional paintings on the walls, but otherwise it looked precisely like a chalet from the southeastern mountains.

"Petunia! Come back at once!"

She stepped into the clearing with Kestilan's voice growing fainter behind her. Despite her reasoning, she still wished she had her pistol or a silver dagger or something. She gave the top of her bodice a little pat, feeling the matches there. At least she had them.

The door of the chalet swung open and someone strolled out onto the porch. Someone tall and slim, dressed in black, and Petunia froze, thinking it was Rionin. How had he gotten through the wood?

"My Petal! Welcome!"

It was Prince Grigori. Petunia felt as though a bucket of cold water had been dumped over her head, and she nearly did run right back to Kestilan then. But anger got the better of her.

"You! What are you doing here?" Petunia demanded. "What is all this?"

He gave her a broad smile of delight. "Have you come to see my grandmother? She has been pining to see you!"

"Your . . . grandmother?" Petunia's knees went weak. The grand duchess was here? In the prison of the Kingdom Under Stone?

"She came right after you did," Grigori said, as though it were the most obvious thing in the world. He came down the steps, holding out his hand. "I am sorry that I tricked you into coming here," he said. "But it was necessary. Here is where you belong, and so do my grandmother and I. In order to get us here, I had to send you first."

Petunia wanted to slap him. How could he bring the grand

268

duchess to this place? She would be trapped here in the middle of the woods forever!

"Your poor grandmother! Take me to her at once," Petunia ordered, even as her stomach tied itself in a knot. Escaping had just gotten even more complicated. She pushed past him and started up the steps.

Looking startled at her vehemence, but nevertheless pleased, Prince Grigori hurried forward to lead her into the chalet. It was all silver and black with violet upholstery, not unlike the Palace Under Stone, but without the seediness and rot that crept around the corners. Prince Grigori led her down the hall and knocked on a tall door inlaid with mother-of-pearl.

"Grandmother? Our Petunia is here," he called through the door.

"Bring her in, bring her in," came the grand duchess's reply before Petunia could protest that she was not his Petunia.

Grigori opened the door on a beautifully appointed bedroom. The black furniture was draped in lacy white. There were white curtains over the windows, a white-canopied bed piled with white cushions, and white lace shawls and antimacassars on every surface.

The grand duchess, sitting up in a froth of lace and pillows on the bed, was also completely in white. She wore a white lace cap over her white hair, and a ruffled white bed jacket. She looked older, and yet strangely more alert than usual, and Petunia wondered wildly if this were the real grand duchess. But who else could she be?

Petunia covered her distraction by dropping a curtsy. "Your Grace, it's such a surprise to see you here!"

"But why shouldn't I be here? Here is where I belong!" The grand duchess smiled at her, and Petunia felt a chill run down her spine. The old lady fingered the coverlet with evident satisfaction.

"I— I don't understand," Petunia stammered. "This is the prison of the King Under Stone! None of us should be here."

"Prison? Only temporarily," the grand duchess said as if it were no great matter. "My only regret is that I was not able to join my beloved years ago, to be his queen before he was cruelly murdered."

"What?" Petunia blinked stupidly at the grand duchess. Was she really saying that the first King Under Stone would have been ... was her ... Petunia just shuddered, remembering that horrible, bone-white *creature* on his throne.

Petunia drew her cloak around herself and studied the old woman in the bed. *Was* this the grand duchess or had Rionin found some woman of the court to disguise? But to what purpose?

"Now, my Petunia," the grand duchess teased. "Why do you look at me so? Come here and sit on the bed with me, and Grigori will bring us something hot to drink."

"Have your eyes always been green?" Petunia could not remember.

"Of course they have! What other color would they have been? There have been sonnets written about my emerald green eyes! And they remain as sharp today as they were in my

youth—I can see farther than many a young girl!" The grand duchess laughed, showing two rows of very fine white teeth.

Had they always been so fine and white? Petunia could not remember that either, and could not shake the feeling that she was looking at something . . . other . . . something that did indeed belong here in the Kingdom Under Stone and not the world above.

"Come, sit here by me, my dear Petunia!" the grand duchess urged her, patting a small space on the cushion-covered bed beside her. "Let me explain it all to you. It's not quite as horrible as you've been led to believe."

Petunia didn't move.

"Oh, come now!" The grand duchess laughed again. "Do you think I bite? Come here, girl, and let me talk to you comfortably!"

The Grand Duchess Volenskaya had shown her nothing but kindness in the past, Petunia reminded herself, had treated her as one of her own granddaughters, in fact. It was not the old lady's fault that her grandson was evil, and he had clearly tricked her into coming here, just as he had tricked Petunia.

Petunia crossed the room and sat on the edge of the bed next to the grand duchess, arranging her cloak around her.

"Don't you want to take the cloak off? You must be warm," the grand duchess said, reaching one hand out for the ties of the cloak.

"No, thank you." Petunia drew back a little.

"Suit yourself, child," said the grand duchess. "Now let me explain.

"When I was a very young girl, younger than you are now, my father shut my eight sisters and me in a high tower. He was afraid that we would be taken advantage of by fortune seekers, or fall in love with unsuitable men, and so he decided to lock us away until he could find worthy husbands for all of us. I spent ten years in that tower," the grand duchess said, her tone bitter, "but toward the end of that time, something happened."

Despite herself, Petunia was leaning closer to the grand duchess. So it was true, after all. This poor woman had been one of the Nine Daughters of Russaka, seduced by the King Under Stone during her captivity.

"A man began to appear to us," the grand duchess continued. "He was made all of shadows, but he was kind and wonderful. He told us of his kingdom, and how he wanted to take us all away from that horrible tower. He taught us how to make a door in our tower to go to his palace to dance. We spent so many happy nights there." She sighed, smiling at the memory. "It was a gift from heaven, to be able to escape that small tower room!

"And soon I knew an ever greater joy, when I realized that I would be presenting my beloved king with a child. I thought that he would marry me then, and make me his queen. But to my anger, my sisters were all also with child! I determined to have my child first, but Tanya and Daniela's sons were born minutes before mine." Her lips twisted, bitterly, and Petunia recoiled a little at the expression. But the grand duchess did not appear to notice.

"We had our children all in the same horrible night," the grand duchess continued, "while a storm raged outside that kept any help from coming. We had a bell outside our window we could ring when we needed supplies or aid, and though we rang it through the night, the wind howled and none could hear it. When the storm cleared, all nine of us had had our babies, sons all. My parents arrived and looked on us in anguish, but before anyone could speak, a shadow covered the room, and my babe was taken from my arms."

"How dreadful," Petunia said, caught up in the story despite herself.

The grand duchess patted her hand. "The worst was to come. We were no longer allowed to join our dear king in the Palace Under Stone, but told that our sons would be raised as princes, and in time we might see them all again.

"Our father married us to whatever fools he could find before the scandal spread. Which is how I ended up in West-falin. A lovely country, to be sure," the grand duchess said, giving Petunia's hand a squeeze. "But so far from my home, and so far from my true king . . . though for that, everything in the sunlight world is." She chuckled a little at that. "And I was right: my king did favor me. He arranged for that silly little earldom to be broken up so that I might live in comfort on my estate, one of his last acts before he was murdered."

Petunia sat frozen. She didn't know which was worse: that this strange person sitting beside her might be a courtier impersonating the grand duchess, or that these words might actually be coming from that respected grand dame.

"Oliver's estate ... the King Under Stone..." Petunia could barely whisper the words.

"And then," the old woman continued as if Petunia hadn't spoken, "after a lifetime of waiting, I was contacted by my son! My firstborn, the son of my heart and soul!" The grand duchess's eyes were shining, and she was looking beyond Petunia now, savoring the memory. "He would come as a shadow to my bedroom window, nightly visits from my dear one after so many years! The sad news that my magnificent king had died was a great blow. But I was consoled when my son told me that his two oldest brothers were also dead, and now *he* is the King Under Stone!"

"*Rionin* is your son?" Petunia's entire body went numb.

The white hair, the green eyes ... Rionin looked so much like the grand duchess. Why hadn't she seen it before?

"Yes," the grand duchess said with great pride. "Though I have always called him Alexei." She sniffed. "It was his father who named him Rionin. A strange name, but I know that my king must have had his reasons for this. Perhaps in his language it had some noble meaning," she mused. "I must ask him."

"Rionin is your son," Petunia said again. The sensation was slowly and coldly trickling back into her body. "Could you not ... can't you tell him ... my sister Lily is already married!" Petunia clutched at the grand duchess's hands desperately. "Please tell him! She doesn't want to marry him! None of us want to stay here and marry the princes! Can't you help us, please?" Tears stung her eyes.

The grand duchess looked at Petunia and smiled, and

Petunia felt relief wash over her. This was the grand duchess, she was sure. And the grand duchess would help them. The tears wobbled and fell from her lower lashes.

"Don't worry, my dear Petunia," she said. "I've been speaking to my son a great deal about you. Kestilan won't like it, of course, but I hardly care. His mother was some feather-brained Belgique countess. He's hardly worth your attention, child." Now the grand duchess squeezed Petunia's hands in both of hers. "No, no, I will have you for my Grigori, the only one of my children or grandchildren who wasn't a disappointment to me, other than my Alexei! And Alexei has finally agreed . . . that's why you are here, isn't it?"

"What?" Petunia pulled her hands free and leaped off the bed.

"Come now, Petunia, I've seen you and Grigori together, you will make a lovely couple. You will live here with me, but of course we shall go to the palace every night for the dancing! And we will have servants, not like those *things* at the palace. The maids from my estate, and Grigori's men."

"Why— No— How could you—" Petunia didn't even know what to say, but the grand duchess just continued to look at her with her bright eyes and her wide smile.

"It will be wonderful, my Petunia. You may call me Grandmother, if you like."

Petunia backed toward the door, her hands behind her. When she felt the latch she fumbled it open.

"You are not my grandmother," she said. Then she turned and ran through the door.

She didn't get far. In the passageway she ran straight into Grigori. He seized her arms, and she screamed and writhed out of his grip. She grabbed the pistol from his belt and stepped back just far enough to aim.

"My petal, what are you doing?"

Grigori snatched at the pistol, fouling her shot in the narrow passageway, and the bullet merely grazed his shoulder and embedded itself in the wall behind. He wrestled with her, and she managed one more shot, which went wild and shattered an ornate mirror on the wall near the door. He tore the pistol from her grip and wrapped his other arm around her waist, lifting her free of the ground and carrying her, writhing and screaming, back to his grandmother.

The grand duchess cried out and rustled her swathes of lace, but Petunia didn't spare the old woman a look. She was more monstrous than Grigori or Rionin, as far as Petunia was concerned, and she never wanted to speak to the grand duchess again.

Grigori threw Petunia onto the foot of the bed and kicked the door closed behind him. Petunia was on her feet again in an instant. She lunged at Grigori, who held the pistol high over her head with one hand and pushed her away with the other. He frowned at Petunia as though her behavior were completely irrational.

"Let me go, you monster!" Petunia spit at him, and a glob of saliva struck the middle of his chest.

He took out a handkerchief and dabbed at it, frowning

even deeper. Behind her, Petunia heard the grand duchess suck in a breath in disgust.

"Such unbecoming behavior, Petunia! And what makes you want to leave? You have already admitted you have no love for Kestilan!"

"I want out of this whole horrid place," Petunia said, panting. She tried for the pistol again.

"I admire your spirit, my petal," Grigori said, stepping away from her. "But this is ridiculous! I am your betrothed, and you must stop—"

There was a shout and a crash from the front of the house.

Petunia used the distraction to punch Grigori in the stomach, and when he doubled over, she snatched the pistol from his hand. She cocked the hammer but didn't know whom to aim at. Grigori? The grand duchess? Or the new threat coming down the passage?

The door burst open, slamming into Grigori, who was just straightening, and knocking him to the ground. Standing in the doorway was a man in a wolf mask holding an ax. Petunia made her decision, crossing to the bed and aiming her pistol at the grand duchess, who began to wail and wring her hands.

"Oliver," Petunia ordered, cutting through the old woman's wails. "Take care of Grigori, I've got my eye on *her*."

Grigori started to scramble to his feet as Oliver brought the butt of his pistol down on the back of the prince's head. Grigori went down like a felled tree, and the grand duchess screamed like she had been wounded herself.

"My Grigori!" She clawed at the lacy bedclothes, trying to rise.

"Madame, please be still," someone said, coming into the room behind Oliver.

"Galen!" Petunia recognized his voice at once and nearly dropped the pistol. She was almost shaking with relief.

"Steady on, Pet," he said, looking around. "Walter?"

A bubble of hysteria formed in Petunia's chest as their old gardener came hobbling into the room, peg leg and all. He raised one eyebrow at Petunia, who was standing over the ruffled bed with a large pistol aimed at the grand duchess's chest.

"Well, Petunia," Walter finally said. "I see you've found us an excellent spot to finish our preparations in."

"It was my pleasure," Petunia said, and couldn't keep the hysterical laughter contained any longer.

Invisible

Oliver followed Petunia silently and invisibly through the silver wood to the path, where four of the dark princes were waiting for her now. They were pacing along the path, occasionally taking a few steps between the trees, then they would leap back with expressions of great pain.

"What are you all doing here?" Petunia glared around at them, and Oliver had to admire her courage. "I hardly need *four* of you to help me break off some twigs."

Just moments before, she had helped to bind Prince Grigori. She had listened, face impassive, as Grigori admitted that he had written in wax on the floor of the hothouse to open a gate between the estate and the Kingdom Under Stone.

Then she had watched as Oliver and Galen had dragged Grigori down the passageway to one of the other bedchambers. She had listened unflinching to the screaming and recriminations of the Grand Duchess Volenskaya while Heinrich had checked the old woman's room for any weapons. He had nailed the window shut before locking the grand duchess into her ornate bedchamber.

Without the slightest sign of fear, Petunia had listened while Galen had told her their plan, nodded, and then swept out of the chalet without even bothering to look back. Not that it would have mattered if she had: both Oliver and Galen had donned their invisibility cloaks so that they could follow her.

When Oliver had led the charge through the silver wood to the source of the screaming and shooting, they had seen the two princes Under Stone who had been with Petunia crossing the lake in their little boat. That had chilled Oliver more than the screams or the gunshot. Were the princes running away and leaving Petunia? What had happened?

But he shouldn't have been surprised to find that Petunia had things well in hand when they arrived.

Oliver did like to think that when she looked up and saw him standing in the doorway, her face had brightened. Not just to have help, but to see him specifically.

When they broke through the woods and found that four princes had returned, Oliver felt a flash of relief. The princes would have had to take more than one boat across the lake, which meant that he and Galen would have an easier time crossing as well.

That had been the one uncertainty in their plan, because the boats were crowded at three passengers, and adding one invisible stowaway would have been dangerous enough, two impossible. Oliver had been prepared to wait on the shore

until Galen could sneak back over later to fetch him, but now it seemed that they would both be able to cross the lake immediately.

"Well? Answer me!" Petunia shook a handful of silver twigs that she had hastily gathered at the princes, who recoiled.

"We thought you had been attacked," Kestilan said. "So we went for help."

"It's really not all that helpful if you stand on the path sulking while some fool with a pistol tries to take me hostage in the wood," Petunia retorted.

They had decided that she had best stick as close to the truth as possible without mentioning Oliver, Galen, and the others. The King Under Stone would know about his mother's chalet in the forest, and there was no sense pretending that Petunia had been lost for an hour.

"What?"

Now Kestilan came forward, concerned, though the twigs in her hands kept him from actually touching Petunia. Oliver was quite pleased by this, and by the way Petunia held them up to fend him off when it looked like he might put his arms around her.

"Did you know that Prince Grigori and the Grand Duchess Volenskaya are living in the middle of the silver wood?" Petunia's voice was sharp.

The princes stared at her.

"You didn't, did you?" Her tone changed and she sounded pitying. "Rionin has brought his mother and his nephew Grigori here and built them a lovely house in the thick of the

woods. I stumbled upon it, and Grigori tried to take me captive. I barely managed to fight my way free."

Kestilan and one of the other princes looked impressed, and Oliver could hardly blame them. The third prince looked suspicious, though, and the last was angry.

"No wonder our palace is falling into ruin," he raged. "He's been using his power to build a pretty little cottage for his mother, has he? And where are *our* mothers?"

"Tirolian," said the suspicious prince. "Stop it. I, for one, had enough parent in our father. I have no wish to bring my mother here."

"If Rionin were to die, Stavian would be king," Tirolian said in a low voice to the suspicious prince. "A not unwelcome change."

"Do you dare to speak treason against our brother Rionin?" Kestilan looked aghast.

"Can we go back to the palace and speak treason in comfort?" Petunia brandished her twigs again. "I would like to return to my sisters."

"We will return, but there will be no talk of treason," Kestilan said.

"What a shame," Petunia said, and began to stroll down the path.

The princes fell into ranks behind her and Oliver came after them. He assumed that Galen was also with him, but the crown prince moved so silently that Oliver had no idea where he was. Oliver stayed as close behind the princes as he dared, straining to hear what Petunia and Kestilan were

saying. But he needn't have worried, Petunia clearly wanted everyone to hear what she said next, and her voice carried down the path.

"You know why Rionin allowed me to come here and gather these twigs, don't you?" Petunia's voice was arch. "He *wanted* me to find his mother's chalet. If I hadn't found it by accident, I'm sure that Grigori would have come to collect me. Rionin promised me to Grigori, you see. Rionin's mother likes me too much to let me marry the son of some feather-brained Belgique countess. At least, I believe those were her words. Grigori's reward for bringing his grandmother here, along with my sisters and me, is that he gets me."

She said it so lightly, as though it were of no consequence, but Oliver's hands curled over his weapons. How could she say and do these things and act like she didn't care whether Rionin gave her—gave her like she was a piece of property—to Grigori or to his brother Kestilan?

Oliver couldn't stand it. He drew his pistol as quietly as he could.

A hand came down hard on his arm.

"She will be all right," said the crown prince in Oliver's ear. "Remember, she has known them all her life." Galen let go of him, and Oliver slowly slipped the pistol back into the holster.

A moment later they were at the shore of the black lake. There were two small boats; it would be a tight fit, but better than they had planned for.

"You ride with Petunia," Galen murmured in his ear.

Oliver relaxed just enough to realize that he had had his jaw clenched shut. He loosened it, trying to breathe normally as he watched Kestilan help Petunia into one of the boats. He would need to get in without making any noise, just before they pushed off.

Just as one of the princes—Blathen—was stepping into the stern, Oliver also got in. Then he discovered a little hitch: he couldn't sit in the middle because he would be cheek-to-cheek with Kestilan, but the bow was very narrow.

"These seats are so uncomfortable," Petunia fussed.

She twisted about in the bow until her skirts were wrapped around her legs. She was leaning on her side, one elbow propped on the gunwale. If Oliver leaned on one hip, he could just fit next to her.

Oliver lowered himself gingerly into the little space beside Petunia. He had to grab hold of the gunwale on his side to stop himself from falling on top of her. As it was, they were pressed very closely together. Her perfume smelled like roses and cinnamon, or perhaps, he thought, that was just Petunia herself.

Blathen pushed them out into the lake with a grunt and nearly fell face-first into the water. He leaped aboard at the last minute, panting, and Kestilan laughed at him.

"Feeling your age?" He began to stroke with the oars.

Oliver looked over and saw that the other boat had also pushed out, with only slightly less effort.

"The boat is heavy," complained Blathen.

"You've crossed this lake thousands of times," Kestilan sniped.

They rowed the rest of the way in silence, and Oliver did his best not to crush Petunia. It was hard not to put an arm around her, both for balance and because he very much wanted to. He did sigh with relief when the bottom of the boat scraped onto the coarse sand of the island, but he didn't think anyone noticed.

Other than Petunia, who gave a small laugh.

"What are you laughing about?" Kestilan turned to help her out of the boat.

"Nothing I'd share with you," she retorted.

She stalked into the palace, Oliver at her heels.

Once inside, she went straight through the main hall and into a smaller corridor. Oliver would have liked to stop and stare: everything was silver and black, blue and violet, muted colors that somehow seemed garish. He could see the resemblance between the decor of the palace and that of the grand duchess's chalet. It was really quite morbid.

But Petunia did not stop. She didn't stop when a courtier popped out of a room and demanded to know what the to-do across the lake had been about. She didn't stop when a very tall lady in a black lace gown stood in her path and asked what she was doing with an armload of filthy branches like a servant. Petunia just walked around these people, and Oliver stayed with her.

At last she had to stop, because they turned a corner and the King Under Stone was there.

Oliver knew at once who he was, and not just because he wore a jagged black crown. He had long white hair with fine

streaks of black, and his face was weirdly ageless: seeming at one moment to be very young, at others, immeasurably old. He stood in the middle of the corridor and stared at Petunia.

"You're back," he said in a hollow voice.

"Yes. I do not wish to marry Grigori," she said. "I don't wish to marry Kestilan, either, but Grigori would be even worse."

"I have promised—"

"I don't care what you promised your mother or your nephew, *Alexei*," Petunia interrupted. "I'm not going to be given as a prize to the man who tricked me into coming here!"

She waved the silver branches in his face and he flinched and stepped aside. At the end of the corridor she went into a room that was full of women—and not just any women, but her sisters—who all greeted her with cries of delight. Oliver slipped into the room and pressed himself against the wall, and felt Galen brush against his arm as he did the same. One of the princesses shut the door and then braced a chair against it.

"Hush, all of you!" Crown Princess Rose called out. When they had quieted she looked Petunia over. "I was going to ask if you were hurt, but by the look on your face, you have good news for us."

"The very best," Galen said, shrugging off his gray shawl.

"Galen!" The crown princess flung herself into her husband's arms with a glad cry.

The other princesses shrieked and threw themselves at their brother-in-law only a moment later.

"Don't scream so," Petunia said to her sisters in a low but carrying voice. "Rionin was right outside this room."

The others calmed down somewhat, and Petunia came and stood against the wall next to Oliver. Even though he was still invisible, she fumbled until she found his hand and gripped it.

"Is Heinrich with you?" Princess Lily—for Oliver guessed that this was she—put a trembling hand on Galen's arm.

"He's waiting for you at the gate, Lily," Galen said, and embraced her. "You'll be with him tonight."

She burst into tears.

"Who's holding hands with Petunia?" The princess with the round spectacles was watching them with a shrewd expression.

Oliver tried to let go of Petunia, but she held on. So he reached up with his other hand and undid the fastening of the cloak. He nodded uncertainly at the princesses, and they all smiled back.

"Oh, good," Poppy said. "We need all the help we can get."

While Petunia told what had happened and Galen explained their plan, they all whittled the silver twigs. They were roughly the length and thickness of knitting needles, but into each one they scratched the name of the King Under Stone.

"Blessed silver will kill any of the princes or courtiers," Galen told Oliver. "But in order to kill the king, you must have his true name on the weapon."

"I could have sworn that I put a bullet into that . . . that . . . *bastard* ten years ago," Lily said as she scraped a long curl of silver from the tip of a twig with one of Oliver's knives.

"I too," Galen said gently. "But unfortunately it was after he was king."

"No, not then," Lily said, and her frantic hands went still. "I shot him. In the boats, as they chased us over the lake. I shot Parian, who had been my partner, and then I shot Rionin for Jonquil. He fell back into the bottom of the boat."

"I remember that," Galen said slowly.

"How did he survive?" Lily looked at Galen, then appealed to Rose and even Oliver, who shrugged uncomfortably. "Illiken was the king then."

Petunia, sitting next to Oliver, suddenly bolted to her feet. "He *does* have a secret name! I'll wager it protected him!" She pointed at Oliver. "You heard me, out in the passageway."

"Alexei?" Oliver had heard her say the name but had had no idea what she was doing. He thought perhaps she was being insulting in Russakan. "His true name is Alexei?"

"His mother wanted to name him Alexei," Petunia said. "She told me that in her heart, she had always thought of him as Alexei."

Jonquil made a sound of disgust. "Are you telling me that I've been scratching the wrong name on all these sticks?"

"Just put Alexei in front of Rionin," Daisy said, and began to do so with the sticks in her lap. "Alexei Rionin Under Stone. A very handsome name."

"Twenty-three years of being my twin and you're just now starting to use sarcasm?" Poppy looked at Daisy for a long minute. "I don't think I like it."

"I don't think I like *this*," Jonquil said, fingering the scratches she had made in a silver twig. "What if it doesn't work?"

"We're going to seal him inside his precious kingdom as well," Poppy said. "So it doesn't matter if he's dead or not. No nightmares, no shadows in the garden." She sighed. "Won't that be a nice change?"

"But what if it doesn't work?" Jonquil fretted.

"It will work," Galen said. "Walter and the good frau have spent centuries studying magic. They are certain it will work."

Oliver saw Lily turn from pale to ghostly white. He got up from the stool he was sitting on, ready to catch her if she fainted.

"The last time they did this, most of them died," Lily whispered. "Oh, Heinrich!"

Rose and Galen exchanged looks. She knows, Oliver thought. She knows that Galen will not make it out alive. Oliver wondered if he would. He would gladly die for Petunia . . . he realized that he would gladly die just to stop the King Under Stone and his brethren.

But now Galen was kneeling down in front of Lily's stool.

"Heinrich will be waiting for you at the gate," Galen said firmly. "He is to make sure you get out. He won't be part of the enchantment."

Lily slumped, putting her shaking hands on his shoulders.

"But *you* will, won't you?" Pansy's voice broke on a sob.

"Yes, Pan," Galen said quietly.

"I don't like that," Pansy said.

Galen stood and put his arms around the fine-boned girl, while Rose continued to comfort Lily. Oliver looked away. It was such a private moment; he hated to intrude on it. Galen was beloved by all of the sisters, but the love between him and Rose was so clear and shining that it hurt to look at them, spending their last hours together caring for the other girls.

Oliver got up, pretending that he needed something from the table near the door.

"Put your cloak on," Petunia said, following him.

Petunia

Petunia looked over her shoulder as she led Oliver out the door. "I left my matches in my room," she said. "I had better make sure no one's found them."

"Be careful," Rose warned.

"We will," Petunia said.

"Remember, Pet," Hyacinth said, "supper is late tonight, and we are to go straight to the ball afterward."

"Yes, yes," Petunia said as she went out, with Oliver invisible beside her. He had one light hand on her elbow, and she did her best not to put her other hand on top of it. "Honestly, they still treat me like I'm six," she complained to him after she had closed the door.

"They probably always will," Oliver offered in a whisper. "I know it drives my brother Simon wild, but I just always see him as a four-year-old swinging a wooden sword at the trees."

There was no further talk until they reached her room.

Oliver unfastened the cloak but left it over his shoulders just in case.

"I know why too," Petunia said, picking up the threads of their conversation. "You're used to looking out for Simon, and you always will look out for him. Especially because he's like me." She made a rueful face. "He's not afraid of being a bandit, and I'm not afraid of this." She waved a hand around at the tatty black furnishings.

"You're not?" Oliver looked at her in amazement.

"I know I should be," she confided, sitting down on the edge of the bed. "I really should. But you have to understand: I came here almost every night of my life from the time I was two until I was almost seven. This was like an extension of my home. They might say mean things, and when I was ill I didn't always *want* to come, but no one ever hurt me directly. And, even though I know now that he's horrible, Kestilan is very handsome, and when you're six and a handsome prince wants to dance with you . . . can you help being flattered?"

Oliver sank down in a chair, staring at her.

Petunia closed her eyes, wishing she hadn't said a word. She'd thought that perhaps he'd understand, considering his own unusual upbringing. Her governess had been fond of the saying "familiarity breeds contempt," but to Petunia familiarity had bred a strange sort of comfort. The clothes were slick and strange, the food tasted like it had been sprinkled with ashes, but she had known Kestilan far longer than she'd known Oliver. Longer than she'd known Galen, even, and he was as dear to her as if he had been born her brother.

She dared to look at Oliver. He was nodding slowly.

"I can see that," he said. "Did you know, we never told Simon why we went out wearing wolf masks until he was twelve years old? My mother was afraid that he would see it as a game, or worse: a normal way to earn a living." He nodded again. "And he would have. But you're really not afraid? Even now?"

"I guess I'm a bit . . . spoiled about it, I suppose is the word. Everyone tells me not to worry, that it will all be fine." She shrugged. "Just like last time. Galen killed the King Under Stone, we locked the gate, and we were safe." She couldn't help but grin at him. "It is the most exciting thing that has ever happened to me. Even more exciting than being abducted by you.

"Galen and Rose got married that summer," she went on. "It was terribly romantic." She shrugged again. "Honestly? I'm having a hard time believing that it won't happen like that again. Galen will work some magic. We'll seal the gate and go home. Poppy and Daisy will have a beautiful wedding."

Oliver got up from his chair and came over to the bed. He sank down beside her and put his arm around her waist. She leaned her head on his shoulder.

"It *will* be all right," he told her. "You shouldn't be afraid. After tonight it will all be over. You will be home, getting ready for Poppy and Daisy's wedding. I promise you that."

"And you'll have your earldom back," Petunia said with total confidence.

"I wish I felt as certain," Oliver said.

293

She pulled away from him. "You will," she said. "It was the King Under Stone who took it from you, to give to the grand duchess."

He gaped at her.

"She just told me," Petunia said. "I didn't know his influence reached so far, but I should have. If he can cause wars and kill our suitors and make it so Mother and Rose and Lily . . . so that they couldn't have children." Her eyes filled with tears, but she blinked them away. "Then it was probably no great feat to destroy your earldom."

"I promise to get you safely home," Oliver repeated, sounding shaken. "And I promise that I will get my father's lands back." He clenched his fists.

His promise hung in the air for a few heartbeats while they sat together in silence.

"Oliver?" Petunia asked after a time. "Are you afraid?"

"No," he said. "I'm not afraid."

Petunia didn't know if it was true or not, but it sounded true. "Thank you," she said.

He leaned around, and her heart started to thump. He was going to kiss her.

But before he could, there were voices in the corridor. He leaped to his feet and fastened the cloak. A moment later, Olga came in, looking sulky. With her was the tall court lady, a triumphant expression on her face.

"Here is your new maid," she announced.

"I'm supposed to be a princess," Olga said.

Petunia felt her skirts move just a little and heard the

scrape of a boot. Oliver was under the bed again. She wondered if he was going to peek while she dressed for the ball. She found that she wouldn't wholly object.

"Olga, don't be stupid," Petunia said. "Haven't you figured out by now that everything they say is a lie? They only brought you here because there are no real servants. So stop sniveling and help me dress."

The court lady went off with a bray of satisfied laughter.

Olga yanked Petunia's cloak off and threw it on the bed, then began to rip at the fastenings of her gown. Petunia felt like a chicken being plucked for dinner.

She twisted away. "I know this is a riding gown, but it's *mine* and I'm going to wear it tonight anyway. I just need you to help me with my hair."

"You'll look like a fool," Olga said.

"Stop being rude and listen to me," Petunia retorted.

"I don't want to listen to you, *Your Highness*," Olga growled.

"Prince Grigori and his grandmother live in a chalet across the lake," Petunia said as though Olga had not spoken. "Prince Grigori wanted to marry me, but I refused."

"So you're saying that I can have the prince, since you've cast him aside?" Olga sounded even angrier at Petunia's proposition.

"What I'm saying," Petunia said with icy patience, "is that you can sulk until they have you beaten, or you can make the best of things. You love Grigori, do you not?" Silence. "Then I'm telling you that you have an opportunity here, if you choose to take it."

"What makes you think he'll even look at me?"

Olga sounded so vulnerable that Petunia pitied the girl, despite her duplicity.

"I did everything asked of me," Olga said. "I kept open your window so the princes had a better chance of reaching you. I spent all night in the cold of the forest, helping Prince Grigori with the spell to create a rosebush in winter. And still I am but a servant!"

"Don't worry," Petunia assured her, "I rejected him in such a way that he'll never look at me again."

"Poor Grigori," said Olga with a sigh.

"Yes," Petunia said, her voice flat. "Poor Grigori."

Once she had her hair put up, Petunia sent Olga to see if her sisters needed assistance and made her own way to the dining room. She couldn't have said anything to Oliver without Olga overhearing, but she supposed she would see him soon enough. He and Galen would stay hidden until it was time for the ball, and then they would begin their plan.

Just thinking of it made Petunia's hands sweat, and she didn't want Rionin to see her nervousness. But Rionin was not at dinner, and the princes were too moody to pay attention to anyone. When Blathen threw down his napkin, they all sighed in relief.

He held out an arm to Poppy, who put her hand on it as if nothing pleased her more than to accompany him to the ballroom. Stavian snarled at his brother, snatching up Hyacinth and moving to the head of the line. Then Kadros and Violet took their place behind Stavian and Hya, which made

Blathen's expression sour further. Daisy went quickly to Tirolian, looking frightened as they joined the line, and Iris shuddered as Derivos clasped her arm. Lilac and Talivor, Pansy and Telinros went to their places, and at last Kestilan reached Petunia. She joined him as Rose, Lily, Jonquil, and Orchid formed ranks behind. The sisters looked odd in riding gowns, standing beside the princes in their faded silk, and the mood was chill as they entered the ballroom.

The same music. The same dances. Petunia could not count the number of Midnight Balls she'd seen. Most of them she'd been too young to remember. She tried to feign boredom, but the knowledge that Oliver might be there somewhere, along with Galen, kept her on edge.

Added to that, Kestilan was paying her special attention. She gritted her teeth. There could not have been a worse time for Kestilan to decide that he truly loved her.

"Petunia," he said, looking down at her with what she assumed was his version of cow's eyes. "We've known each other so long," he said.

"Yes," she replied crisply. "Since I was two years old."

"And you were such a small girl then," he went on.

"Yes, I was *two years old*," she repeated.

She remembered him having to essentially carry her through the steps of the dance, or bend almost double to reach her waist, while on the black throne the King Under Stone watched and wallowed in the power that he gained from the dancing.

"So it has been inspiring to see what a beautiful woman you have become," Kestilan soldiered on.

"That's repulsive," Petunia replied. "First, that you've been dancing with me since I was a small child, planning to marry me all that time. And now you've only decided that you really want to marry me because someone else wants me. Petty and disgusting, Kestilan. Petty and disgusting." She shook her head.

"What would you have me say?" He glared down at her.

"I would ask for the truth from anyone else," she said. "But I think I just heard it, and I don't want to hear any more."

"Petunia, are you all right?" Pansy asked as she and Telinros danced near them.

"I'm fine," Petunia said. "But I'm going to sit out the next dance."

"You are?" Kestilan looked surprised.

"Yes," Petunia told him. "We are still allowed to sit out at least one dance, I believe."

When the music ended, she pulled free of Kestilan and hurried to one of the chairs lining the wall before they were caught up in the next dance. He started to follow, but she gave him a look that sent him to the refreshment table instead.

Pansy sat down beside her. "I cannot bear another minute!" She looked as if she were going to burst into tears.

"Paaansy," came a hollow voice from Pansy's other side. "I am a gooood spirit!"

"Galen," whispered Pansy in delight.

Petunia almost laughed out loud in relief. It was just like ten years ago, when Galen had pretended to be a ghost so that Pansy would help him set up the escape. Petunia felt someone

take her hand. The hand was warm and calloused and already so familiar. Oliver.

"Oliver's going to take you across the lake," Galen said. "Remember: leave youngest to oldest."

"I still think Lily should go first," Petunia argued. "It would be just our luck to have Rionin decide to marry her tonight."

"Getting Lily out is going to be quite a trick," Galen said. "I may have to create a diversion, which would scotch everyone else's chances."

"Fine," Petunia agreed. "But we're taking Jonquil now."

"Definitely," Oliver whispered. "Poor girl."

At the beginning of the ball, Rionin had given Jonquil to the fox-faced man. Now he was dragging her through the steps of the dances despite her weeping. In fact, he seemed to enjoy the weeping, which made Petunia wish she still had her pistol.

"Follow me," Petunia said, rising to her feet.

Kestilan appeared before she had taken two steps.

"No, I'm still not ready to dance," Petunia told him, watching the dancers for a break in the pattern so that she could walk through without getting trampled.

"You've sat out an entire dance almost," Kestilan said.

"And I'll sit out another if I have to," Petunia said without looking at him. "Jonquil needs us. Just look at the state of her! Pan and I are going to help her get herself together."

With that she began weaving her way between the figures of a particularly wild gigue. She hoped that Pansy and Oliver were

299

able to stay with her. The sooner they got Jonquil out, the sooner Galen could send Orchid and Lilac, and then the others.

When she reached Jonquil and the fox-faced man, Petunia stopped them with a firm hand on Jonquil's arm. "Come, darling," Petunia said, "let's get you freshened up."

"She must dance," said Jonquil's partner, leering down at her.

"She needs to retire for a moment," Petunia said, trying to pry the courtier's fingers from Jonquil's thin arm.

"No," the foxy man snarled.

"Say no to me one more time," Petunia snarled back, "and I will have you killed. And if you think I won't, and if you think Rionin won't, then you don't know either of us very well."

Petunia caught Jonquil around the waist as the fox-faced man pushed her away. At the archway that led to the hall, Tirolian had his hands locked around Daisy's waist as though preventing her from fleeing.

"Daisy doesn't need freshening up," he said. "She's just come back from the retiring room, haven't you, my pet?"

"Pet is *my* nickname, if you must know," Petunia told him. "Now make way; Jonquil is faint."

As they walked around Daisy and Tirolian, Petunia had to fight the urge to give Daisy some sign that all would be well. But she could feel Oliver's hand on her back, urging her on, and knew that the least hint of something amiss would ruin their chances. Tirolian was watching, so they went quickly into the retiring room.

"I can't take it," Jonquil said, bursting into fresh tears. She sank down on a stool covered in threadbare velvet.

"Shhh," Pansy said, wiping at their older sister's face with her handkerchief. "We're going now, please don't cry."

"Now?" Jonquil gulped, looking around. "Are Galen and Oliver . . . ?" She stopped crying and got to her feet with visible effort. "I'm ready."

Petunia had stayed near the door while Oliver kept watch just outside. The door opened a crack and his voice came in softly.

"It's clear."

"Let's go," Petunia whispered.

They walked swiftly through the front hall to the palace doors. One was ajar, but Petunia didn't have time to wonder about it, just kept going as she half carried Jonquil.

"The boats are there," Oliver whispered. "I'll row you across and—"

"Hello, Olga," Petunia said.

They stopped short a few paces from the boats. Olga was sitting in one, trying to row even though the boat was too far out of the water to actually move.

"Where are you going?" Olga eyed them suspiciously.

"We were going to hide in the silver wood, to get away from our princes for a time," Petunia said. Jonquil let out a little moan, and Petunia squeezed her waist to make her stop.

Olga looked outraged and started to say something, but Petunia cut her off.

"Do you want us to help you across? You're not going to get far, otherwise," Petunia said.

"What are you doing?" Oliver whispered in her ear.

"Pan and I will row Jonquil and Olga across," she murmured, trying not to move her lips. "You get Orchid and Lilac."

"Are you sure?"

Petunia decided that she had had quite enough of everyone doubting her.

"Come on, Jonquil," she said, pulling her sister toward the boat. Pansy trailed behind, looking uncertain. "We'll help you get to your darling Grigori," Petunia told Olga, "but you keep your mouth shut about what we're doing, all right?"

Olga still looked suspicious.

"Do you love Grigori or not?" Petunia wanted to slap the girl. How dare she sit there like a mule; did she not realize that Petunia and her sisters were in grave danger and it was partially her fault?

"Get in," Olga said. "I'll keep quiet."

Petunia installed Jonquil in the bow, and Olga moved to the stern. Petunia sat in the middle and Pansy pushed them easily down into the water. Petunia could tell that Oliver was helping her, and just hoped that Olga wasn't looking when Pansy miraculously leaped into the boat without getting her skirts wet.

"It's too easy," Jonquil whispered.

Rescuer

Once Petunia was well under way with Pansy and Jonquil, Oliver ran back to the ballroom. He scanned the room, but of course there was no sign of Galen. Then Oliver realized: they were supposed to take the princesses out youngest to oldest, to avoid confusion... but he didn't know who came after Pansy. Iris? Lilac?

Then he saw one of them coming his way. It was Orchid, with the spectacles. She had spilled something purple on her skirt and was holding it up so it wouldn't drip on the floor.

"Clumsy me," she called almost gaily over her shoulder. "I'll be right back."

"I'll help you," said another one. Lilac?

"Hurry," Oliver muttered as they passed him.

The other one—Lilac, he was almost certain—jumped.

"Sorry," Oliver muttered.

"Galen's bringing Violet," Orchid whispered. "See if you

can get Iris away from Derivos." She gave a little flutter with her free hand in the direction of the dais.

"Thanks," Oliver murmured.

Iris was engaged in heated debate with her prince right at the foot of the dais. Lily had gotten up from her throne, and Rose was moving toward them as well.

"It's just not fair," Iris was saying shrilly. "Why can't I be with Blathen? And you've always had your eyes on Rose, Derivos, don't deny it!" She jabbed Derivos's chest with one finger.

"You *want* to marry Blathen?" Derivos was plainly baffled by this turn of events.

The King Under Stone sat on his throne, laughing.

Oliver could see what Iris was doing. She was causing a diversion so the others could slip away. But he'd heard about their escape ten years ago, and that diversion. When it had ended, the king had seen immediately that the most of the princesses were gone. If Rionin saw through Iris's ploy before the others were out . . .

"It's just not fair," Iris said, beginning to cry. "You get to trade us or cast us aside! And we're stuck with your decision! It's just not fair!"

"Of course it's not fair," said Poppy, coming forward and putting her arm around Iris's waist. "When have they ever been fair?" She glared at Rionin.

"Come, dear, you're not yourself. Let's go get something to drink," said Daisy, coming up on Iris's other side.

That was nine of them, Oliver calculated. Nine of them out safely, if the twins managed to sneak Iris out now. Leaving

Hyacinth, Rose, and Lily. There would have to be another diversion, Oliver realized. A big one. They'd hoped to slip the princesses out without resorting to extreme measures, but Oliver's stomach was twisting with fear and he knew they needed to go, now.

Galen had the same thought.

"Grab Rose, Lily, and Hya," came the crown prince's voice in his ear. "I'm going to make some noise."

"Right," Oliver whispered.

Galen didn't wait long. Oliver was just reaching for Rose's arm when the far wall of the ballroom exploded outward in a maelstrom of black shards. Everyone screamed, including Oliver, much to his embarrassment. He was fortunate that no one noticed the extra voice in all the confusion.

Rionin stepped down from the dais and strode toward the explosion. Rose had Lily by one arm and was calling for Hyacinth. Oliver could see her, caught in the melee in the middle of the dance floor. He tugged at Rose's sleeve to get her attention.

"What is it?" She looked around, irritated.

"It's Oliver," he said, speaking normally so that he could be heard over the din. "I'll get Hyacinth, you and Lily run for the boats."

"All right," she said reluctantly.

Oliver dodged through the crowd to Hyacinth. She was looking around for her sisters, but her partner wouldn't let go of her elbow. Oliver took her free hand in his, leaned close, and whispered. "It's Oliver, come with me."

"I have to find Violet; she hates loud noises," Hyacinth babbled to her partner.

She yanked free of her prince, and then Oliver was leading her through the throng as swiftly as he could. They were in the main hall, and he saw tears streaking Hyacinth's face, when they heard the cry.

"Our brides!"

"Run!" Hyacinth screamed.

She let go of Oliver's hand and raced for the doors. Oliver stayed close on her heels. When they were through the enormous front doors, he barred them with a silver twig. It seemed foolish: so small and fragile, balanced between the two great latches. But when their pursuers rattled the doors, the silver glowed and no one came through.

"Hya! Hya!" Rose called.

"Come on," Hyacinth said blindly to Oliver.

He unfastened the short purple cape and gathered up the longer cloak he wore beneath it, following her to where Rose and Lily were waiting in one of the two boats left. He pointed Hyacinth toward the empty boat, but Rose stopped him.

"Don't," she said, "Galen . . ."

"I'm sorry," Oliver said, stepping back.

Hyacinth climbed into the other boat with Rose and Lily, and Oliver pushed off, leaping into the bow at the last moment. Hyacinth and Rose were in the rower's seat, and Lily was in the stern. In her hand she clutched two silver knitting needles, and her face was beautiful and strained.

The princes had broken the door to the palace open before their boat reached the other shore, the silver twig proving to be a temporary lock. The princes came down to the

water, the courtiers following behind, and four of the princes jumped into the remaining boat.

There was no sign of Galen.

When their boat crunched onto the far shore, Oliver leaped out and dragged it farther up the sand. The three princesses climbed out and began to run up the path. Rose had tears streaming down her cheeks, but she didn't look back.

"Are you wearing Petunia's cloak?" Hyacinth said suddenly, slowing down a little to stare at him.

"Yes," Oliver said, taking her arm and hurrying her along. "I knew she'd want it, and she left it in her room. I couldn't think of how else to carry it."

"You're a good boy," Hyacinth said.

They reached the gate at last, and the others were waiting. As soon as he saw Oliver, Heinrich opened the silver-and-pearl gate to reveal a golden staircase. Lily and Rose stayed back, and so did Petunia, but the others began disappearing up the shining stair.

Oliver took off both cloaks and helped Petunia into hers. She stood on tiptoe to kiss him on the cheek, and then Heinrich was telling her to hurry.

"I don't think so," said a voice, and there was the sound of a pistol cocking.

Oliver turned, one arm still around Petunia, and found Prince Grigori only a few paces away. He was holding a pistol and smiling. Behind him stood Olga, her face blotchy from crying.

"Petunia stays with me," he said. "The rest of you must go back to the palace."

307

Violet, on the lowest stair, called out. "I have a husband waiting for me!"

"Your husband is waiting for you back there," Grigori said, jerking his head toward the Palace Under Stone. "When your children are grown they will break the king free of this prison and we will rule Ionia together!"

Poppy snorted. "I'm sure Rionin will be delighted to share his throne," she muttered.

Petunia couldn't take it anymore. "When will you stop?" She stepped forward, anger clear in every line of her body. "When will any of you stop?"

And on the last word, she threw her red cloak at Grigori. It went over his head and down over his upper body, covering the pistol. He struggled and fired a shot. The bullet tore through the velvet and went wild past Oliver's shoulder.

"Run," Oliver said.

But they never reached the stair. Crumpled on the black soil just inside the gate was Rose, her hands clutched to her left side. Heinrich knelt over her, and Lily held her head.

"Not Rose," Petunia whispered, and her lower lip began to tremble.

"One less to plague me," Prince Grigori said, freeing himself of the cloak.

Oliver didn't hesitate. He drew his own pistol, aiming for the Russakan prince's heart. But before he could fire, someone else did. The bullet found its mark and Grigori fell without a sound. Screaming, Olga threw herself on the fallen prince.

Oliver wheeled and saw Lily lower one of Heinrich's pistols. Petunia knelt on Rose's other side, sobbing in great gulps. Over the sound of her weeping, Oliver could hear booted feet stomping up the path toward them.

He met Heinrich's gaze.

"Take them up the stairs," Oliver ordered in a voice that was suddenly not his own. It was Karl's and Johan's, and even his father's half-remembered bark. "Carry Pet if you have to."

"But Rose—" Petunia began.

"More power for the spell if I stay," Rose murmured.

"She's right," Oliver said. "Give the signal, Heinrich. We have to start now."

Lily and Petunia kissed Rose as Heinrich pulled them away. When Petunia's foot was on the bottom stair, Heinrich tookout a pistol and fired two quick shots in the air. Oliver knelt by Rose and raised her up to lean against his chest.

"You know what to do?"

"Yes," she whispered. "I helped Galen in his studies."

Oliver began pulling things out of his pockets: a wand of silver, a bag of black soil mixed with powdered diamonds, an intricate knot of unbleached wool. He laid the knot on Rose's lap and scattered the soil and diamond dust around them both. Then he helped her take a silver knitting needle out of her bodice. It was red and sticky.

"I never meant to leave Galen behind, anyway," she whispered. "Not when he came back for me. He always comes back for me." She gripped the bloody needle, looking like a sorceress from a story, all terrible beauty.

He took out a long silver branch of his own and held it up like a sword. He was ready.

The dark princes rounded the corner of the path and headed for Oliver and Rose, their faces twisted with rage, but it didn't matter. There was a strange tug in Oliver's chest, and then he heard a voice that boomed over the sound of the princes' shouts, over the wails from Olga as she crouched over Grigori's body, over the sound of Rose's quiet tears.

The voice was that of the good frau, and yet it could not be the good frau, for it was so loud that it made Oliver's ears hurt, and so beautiful that it brought tears to his eyes. It was old and young and beyond time itself. He loved the voice, and feared it too.

The voice went on and on for an age, and all the while Oliver forced himself to think, as he had been told, of a wall of silver without door or break, a wall that ran around the Kingdom Under Stone. He had no magic of his own, but Walter Vogel had told him it wouldn't matter: the strength of his spirit, his conviction, would be enough.

Oliver thought so hard about this wall, and held so tightly to Rose, that when the wood began to burn he never noticed. His eyes were shut anyway, and the pulling in his chest was so strong that when hands began to drag him backward through the gate, he only held tighter to Rose. They must not be separated. Together they would let the good frau draw all the strength she needed from them, and then the silver wall would have no seam.

The voice stopped, and Oliver fell into darkness.

Cloaked

Petunia only paused long enough at the top of the stair to see that her sisters and Heinrich were safe. Then she picked up her skirts and started back down.

"Petunia, no!" Pansy wailed.

"Wait," Heinrich said, and she heard his boots hit the first step. "Take this."

She looked back and he was holding out a pistol. She grabbed it and then flew down the stairs, leaving it to him to stop the others from following. She was not going to leave Oliver and Rose to die.

At the bottom of the stairs a great voice suddenly overtook her. She staggered to Rose and Oliver, who were in the gateway. She stood behind them, bracing her upper arm against the side of the gate as Telinros came howling toward them.

She shot him.

His body jerked and then tumbled to the ground, nearly

tripping Blathen who was right behind. Petunia aimed for Blathen next.

"Mine!" Poppy said from behind her.

Petunia leaped aside as Poppy leveled her pistol and shot Blathen through the heart. "Bastard," she muttered as his body crumpled atop Telinros's. She exchanged a fierce smile with Petunia.

And then there was the king. The King Under Stone stepped toward them, his face taut with rage.

"Come with me now and your punishments shall be lessened. Unlike your sisters'."

"No," Petunia said. She leveled the pistol at him, but her heart quailed. Heinrich didn't know that the grand duchess had called her son Alexei. If his bullets were marked, they would be marked only with the name Rionin.

"Ha!" Poppy fired her pistol, but the king swiveled, bending backward in a way no human could have done. The bullet struck Derivos, and he dropped with a scream, clutching his side.

"I am not so easy to kill as my brothers," the king purred.

"That's what you think," Poppy snarled, and cocked her pistol again.

"Alexei," Petunia said, suddenly.

The king's gaze snapped to her. "What did you say?"

Petunia reached up to her elaborate coiffure. After Olga had left she had nestled several silver needles into it. All had been etched with the name *Alexei Rionin Under Stone*. She handed one behind her to Poppy, then rolled the others between her fingers.

"Alexei," Petunia said again. "Catch!" And she tossed the needles like darts.

They struck him in the chest, not hard enough to wound, but he hissed and swatted at them. While he was distracted Poppy shoved the last needle down the barrel of her pistol and then took her shot. A black flower blossomed on the white breast of the King Under Stone's shirt. He looked up at the sisters with horror.

His scream tore at their ears.

"Ha!" Poppy shouted again. There were tears on her cheeks.

Rionin's scream went on as he crumpled in a hideous, boneless way. When Petunia tore her attention from the king, she saw the remaining princes slinking away, hands to their ears, as the voice of the spell grew. Petunia and Poppy shot at them, but their shots went wild, as though the air were warping inward toward the palace. Petunia thought with horror that Rose and Oliver might be trapped half-inside and half-outside the new wall when the spell finished.

"Go," she shouted to Poppy. "I'll help Rose and Oliver."

"But I can't let you—"

"Yes, you can," Petunia said. "Christian is waiting."

Poppy grimaced, but then she turned and ran up the stairs.

Petunia went to the pair slumped between the gateposts. They were so caught up in the spell that Petunia doubted either of them knew she was there. But as she leaned down to

get a grip under Oliver's arms, Rose's voice brought her up short.

"Galen. He always came back for us, Pet," Rose said. Her eyes pleaded with Petunia as she continued to hold her wand steady in front of her.

Looking up, Petunia saw that Kestilan had turned back and was coming toward her, straining against the onslaught of the voice. There was a black dagger in his hand.

"Mother, please protect us," she whispered.

Then Petunia reached into the bodice of her gown for her matches. She lit one and dropped it back into the box. The matches flared and she tossed the tiny ball of flames into the woods at her right.

The silver wood went up in a great sheet of blue-white flame. Kestilan and the tattered remnants of the court of the King Under Stone fled back to the lake. Petunia grabbed Oliver under the arms and dragged him to the foot of the golden stair, grateful that he was holding so tight to Rose.

The heat from the fire was intense. Petunia drew her cloak around her, gathering what little protection she could. Then she took a deep breath and plunged into the smoke and flames, looking for any sign of Galen or Bishop Schelker or Walter Vogel and the crone.

There was nothing, nothing but silver trees burning white and blue. She reached the shore and saw that the court had taken all the boats. They were well on their way back to the palace, and Petunia was alone. She swayed and nearly went to her knees at the edge of the lake. But the oppressive heat from the burning wood drove her on. She ran along the shore, call-ing out for Galen and Bishop Schelker.

When she found them, she hardly knew what it was she had found.

In a sudden clearing in the wood were four figures made of light, and for a moment she thought they were just more burning trees. But this light was green, as green as new grass or tulip leaves or the glass of her father's hothouses. It rose up like four shining columns in the clearing. She stopped, gasp-ing for breath, and through the intense glow she could make out the dear familiar face of Galen, and beyond him Bishop Schelker, Walter Vogel, and a tall, beautiful woman who was speaking the endless words of the spell.

"The *crone?*"

The words burst out before she could stop them. Galen and Oliver had told her of the toothless old woman, but the face she could see through the green was wrenchingly beauti-ful. Long, dark hair fell on either side of the serene features, and a crown rested on her brow.

"My queen," said a familiar voice, and Petunia looked and saw that through the green, Walter was also young, and handsome, standing straight on two strong legs.

"Your queen?"

The heat forced her farther into the clearing, until she stood in the cool protection of the four columns of green light. Galen and the bishop smiled at her, though their faces were otherwise rigid with the intensity of the spell.

"One of the greatest queens Westfalin has ever known,"

Walter said. "Beautiful, brilliant, and just. When Ranulf, her husband, was killed by Wolfram von Aue, she learned magic that she might bind him in this prison. And I learned it, too, so that I might help her."

"Then she was . . . Oh!" Petunia put a hand to her mouth in awe.

"Ethelia," Walter said. "Blessed Ethelia, they called her. And I was her knight."

Petunia did not know what to say. The grizzled old gardener who had shown her bird's nests when she was a child had been the knight protector of a queen? And one of the great wizards who had bound the King Under Stone?

"Pet, you have to go," said Galen, his voice strained.

"Come with me," she begged.

"I can't, not alone."

Queen Ethelia's voice was rising, and the figures in the columns of green light were stretching and wavering with the force of it.

"Go, Petunia," said Walter. "Go and save the others."

"Get Rose out of here," Galen said.

Petunia whirled and ran, racing along the shore until she reached the path. The flames rose ever higher, and the smoke choked her. She ran down the path, pulling the hood of her cloak up over her hair as sparks and burning leaves rained down.

Just before she reached the gate, a tree fell across the path.

The blue-white flames were staining her vision, and the heat made her cloak feel like it was made of lead. Beyond the fallen

log she could see Oliver and Rose, huddled at the very foot of the stair. She turned, seeing nothing but flames and more trees falling as the fire tore away their roots.

"There's nothing for it," she said. She pulled the cloak even tighter around her. "This velvet was once a gown worn at the Midnight Ball. The silver was given to me by Bishop Schelker for my nameday. It's all I've got, and it had better be enough."

Petunia rose up on her toes, took two quick steps, and then leaped through the flames.

The fire did not touch her. She landed within the arch of the gate and dropped to her knees beside Rose.

There was no movement from Oliver or Rose, save for the blood that continued to ooze from Rose's side. Petunia tore off a strip of her skirt and pressed it against the wound.

The powerful voice of the ancient queen rose to a crescendo, and Petunia swayed on her knees. And then there was a sound that seemed to come from everywhere and nowhere. Petunia wasn't even sure she had heard it with her ears; it might have come from inside her body for all she could tell.

The darkness overhead glowed green, and within the green Petunia thought she saw a face of ineffable beauty smiling down at her. From the ground at the outer edge of the burning forest, a band of silver light stretched upward and became a massive wall without a door or gate as far as she could see in either direction.

It was done.

Tears slipped down Petunia's cheeks, and she keeled

forward over Rose for a moment in sheer relief. Her ears felt like they were full of cotton, and she wondered if the spell had damaged her hearing for good. She freed her sister from Oliver's grip and began to drag Rose up the stairs. Halfway to safety her burden was lifted by a pair of large, rough hands, and there was the giant bandit Karl, grinning at her.

Petunia hurried back for Oliver, but when she reached him someone stopped her with a hand on her shoulder. The older bandit, Johan, had followed her and was saying something, but she could hear only her own heartbeat. Seeing that she didn't understand, he just smiled and leaned down to hoist Oliver across his shoulders. Then he began slowly climbing the stair.

Petunia stood shaking at the bottom for a moment, wondering if Karl or Johan would carry her up. For the first time, she understood: they were safe. It was over. And they would always be safe from the King Under Stone.

The new king, whoever he was, could not leave his shining prison. If the fire did not destroy them all . . .

Her knees buckled.

"Come on, Pet," Galen said as her ears finally cleared. "I don't think I can carry you under my arm this time."

Epilogue

The twins' wedding was such a grand affair that two days later there was a small party in the gardens, just for the royal family. Spring was always unpredictable in Westfalin, but that day the sun shone and it was warm enough to be pleasant, though still cool enough for cloaks and muffs.

"I shall buy you a new red cloak," Oliver promised Petunia as they sat on a small bench to one side of the lawns.

Christian was attempting to put a rosy glow in everyone's cheeks by teaching them a game featuring several wooden balls and a child's hoop he'd found somewhere. Petunia was fairly certain that he was making it up as he went along, but Poppy didn't seem to mind even though she was losing badly. Hyacinth was fairing rather better, though her husband kept breaking her concentration by trying to kiss her.

"I like my old one," Petunia said.

"It has a bullet hole in it," Oliver said, "and I understand that it still smells of smoke."

"Any cloak that can save you from a fire so hot it can melt silver is worth mending," Petunia said primly.

"That is true," Oliver agreed, his gaze on a sofa near the mouth of the hedge maze.

On the sofa, covered in a beautifully knitted throw blanket, Rose reclined like an exotic queen. Her side no longer pained her, but Dr. Kelling had insisted that she rest after the rigors of the wedding, hence the sofa in the gardens. It worried Petunia that Rose hadn't objected to this, but it soothed some of her worry to know how much worse things had almost been.

Galen sat on the end of the sofa by Rose's feet, knitting something that Petunia had thought was a hat but now seemed to be much too large. White frosted his hair on the sides, and there were new lines around his eyes, but otherwise he seemed well enough. They were all mourning the loss of Bishop Schelker, Walter Vogel, and the good frau, but every time she looked at Galen, Petunia wanted to cheer. With her last ounce of power, the good frau—Queen Ethelia, Petunia had to remind herself—had pushed Galen out of the silver prison wall.

Jonquil went by with a full plate of food, and Petunia reached out and tried to snag a small cream puff from it. Jonquil lifted it over Petunia's head before she could, and clucked her tongue.

"These are for Lily," she said.

"Oh, really?" Petunia gave her a look.

"And possibly some are for that Analousian duke Jacques

invited," Jonquil said with a sparkle in her eyes. "But none are for you."

Then she flipped one to Oliver.

"You can have one, my lord earl," she said, and twirled away.

"These are excellent," Oliver said, eating half of it in one bite. He fed Petunia the other half so that she wouldn't get cream on her knitting. Oliver was just leaning in to steal a kiss—

"I hope this means you're planning on marrying her, boy," barked King Gregor.

Oliver leaped to his feet. "Sire! Yes! I mean . . . I . . . sire!"

"I didn't pardon you and restore your earldom so that you could loll around in my gardens flirting with my daughters," King Gregor said. Then he bent down and gave Petunia a kiss on the cheek. "I like him," he whispered loudly in her ear.

"Me too," she whispered back, blushing.

"What are you knitting? Something for Lily's baby?" King Gregor beamed down at the white wool in Petunia's hands.

"Er, actually, it's a muff," Petunia said. "For me, but . . ."

"I can see your point," Dr. Kelling said, while Oliver continued to stand awkwardly next to the bench, turning red and white in turns. "The weather continues to be cool." The doctor gave Oliver a sympathetic look from beneath his bushy brows.

"Go over and speak to Galen, would you?" King Gregor pleaded. "He and Rose are being coy about something and I don't like it."

"Sire," Oliver said as he helped Petunia to her feet, "I'd like to marry Petunia."

"Of course you would," retorted King Gregor. "But not right now! We just got those two taken care of." He pointed to the twins who were still trying to play Christian's odd game. "And weddings are expensive!"

He and Dr. Kelling walked off, leaving Oliver standing, stunned, beside Petunia.

"You'll have to get used to Papa," she told him, dropping her knitting on the bench and taking his arm.

"Indeed I will," he said faintly as they crossed the lawn.

"Does this mean I can finally go see how Lady Emily has redecorated the manor?" Petunia asked.

"I suppose so," Oliver said.

"Perhaps we can go when my sisters aren't around . . . just the two of us?"

"Yes, we should," Oliver said with more enthusiasm this time.

"You should what?" Rose looked up at them from the dish of hothouse strawberries she was eating.

"Ask Galen what he's knitting," Petunia said.

"It's a baby blanket," Rose said.

"It's round." Petunia squinted at the thing her brother-in-law was holding. "It looks like a mushroom."

"Wait and see," Galen said.

"Is it for Lily's baby?" Petunia asked.

"No," Rose said, looking up from her strawberries with a broad smile. "It's for mine."

Petunia's Fingerless Gloves

Materials:

1 skein medium-weight yarn

Size 8 (US) double-pointed needles

Instructions:

Cast on 40 stitches, dividing between three of the needles. Place marker at beginning of row and join for working in the round.

Knit in a 3×2 rib (knit 3, purl 2) for 1 inch.

Thumb: Bind off the first 6 stitches, continue working the row in pattern. On the next round, loosely cast on 6 stitches, continue working the row in pattern.

Work the 3×2 rib for 5 inches, or as long as desired. Bind off loosely in pattern, weave in ends.

Cast on the second glove immediately.

Rose's Baby Blanket

Materials:

140 yards medium-weight cotton yarn (approximately)

1 skein novelty yarn such as pompom or faux fur

Size 10½ (US) double-pointed needles

Size 10½ circular needles in 16" and 32" lengths

Instructions:

On one double-pointed needle, cast on 4 stitches.

Row 1: (Knit 1, yarn over) repeat to end. You now have eight stitches. Divide them onto three of the double-pointed needles and join for working in the round.

Row 2: (Knit 2, place a marker) repeat to end.

Row 3: (Knit to marker, slip the marker, yarn over) repeat to end.

Row 4: Knit all stitches, carefully slipping markers.

Repeat rows 3 and 4, switching to circular needles as needed.

When you can no longer fit more stitches onto the 32" needle, the blanket will be large enough. Switch to the novelty yarn and bind off all stitches. Weave in ends.

Acknowledgments

Great things come in threes, so as soon as I started working on *Princess of Glass*, I knew that I would need to write a third book about the Westfalian princesses or it just wouldn't feel right. But in order to write Petunia's story I was going to need some help, especially since I was expecting my third child during the initial writing stage and caring for a newborn during editing!

Help came, as it always does, in the shape of friends and family who loved, supported, and fed me (and my children!) while I was working. Thank you all so much! In particular, my stalwart husband cooked, cleaned, took the two older children on long car rides, and held the baby late into the night so that I could work. Our favorite babysitter spent hours playing "restaurant" and Indiana Jones (thanks, Miranda!), while I hunched over my trusty laptop in the library. Thanks, too, to our local librarians, for providing me with a lovely place to work. (And, occasionally, nap.)

Special thanks to everybody at Bloomsbury for all their hard work and tireless cheerleading. Melanie Cecka, my beloved editor on seven previous books, gave advice and feedback in the early stages of this book. Michelle Nagler is due for some custom knitwear as thanks for leaping into the breach with me when it came time to edit. Tim Travaglini, he of the dapper bowties, got roped into the editing party as well, making this book truly a team effort.

But very special thanks go to Amy Jameson, my fantastic agent. Seven years ago I didn't know what a literary agent *did*; now I couldn't imagine the world without her. Her unflagging support, friendship, editorial feedback, and generally soothing presence make my books possible. And so, with great pleasure and the most sincere affection, I dedicate this book to her.

Read on for a selection from . . .

Sun and Moon, Ice and Snow

The secrets of a frozen palace reveal a love she never imagined . . .

NEW YORK TIMES BESTSELLING AUTHOR

JESSICA DAY GEORGE

BLOOMSBURY

When a great white bear promises untold riches to her family, the "lass" (as she's known) agrees to go away with him. But the bear is not what he seems, nor is his castle. To unravel the mystery, the lass sets out on a windswept journey beyond the edge of the world. Based on the Nordic legend "East of the Sun, West of the Moon," with romantic echoes of "Beauty and the Beast," this reimagined story will leave fans of fantasy and fairy tale enchanted.

L ong ago and far away in the land of ice and snow, there came a time when it seemed that winter would never end. The months when summer should have given the land respite were cold and damp, and the winter months were snow filled and colder still. The people said the cold had lasted a hundred years, and feared that it would last a hundred more. It was not a natural winter, and no one knew what witch or troll had caused the winds to howl so fiercely.

There was nothing to do in the long nights when the sun never rose and the day never came but huddle together by the fire and dream of warmth. As a consequence, many children were born, and as food grew scarcer, the people grew even more desperate.

It seemed that there was no bleaker place than the house of the woodcutter Jarl Oskarson. Jarl himself was a kind man, and devoted to his family. But Jarl and his wife, Frida, had been blessed, or burdened, depending on one's outlook, with nine children. Five of them were boys, who were a help to their parents, but four were girls, which displeased Frida greatly. She had no use for girls, she would say with a sniff as she sat by the fire. They were empty-headed and would one day cost the poverty-stricken family the price of a dowry. No one dared point out to her that the four girls did all of the cooking, washing, and mending, leaving Frida with ample leisure time.

So disappointed was Frida at seeing that her ninth labor had resulted in yet another worthless girl that she thrust the screaming baby into the arms of her eldest daughter, Jorunn, and refused to give her a name. Because the naming of daughters was a task for mothers, and her mother had refused that task, the ninth child of Jarl Oskarson remained nameless. They simply called her *pika,* which meant "girl" in the language of the North.

The nameless state of their last child worried Jarl. Unnamed children could not be baptized, and the trolls had been known to steal unbaptized babies. Jarl loved his children despite the family's poverty, and so he set out gifts to appease the troll-folk. Cheeses, honey-sweetened milk, almond pastries, and other delicacies that they could barely afford. Frida called it a waste, for she did not believe in trolls, but Jarl spent most of his days deep in the forest, and he had seen troubling things there. When the food disappeared, he held it up as evidence that such creatures were real, but Frida just sniffed that it was more likely their neighbors' dogs were growing fat while she starved.

When the pika was nine, the eldest child, Hans Peter, came home from the sea. He was a tall young man, blue-eyed and handsome, or at least he had been handsome before he left. Now, after five years aboard the merchant ship *Sea Dragon*, he was stooped and tired, his hair more silver than gold, and his blue eyes had a haunted look. He had traveled far, he said, and seen some things more wonderful than he could describe and others too terrible to relate. He had been injured on a journey so far to the north that sun and moon seemed to touch in the sky as they passed, and now he was home to stay.

This vexed Frida greatly, because she had been very pleased to send her eldest son into the world. There had been one less mouth to feed and the promise of wages sent home. But now Hans Peter sat all day in their cottage, carving strange figures on the firewood before dropping it into the hearth. Hans Peter's injury must have been healed before he returned home, or perhaps, Jarl told the others, it had not been an injury of the body. Whatever it had been, there was no sign of it now, save for the young man's melancholy.

But the pika worshipped him. She thought that her brother was still the handsomest man in the district, even though everyone else said that title had surely passed to the next brother down, Torst (for all the woodcutter's children were fair). But Torst liked pulling the youngest girl's braids and teasing her, while Hans Peter was soft-spoken and kind.

He had learned some of the language of the Englanders on his travels, and he called the youngest girl "lass." It still meant nothing more than "girl," but it sounded prettier than "pika."

"Aye, lass," he would say, holding up a piece of wood he had been carving, to show her the strange, angular marks upon it. "This is 'bear.' And this here"—pointing to another—"is 'whale.'" And then he would cast the wood into the fire. And the lass would nod solemnly and snuggle close to listen to one of his rare stories about the life of men at sea.

Jorunn, who, as the eldest girl, had the charge of teaching the younger children their letters, scoffed at the lass when she insisted that Hans Peter's carvings were a sort of language. "It's not the language of England, that's for sure," she retorted, tossing another one of the carvings into the fire and using a bit of charred stick to write the alphabet on the scrubbed table. "For the priest says that every Christian land uses the same letters. And the priest went to school in Christiania." Her words carried a solemn weight: Christiania was the capital, and the priest was the only person for miles around who had been there.

But Hans Peter continued to show his little lass the carvings, and she continued to study them with big, solemn eyes. Of all the children, she alone had dark brown eyes, though her hair was more reddish than gold, which was not uncommon in that family. Before it went gray, Jarl had boasted the same color hair, and four of the nine children had inherited it.

When the lass was eleven, Jorunn married a farmer's son who was too poor himself to expect much in the way of dowry, and they moved into an extra room in his father's house. That same year, Hans Peter traded some of his more commonplace carvings to a tinker from the south, so the family got the flour and salt they would need to last another winter. He hadn't particularly enjoyed making wooden bowls and spoons, but the patterns of fish and birds he had carved around the edges of the bowls had made the lass clap her hands with pleasure.

Frida was marginally appeased, and a little of Jarl's burden was eased. And the lass grew, and Hans Peter carved. And the winter continued, without sign of spring.

In the North, they say that the third son is the lucky son. He is the one who will travel far, and see magic done. The third son of King Olav Hawknose had ridden the north wind into battle and returned home victorious, weighted down with gold and married to a foreign princess. In tales the third son is called the ash lad, or Askeladden, and he is both clever and lucky.

Hoping to inspire her own third son to such heights, Frida had named the boy Askeladden. The woodcutter's wife dreamed of one day going to live in the palace her own ash lad would build for her with the gold he found in a hollow log. Then he would save an enchanted princess and bring her to the palace to live with him and his doting mother.

Askeladden Jarlson was not the hero of legend and tale, however, and everyone but his mother knew it. He preferred drinking the raw ale of the mountains and dodging work to living off the land or his wits. And, as he told the young lass with a wink and a nudge, he much preferred saucy farmers' daughters to icy princesses.

This particular afternoon, Hans Peter had moved over on the bench and given the lass the place closest to the fire. He usually sat there for the convenience of the light and so that he could throw his shavings into the fire with an easy toss, but he did not need the heat. The cold did not seem to bite into his bones as it did to the rest of the family. He said it was because he had been to a place that was colder than hell, and nothing after that would ever be as chill.

"Here, lass," her eldest brother said, holding up a bit of wood. "What's this then?"

By twelve she could recognize many of the strange symbols. "Reindeer," she replied promptly. "But don't show Mother; she'll be so angry."

Hans Peter winked at her, in a much friendlier way than Askel had. "Don't you worry. Before you can wrinkle your pretty nose, this will be a spoon with flowers 'round the handle."

The door of their small cottage burst open, and fifteen-year-old Einar came rushing in. He left the door open in his haste, letting in the wind and snow. He stood in the middle of the main room, hands on knees, and wheezed for a few minutes.

The rest of the family, those who were at home at any rate, stared at him. It was some moments before sixteen-year-old Katla ran to close the door. She wheeled around to continue staring at Einar as soon as the heavy door was safely latched.

"In—in—in the vill-village," he gasped. "Jens Pederson said he saw it."

"Saw what?" Askel looked up from the corner where he was polishing his worn boots.

"Saints preserve me from half-witted children," Frida murmured to herself, and pulled her tattered shawl tighter about her shoulders. She picked up her knitting, ignoring Einar.

"The—the—the—," Einar stammered.

"The—the—the," Askel mocked, and went back to his polishing.

"The white reindeer," Einar spit out, making his family freeze in astonishment.

Stories of the white reindeer were as plentiful as stories of lucky third sons. Everybody knew that if you found the white reindeer, it would give you one gift. And what wonderful gifts the reindeer had granted! Fabulous dowries for poor fishermen's daughters, sacks of gold, new houses, kettles that were always full to the brim with delectable foods, seven-league boots, golden ships . . . and many more wondrous things.

Everyone was on their feet now, jaws agape. Everyone except for Hans Peter, who shook his head and went back to carving. Askeladden crossed the room in two strides and grabbed Einar by the shoulders, shaking the younger boy.

"You are certain? The white reindeer was seen?"

Einar nodded, struck dumb once more.

"Where?"

"To—to the east, past Karl Henrykson's farm. By the three waterfalls."

Askel released his brother and grabbed up the boots he had been polishing. Thrusting his feet into them, he pulled on one of the patched parkas that hung by the door. Then he took down a pair of skis and poles.

"Don't wait up, Mother," he said gaily, and went out into the snow.

The other children, who until now had not said a word, all scrambled to follow. Frida made no remark as all her remaining children save Hans Peter and the lass divided up the warm clothes and skis and went out into the cold. When the last of them were gone, she turned to Hans Peter and the lass, displeased.

"Well, your brothers and sisters are determined to make this family's fortune, but I see that you are not," she snapped. She stalked over to the hearth and took up the spoon that Katla had been using to stir the soup.

"The little one is too young to be off in the forest chasing moonbeams," Hans Peter said. "And a nameless child should never wander in the woods."

"And what's your excuse, a great big man like you? Rather sit all day by the fire like an old woman warming your lazy bones?"

"The lass is too young, and I am too old," Hans Peter

said mildly. "I went chasing moonbeams aboard the *Sea Dragon*, and I have always regretted it."

The little lass looked from her grumbling mother to her sad-eyed brother and didn't know what to do. She could remain here, she supposed. As Hans Peter had said, she was too young to be out in the cold, and night was falling. But what a glorious thing it would be to catch the white reindeer, the lass thought, and to ask it to make Hans Peter happy again.

"I'm going too," she announced, and got up from her place by the fire. She felt a little thrill of fear, but thought that if any trolls confronted her, she would claim to be her sister Annifrid.

"What?" Hans Peter looked startled. He dropped the piece of wood he was carving and took one of her hands in his own. "My little lass, this is not a good thing to do."

"I'll be all right," she told him, mustering confidence she did not feel.

"There are no parkas left," Hans Peter pointed out.

"I'll use a blanket," the lass said after a moment's consideration. She had set her mind to finding that reindeer, for Hans Peter's sake, and nothing would deter her.

"You'll freeze to death," their mother said shrilly. "If you'd wanted a parka to wear, you should have moved faster. Come and stir this soup; I still have stockings to darn."

"No." The lass put her chin up. "I will find the white reindeer."

"Then wear mine," Hans Peter said. He climbed up to the loft and the lass heard him rummaging in his sea chest. He rarely opened it, and she could hear the hinges squeak in protest when the lid closed. Hans Peter descended the ladder and held out a parka and a pair of boots. "These will keep you warm. And safe."

"Oh, I couldn't!" Her hands rose to her cheeks, stunned by the beauty of the items he held before her.

The boots and parka were lined with the finest, whitest fur she had ever seen. On the outside they were of softly felted wool as white as new snow, embroidered with bands of bloodred and azure blue. The spiky patterns of the embroidery matched the style of the carvings that Hans Peter made, but none of these symbols were familiar to the lass.

"You can and you will," he said, holding them out. "The boots are too big for you, of course. But if you keep your old boots on underneath, they'll work well enough. Strap on some snowshoes and you'll be able to walk like a bear. And the parka will cover you from stem to stern, which is a good thing in this cold."

"Those things are too fine for her," their mother snapped, her gleaming eyes checking the seams and verifying the quality. "We could sell them to the next trader for a pretty penny, and no mistake." She crossed her arms under her bosom. "Why did you not say before that you had such things to trade? And here the family is going wanting!"

"I'll not sell these for love nor money," Hans Peter said. His eyes held the dead look that they'd had when he first arrived home, the look that was only now beginning to fade.

"But," Frida began.

"I'll not sell these for love nor money," her eldest son repeated. "I earned them with blood, and I'll part with them when death takes me, but not before. The lass shall have them tonight, and after that, back into the chest they go!"

Not wanting to argue with him in this strange, fierce mood, the lass took the proffered clothing and put it on. The parka extended well past her knees and the boots rose to meet it. With her own scuffed boots underneath, they were just snug enough, and she had to push the heavy sleeves of the parka back in order to use her hands.

"I've never been so warm," she said in wonder. She had never known what it was like to feel the glow over your whole body that you felt on your cheeks and hands when you sat close to the fire.

Her brother pulled the hood up, tucking in her hair, and pulled the ribbons to tighten it around her face. "God willing, one day you shall be this warm all the time," he told her, his voice gruff with emotion. Then he held back the sleeves while she tugged on her mittens, and she went off in search of the white reindeer.

Jessica Day George

is the author of many books for young readers and teens, including *Princess of the Midnight Ball*, *Princess of Glass*, and *Princess of the Silver Woods*; *Sun and Moon, Ice and Snow*; *Tuesdays at the Castle* and the *New York Times* bestseller *Wednesdays in the Tower*; and the Dragon Slippers trilogy. Originally from Idaho, Jessica studied at Brigham Young University and worked as a librarian and bookseller before turning to writing full time. She now lives in Salt Lake City, Utah, with her husband and three children.

www.JessicaDayGeorge.com